Double Crossing

Double Crossing

EVE TAL

Cinco Puntos Press   El Paso

FIRST EDITION
10 9 8 7 6 5 4 3 2 1

Library of Congress Cataloging-in-Publication Data

Tal, Eve, 1947-
  Double crossing / by Eve Tal.— 1st ed.
     p. cm.
  Summary: In 1905, as life becomes increasingly difficult for Jews in
Ukraine, eleven-year-old Raizel and her father flee to America in hopes of
earning money to bring the rest of the family there, but her father's health
and Orthodox faith become barriers.
  ISBN 0-938317-94-6
  [1. Emigration and immigration—Fiction. 2. Fathers and daughters—
Fiction. 3. Jews—Ukraine—Fiction. 4. Ukraine—History—Revolution,
1905-1907—Fiction.] I. Title.
  PZ7.T14138Do 2005
  [Fic]—dc22
                         2005008188

Cover painting by Susan Klahr *acrylic and oil on pastel board*
Photograph of author by Tal Bedrack
Book design by JB Bryan / La Alameda Press

Thanks to Debbie Nathan for her careful historical edit, the helpful
librarians at Ellis Island and YIVO, Briana Simon, and the warm support
of the students and teachers in the Hollins University Children's Literature
Graduate Program.

Thanks to the Lannan Foundation for their support and encouragement.

In loving memory of
Rose, Louis, Shalom, and Sima Altman,
and for my mother, Hannah:
I wish you could have read this book.

Contents

1

Telling Tales

Papa didn't come home that Friday. I waited at the gate as dusk swallowed house after house along the street. My brother Lemmel left for the prayer house with the men and older boys of the village. Inside the house, Mama prepared to light the candles to welcome in the Sabbath.

But where was Papa?

He never came home so late. All week he peddled his goods among the Ukrainian peasants, but Friday afternoons he returned early, went first to the bathhouse and then to the prayer house to welcome in the Sabbath.

"Where's Papa?" asked Shloyme, my younger brother, as he plopped onto the doorstep. Baby Hannah tugged me down beside her.

"Soon, he'll be home soon. Shall I tell you a story?" I suggested to take my thoughts away from the worry mouse gnawing in my mind.

"Tell me about America," begged Shloyme.

"In America the streets are paved with polished marble," I began, thankful Shloyme had asked for his favorite story so I wouldn't have to think too hard. "The people ride in silver carriages. In winter, it snows goose down. They gather it to make feather pillows. And when it rains, it rains . . . can you guess?"

"Honey!" Shloyme bobbed up and down.

"Hunna!" Baby Hannah clapped her hands.

"Yes, honey," I said, licking my lips.

Would I ever see America?

Many people in Jibatov had gone to America. Mottel, the tailor's son, ran away to America to escape the Czar's army and the Russian-Japanese War. The widowed dressmaker's sister sent her a ticket and she disappeared the next day. Hirshel, the shoemaker, left his wife and six children. Five years later they still waited for him to send steamship tickets.

Nobody who went to America from Jibatov ever came back.

But they wrote letters. We would be sitting at the kitchen table peeling onions and Freida would stick her head in the window.

"Havaleh, have you heard?" she shouted to Mama. "Yente got a letter from her brother, that good-for-nothing in New York. You won't believe what he wrote!"

And the stories came pouring out. By the time I was eleven in 1905, I knew all the stories about becoming rich in America. When I wasn't too busy helping in the house, I loved telling tales to Shloyme and Hannah. Mama said my stories were a lot of singing and not enough noodles, but I didn't care. Even if they weren't true, they were good stories.

"Raizel, tell me about the food." Four-year-old Shloyme always wanted to hear about food.

"Every day in America they eat roast chicken for dinner, not only on holidays," I continued. "And for dessert they eat honey cake and poppy cake and oranges. You remember how we ate oranges at Uncle Nahum's? They came all the way from Palestine." Uncle Nahum, Mama's brother, was the richest man in our little town in the Ukraine. The memory of the sweet-sour orange taste brought juice to my mouth.

"Raaai - zel, where are you?"

"Outside with the little ones," I called to Mama. "In America, no one has to work. Gold and silver coins grow on the trees. Everyone lives in a fine stone house as big as a castle and . . . "

"Raizel, are you telling those silly stories again? Such nonsense you have in your head." Mama stepped outside and shivered in the late spring chill. She pulled her gray woolen shawl tightly around her shoulders. "It is time to lay the table. The sun will set any minute."

"But Papa isn't home yet." The worry mouse gnawed harder. So many bad things could happen to a Jew in the Ukraine. A drunken peasant might rob and beat him. Hungry wolves might attack him in the forest. The Czar's soldiers might kidnap him into the army and send him to fight the war in Siberia. "Mama, do you think he had an accident?"

"Hush, child." Mama spat three times to ward off the evil eye. "When a fool is silent, he is counted among the wise."

"Is Raizel a fool, Mama?" Shloyme dug his fat fist into his chin and stared at me.

"Of course not. Raizel is a little girl with a too-big imagination. No, she's almost twelve. She's a big girl who should know better." Mama hugged Shloyme and scooped Baby Hannah from my lap.

I followed them into the house half-wishing I was still small enough for Mama's hugs. Mama was always so busy! There was shopping to do in the town market, the house to clean, chickens to feed, laundry to wash by the river, bread to bake in the iron oven. By the time she finished cooking our dinner, putting the little ones to bed and doing the mending, she had no time left for me, not even to teach me to read like she had promised.

Maybe when the little ones were older she would have more time. I yearned to read like a cow longs to graze in a field of summer wheat. Every time I thought of the stories hidden within those crooked Hebrew letters, I felt like a seed pod about to burst open. Bobbe, my grandmother, had taught me to read my prayers in Yiddish, the language spoken by the Jews of Europe, but that wasn't enough. Books. I wanted to read books. But the only book we owned was the Bible, and I couldn't read the Hebrew words. How I envied Lemmel, my brother.

I sighed. Mama had explained it to me many times. Boys go to school because they must read the Torah in the synagogue. Women take care of the house and have babies, so reading isn't important. Sometimes I wished I had been born a boy, but I kept my thoughts to myself! Whenever I told Mama that I wanted to be something other than what I was, she said, "And if grandma had wheels, she would be a wagon!" So maybe if I was a boy, I wouldn't want to study Torah, who knows?

I smoothed the white tablecloth over the wooden table while Mama made sure Shloyme and Hannah wore clean clothes and faces. The plates were cracked, but I had polished the silver wine cup until it shone. I set the brass candlesticks at the head of the table and brushed off my navy wool dress, a hand-me-down from cousin Leah. It was getting short on me. If Leah would only grow faster, I might have a different holiday dress for the New Year next fall.

With candlesticks and wine glasses, the house seemed more festive. We might only have three little rooms, but when we all sat around the table for the Sabbath meal, I wouldn't trade our home for anyplace in the world, not even America.

The first stars peeped through the inky sky. "Mama, it's time to light the candles." Even without Papa, we had to welcome in the Sabbath.

Mama put a square of lace on her head and raised her hands to shelter the candle flames from sudden drafts. "Blessed art thou, Oh Lord our God, King of the Universe, who blesses us and commands us to kindle the Sabbath lights." Her lips moved silently for a moment. I knew she was praying for Papa to come home safely. "Amen."

"Amen," I whispered.

"Good Shabbas. Good Shabbas." Mama turned to me. "Now Raizel, run down the street and see if Lemmel is out of synagogue yet. Maybe Papa went straight to the prayer house. And don't forget your shawl, you shouldn't catch a chill."

My shawl fluttered around me like butterfly wings as I ran from the house. Sabbath candles glowed orange in the windows of the low wooden houses along our street. I leapt over a puddle and turned the corner where the men were just leaving the prayer house.

"Good Shabbas!" They greeted each other, tucking their prayer books under their arms. I searched the crowd of men in long black coats and black hats for a glimpse of Papa, short and thin, his eyes sparkling behind wire-rimmed glasses.

"He's not here," a voice shouted in my ear.

I jumped.

Lemmel grinned as he stepped from behind me. He was nine and the oldest boy in the family. That meant he should be serious and responsible, but to Lemmel everything was a joke, even his studies.

"You scared me!" I snapped at him. "Papa isn't home yet and Mama sent me to look for him. Do you think the wagon broke down?" All week Papa traveled around the countryside selling pots and pans and old clothes to the peasant farmers. Once Papa's wagon had fallen into a ditch, but he had fixed it and come home in time for the Sabbath services.

Lemmel hopped down the street, first on one foot and then the other. "Papa's smart. Nothing will happen to him. He probably stopped at Uncle Nahum's house." Uncle Nahum's big wooden house and sawmill were just outside of town.

"Even if he stopped at Uncle Nahum's, he should be home by now." I skirted a deep wagon rut in the road. In the winter the streets of Jibatov were clogged with snow and ice. In the spring they turned into a river of mud and in the summer to dust. No one ever had clean shoes in Jibatov.

"Worry mouse, worry mouse, big fat pig will eat your house!" Lemmel chanted in a singsong voice. If it hadn't been the Sabbath, I would have punched him. Lemmel thought he knew everything, just because he could read. It wasn't my fault there was no school for girls in Jibatov and no one had time to teach me.

"Don't talk like that on the Sabbath," I said in my best grown-up voice. "Papa never came home so late before. You know it's forbidden to travel on the Sabbath. What if something terrible happened and he can't even send for help? What if . . . ?"

"Worry mouse!" Lemmel began to run, the fringes of his undershirt flapping beneath his short black coat. I plodded after him. I felt like my woolen stockings were stuffed with stones.

I knew from the tight line on Mama's forehead that Papa hadn't come home yet.

"I'm hungry." Shloyme tugged at Mama's long skirt. Baby Hannah was sucking her thumb and staring at the fresh challah loaf sitting in a basket on the table. The smell of roasted chicken filled the house.

Mama glanced out the window. "Let's wait a few more minutes. Perhaps Papa stopped at Uncle Nahum's."

Lemmel stuck his tongue out at me.

"But I'm hungry now!" Shloyme stomped his foot on the wooden floor.

"Come, I'll tell you a story about the Sabbath," I whispered in his ear and dragged him into the bedroom. Baby Hannah toddled up to my knee. Even Lemmel, who always claimed he was too big for stories, leaned against the doorframe and pretended to study his chewed-up nails.

"Once upon a time, a traveler went searching for the Ten Lost Tribes who vanished from the Land of Israel. To this day no one knows where they disappeared to." I put my arm around Shloyme's shoulders. "For months the traveler trudged through deserts. He crossed the deepest seas and climbed the highest mountains. After many years, he came to a great city located near the River Sambatyon. The people of the city told him that the Ten Lost Tribes lived on the other side of the river. They wore clothes made of silk and even the poorest lived in houses built of diamonds and emeralds. They spent their days studying and praying for the Messiah to come and save the world.

"'Then I will cross the river at once!' cried the traveler. When the people in the city heard this, they burst out laughing.

"'What a fool you are,' they said. 'No one can cross the River Sambatyon. It is impossible!'

"'I will cross it,' said the traveler and left the city.

"As he approached the river, he heard a noise like the sound of a thousand tons of rock rolling down a mountain. A dark black cloud surrounded the river. Huge boulders shot into the air and landed with an awesome crash on the shore. The traveler shook with terror. 'If I approach the river, a boulder will kill me,' he said.

"Not far from the river he saw a tiny hut. He knocked on the door and an old woman opened it. 'I want to cross the River Sambatyon to visit the Ten Lost Tribes,' he said.

"'Then you must wait until Friday evening,' said the old woman and closed the door.

"'All week the traveler waited while the river raged and hurled boulders on the shore. As the sun set on Friday evening, a sweet silence descended on the land. No more rocks fell. The river grew calm and peaceful. In the morning its waters flowed gently as a brook. The traveler saw people standing on the far shore. They wore long flowing robes of the purest white, embroidered with gold and silver.

"'Who are you?' called the traveler.

"'We are the people of Dan and Menashe and Reuben, of the Ten Lost Tribes. How goes the world?'

"'Times are hard,' said the traveler. 'The Czar is cruel. There is hunger and sickness.'

"'Here all is good,' called the people on the shore.

"'I will bring the Jews to you,' said the traveler. 'Then we can be together again and live in peace and harmony.'

"'It cannot be done.' The people shook their heads sadly. 'Only on the Sabbath, when the River Sambatyon rests, can you cross. But on the Sabbath it is forbidden to travel. You may not cross over.'

"All day the traveler waited on the riverbank. As the sun set, marking the close of the Sabbath rest, the river swelled and stormed and turned black as coal. Huge waves crashed on the banks and boulders thudded on the earth. The traveler ran away in fright. With a heavy heart, he returned home."

"You mean he didn't cross over? Why not?" Shloyme demanded.

"Because Jews are forbidden to work on the Sabbath. Traveling is work."

"Where is that river? I'll jump right over it. Papa lets me jump on the Sabbath."

"Baby." Lemmel sneered at him. "That's a stupid story. Raizel only knows stupid stories."

Shloyme's lip trembled. He looked from Lemmel to me.

"Bobbe told me that story," I said. Shloyme smiled. He still remembered our grandmother, Bobbe, who had died last year. Papa's mother had lived with us since I was a baby. She was even smaller than Papa and always smelled like the almond cookies she loved to bake for the holidays. Mama said Bobbe had infected me with her storytelling sickness. Bobbe told stories while she shelled peas and peeled onions. She told them while she kneaded bread and fed the babies. She told them to me every night in the bed we shared, until the morning she didn't wake up.

"Time to eat, children." Mama's voice sounded tired. This time she didn't scold me for telling stories.

We all stared at Papa's empty chair. Without Papa, our home felt like a house with no door. As the oldest male present, Lemmel said the blessings instead of Papa. He lifted the cup of raisin wine in his hand. In a loud voice he recited the blessing, took a sip, and passed the cup around the table. After we had all washed our hands, he said the blessing over the two loaves of braided bread and broke off pieces.

The sweet white bread melted in my mouth. I had been too busy today to eat lunch. First Mama had sent me to the baker to put the barley and potato cholent in his oven to keep it warm for the Sabbath. Then she sent me to Lyuba's to borrow sugar for carrot tzimmis. Then I helped her dust the rooms, polish the wine cups and candlesticks, and carry water from the well in the market square. In between errands, I watched Shloyme and Hannah. So why did the bread stick in my throat after the first bite?

We had just finished the steaming hot chicken soup when the door opened.

"Papa!" Shloyme flung back his chair and threw himself into Papa's open arms. Lemmel's freckled face broke into a grin. Baby Hannah beat the table with her spoon, and Mama burst into tears. A huge boulder rolled off my heart.

"What is all this fuss? My house sounds like market day the week before Passover. Can't a man come home to his family without everyone making a tumult?" Under his black beard, Papa was smiling so hard his glasses pinched his forehead. "Haveleh, are those tears? Has someone died?"

Mama wiped her eyes on her napkin and threw her arms around Papa's neck. "No, Binyumin, someone is alive. Good Shabbas."

"Now Haveleh, I told you I might go to Lubov. It took longer than I thought. I stopped at Nahum's on the way back and left the horse there, I shouldn't have to ride on the Sabbath." Pavel, Uncle Nahum's Christian servant, would take care of Bunchik, the horse.

Mama raised her head from Papa's shoulder. "Did you get . . . ?"

"Not now. I am hungry. I want to greet the Sabbath with my family. I will wash up and join you in a moment."

Suddenly the food tasted better than a New Year's feast at Uncle Nahum's. I heaped my plate with sweet boiled carrots, barley, and a succulent hunk of chicken. In a few moments Papa joined us, said a brief prayer, and began eating so fast it looked like the food was disappearing into the air.

Mama leaned back in her chair and smiled. "What, you didn't eat all week, Binyumin? You eat like a starving man."

"I ate. But nothing tastes as good as your cooking. And outside this house I cannot be sure the food is kosher."

After dinner, Mama and I cleared the table. Soon the familiar Sabbath melodies filled the house. Mama joined in as she put away the food, her high sweet voice mingling with Papa's bass like cream in a cup of coffee. When was the last time I had heard Mama sing? All winter a line of worry had stitched itself across her forehead like a tight seam.

"Mama, why did Papa have to go to Lubov? And why did he come home so late?" I asked as we finished wiping the dishes.

Mama's worry line returned. "Raizel, God gave us two ears and one mouth, so we might hear much and say little. Papa will tell you in good time."

I shut my mouth. Pestering Mama never did any good.

The candles had burned halfway down before Papa finished singing. Usually he told us about his adventures in the countryside—about the inn keeper who charged so much for vodka that his customers went on strike and drank nothing but water for a week, or the peasant woman who always bought two of each 'just in case.' But today he sat back in his chair and smiled.

"Papa, did you bring us something from Lubov?" I knew Shloyme was thinking of sugar candy.

"Yes, but you cannot eat it." Shloyme's mouth fell like a cake without leavening.

"Can you wear it, Papa?" Lemmel took up the game, glancing at his shoes, which were coming apart at the soles.

Papa shook his head and looked at me.

"Can you . . . read it?" At Passover, Papa had promised to buy me a book so Mama could teach me to read.

"You can read it, but it is not a book."

I sighed. We had no money for luxuries like books.

"So what is it, Papa?" Shloyme rubbed his eyes with his fists. Hannah was already dozing on Mama's lap.

Papa took a thick wad of paper out of his coat pocket and carefully unwrapped the oilcloth covering. "Now can you guess?"

Lemmel took the paper in his hands. He examined the black letters and traced them with his finger. "This is Russian, this is another language, maybe German. Nu, Papa, what is it?" He handed it back to Papa.

"Stop teasing them, Binyumin." Mama's fingers played with Hannah's curls.

Papa leaned forward. "I will ask you a riddle. This, my children, is the key to a magic land. This is a doorway to a new life, a life without hunger, Czars, or Cossacks, a life without pogroms or policemen who spit in your face because you are a Jew." Papa's eyes blazed behind his glasses and his voice boomed like the rabbi explaining the Torah portion. "Children, this is life itself! Now can you guess?"

Lemmel shook his head. Papa looked at me.

What could give us a new life? What could take us away from all the bad things in Russia? What . . . ?

Suddenly I knew as surely as if I could read the black letters. It must be. It had to be.

"Papa, are we going to America?"

2
The Second Ticket

"We're going to America! We're going to America!" Lemmel shouted.

"Will we eat honey and roast chicken and oranges every day?" Shloyme asked.

Papa grabbed Shloyme and danced him around the room like a Torah scroll on Simchas Torah. Mama rocked Hannah back and forth, smiling and laughing.

I didn't know which question to ask first. When were we going? How would we get there? Where would we live in America? Were Uncle Nahum and Aunt Freida and the cousins going, too? Where did Papa get the money to buy the tickets?

"Papa . . . ?" I began.

Mama put her finger to her lips. "Shush! Sit down all of you. Such behavior on the Sabbath! It isn't right." When Papa had sat down again with Shloyme on his lap, she said, "Binyumin, they think we're all going. Children, we don't have money for tickets for the whole family. Only Papa is going to America. When he earns enough money, he will send our tickets."

Lemmel sat down with a thud. "Then I still have to go to cheder?"

"Of course," Mama said. "And in America you will go to cheder, too. Otherwise how will you become a learned man and a great rabbi?"

"But Mama, I don't want to be a rabbi. Reb Yankel beats me. I hate studying all day. I want to be a carpenter."

"Enough!" Mama put her hands over her ears. "You will do as you are told. Your great-grandfather was a scholar. People came from all over the Ukraine to learn from him. Learning is a wonderful thing and all my sons will go to cheder and yeshiva, right Binyumin?"

Papa nodded. "Of course. I would have given anything to study. The day my father, blessed be his name, died in the pogrom, and I had to go to work to support my family, was the saddest day of my life. But Havaleh . . . "

"So that's settled," Mama continued. "I don't want to hear any more about not going to cheder. You think Reb Yankel beats you hard? Just wait until you see how hard your Papa will beat you!"

I hid a smile behind my hand. Papa never beat anyone, not even Bunchik, his horse.

"Havaleh, there's something I have to tell you." Papa spoke loudly. "My ticket cost less than we thought and I had enough money left over to buy a child's ticket. I have two tickets to America."

"B-but we never talked about that! Why didn't you save the money for the journey? Remember how expensive passports are."

"The ticket was very cheap because the child will share my bed. Don't worry, Havaleh, I have enough money for the journey."

"Then I am going to America!" Lemmel jumped up from his chair. His long orange side curls bobbed up and down as he hopped from one foot to another. "Good-bye, Reb Yankel! Good-bye, Jibatov! Hello, America!"

Lemmel looked like a baby goat prancing in a meadow. I felt happy for him. As the eldest son, it was right for him to go.

"One moment," Mama said. The worry line bit deep into her forehead. "I am not sure about Lemmel."

"But Mama, I'm the oldest!"

"There are many things to consider," Mama continued as if Lemmel had said nothing.

"But Lemmel is right. He is my first-born son," Papa said.

"I know. That is why it is so important he should go to school. Who can tell what will happen in America? You will be working all day. You will not have time to make Lemmel go to cheder."

"I did not think of that," said Papa.

I could guess what Mama was thinking. Without Mama to watch him, Lemmel would play all day and never become a great rabbi. But if Lemmel didn't go with Papa, who would?

"Children, the candles have almost burned down." Mama picked up Baby Hannah and took Shloyme by the hand.

"But Mama . . . , " Lemmel looked like a pot of soup about to boil over.

"Enough, I said. In the morning we have time to talk. Now we go to bed!"

"Papa, please . . . , " Lemmel wouldn't give up.

"Listen to your mother. To bed. Now!"

I undressed Hannah while Mama tucked Shloyme into bed. He was so tired he fell asleep without asking for a story. Shloyme and Lemmel slept in one bed and I slept in the second. Mama, Papa and Baby Hannah slept in the other room.

"Do you think Mama will let me go?" Lemmel asked after Mama left.

"Papa wants you to go."

"I must go! Reb Yankel pulled my ears so hard this morning I thought they would come off. They still hurt." He rubbed his ears.

"Maybe if you studied harder, he wouldn't punish you so much." If I went to school, I would study every day.

"But I hate studying. The words jump around on the page and all I think about is climbing trees and running in the fields. Even when I try, the words won't stick in my head."

I curled under the feather comforter remembering Lemmel's first day at school. Mama had taken me along when she brought him to the tiny crowded room where Reb Yankel taught the boys of Jibatov to read and write. Bobbe had baked special honey cakes in the shape of the Hebrew letters. Lemmel ate the cakes, but cried when Mama left him. The next day he refused to go to cheder, and Mama had to carry him.

"It's not fair," I said. "You go to school and hate it. I can't go to school and love it. If only Jibatov had a school for girls, or I could take lessons from a private tutor like Leah does. I would love to read the stories about David and Goliath, Ruth, and Esther."

"We never read stories. All we read are prayers. It's boring."

"Still, you can read them if you want to. And you can read Sholem Aleichem and . . . "

"Who wants to read them? If I promise Mama to go to cheder in America every day, do you think she'll let me go?"

"Well . . . remember that time you hid in the woodshed? Mama doesn't forget things like that."

"I'll never forget the beating she gave me! Luckily the broomstick broke!"

Lemmel was silent a moment. "I guess that means Shloyme will go!" Lemmel jabbed Shloyme with his elbow. Shloyme sighed and turned over.

"Stop that! Shloyme is too little to go. Maybe Papa can return the ticket. Or maybe I . . . " I shut my mouth as the cold hand of fear squeezed my throat.

"You? But you're a girl!" Lemmel hooted with laughter. Mama banged on the bedroom wall, but Lemmel was laughing too hard to stop. "Nobody would let a girl go to America. You're so dumb, Raizel."

I threw my pillow at Lemmel. Hard. "Why shouldn't a girl go to America? I can keep house for Papa and cook his food. Why, Papa forgets to eat if you don't remind him!"

Lemmel threw the pillow back at me. "Forget it, Raizel. I'm going to America, even if I have to travel inside Papa's hat!" Lemmel spit the words from between his teeth. He wasn't laughing now. "I'm tired. I've been studying all day. I don't sit home and do nothing like girls."

"Nothing?" I wanted to jump on Lemmel and pound him with my fists. "I help Mama all day. I never have time to play with other girls. Why, ever since Bobbe died, I barely have time to make up stories!" I rubbed away a tear. I certainly had no time to learn to read.

"Crybaby! All you care about are your stupid stories!" Lemmel turned his back to me and pretended to sleep.

Moonlight cut through the shutters like knife blades. I could hear Mama and Papa murmuring on the other side of the wall. What were they saying? Lemmel was the eldest son. In the end Mama would have to let Lemmel go. Anyway, she needed me at home.

I tossed back and forth, too angry with Lemmel to fall asleep. The straw mattress was lumpy and smelled stale after the long winter. What if I was a girl? Girls were important, too. Girls had babies and kept house and cooked the meals. So why did men think they were more important?

"Because a boy must study Torah and pass on the Jewish laws to his sons," Bobbe had said when I asked her. "And when he grows up, he must work to support his family." She winked at me. "Unless he has a rich father-in-law who supports him while he studies."

"But, Bobbe, Lemmel says every morning in their prayers men thank God that they weren't born a woman. He's just making that up, isn't he?"

Bobbe laughed. "Women thank God for making them according to His will and there are those who believe women are actually an improvement. In fact, that reminds me of a story."

Everything had reminded Bobbe of a story. But even though her hands were busy, she always had time for me. She saved me the crunchy scraps of fried chicken fat I loved or kept raisins for me in her apron pocket. Mama said she spoiled me.

Thinking about Bobbe made me warm and sleepy, but something held me from slipping over the edge of sleep. It was something about America I didn't want to think about it. I wouldn't think about it. I wouldn't. I wouldn't . . .

3

Lemmel refused to talk to me in the morning. He went with Papa to the Sabbath morning services while Mama set the table for a late breakfast. I glanced at Mama as I carried the two challahs to the table. Her face was pale and dark clouds seemed to have settled under her eyes.

"Mama . . . ?" I began.

"Not now, Raizel. I have a headache."

I brought Mama a cup of lukewarm tea from the samovar. It was forbidden to light a cooking fire on the Sabbath. When Papa and Lemmel returned, Papa said the blessing and we ate bread and cold barley from dinner the night before.

"It is a beautiful spring day," said Papa, wiping his mouth. "Who wants to go for a walk?"

"Yeah!" Shloyme clapped his chubby hands. Mama got Shloyme and Hannah ready while I cleared the table.

Usually Lemmel was thrilled to walk in the woods, but today his freckled face was serious. "Papa, have you decided if I can go to America?"

"Your Mama and I still have to talk," Papa began.

"But Papa . . . "

"God gave man two ears and one mouth so he might hear much and say little," Mama called from the next room. "Children do not question their parents."

Lemmel shut his mouth and ran outside. You couldn't argue with Mama.

Outside the air smelled like freshly plowed earth. Clouds pranced across the sunny sky like playful lambs. I gave a little skip of happiness and forced myself not to run. What would the neighbors say if they saw me running on the Sabbath?

"Good Shabbas, Reb Binyumin! Good Shabbas, Havaleh!" called Mrs. Stein from across the street. "Going for a stroll?"

Mama hooked her arm through Papa's and nodded. All along the street people were sitting on their stoops warming themselves in the sun. They looked like bears emerging from their dens after a winter of snow and ice.

We passed the synagogue and the butcher's house. After Uncle Nahum, the butcher was the richest man in Jibatov, but he lived in a one-story wooden house just like everyone else. Outside the Jewish quarter, the houses of the Ukrainian peasants had big yards and cow barns. Ducks and chickens scurried around the vegetable gardens and pigs wallowed in the mud. I moved closer to Papa. This part of town always frightened me. I had heard stories of Christians attacking the Jews in other towns, stories about women and children being killed, stories I hoped Shloyme and Hannah wouldn't hear for many years.

"Look at that pig!" Shloyme pointed at a huge sow nursing her piglets. "She's all muddy."

"Ugh. How can anyone eat pigs?" I asked. "They're so dirty."

"And chickens are clean?" Mama asked. "Every religion has its own laws. For Jews, pigs are tref, forbidden; for the Christians, they are a delicacy."

"Would you eat pig meat if you were hungry, Raizel?" asked Shloyme.

I stared at the enormous sow with her tiny little eyes. My stomach turned over. "Even if I were starving, I wouldn't eat pig. I would be sick."

"You're just a baby, Raizel." Lemmel sneered. "If I were starving, I would eat anything."

"God wouldn't want you to eat pig. Right, Papa?"

Papa stroked his beard. "It depends. If you are starving to death and eating tref can save you, then it is allowed. Do you know what that is called, Lemmel?"

Lemmel kicked a clod of dirt and pretended he hadn't heard. Mama sighed and shook her head.

"It is called pikuekh-nefesh. You're allowed to break the Jewish laws if your life is in danger."

"Is that why Bobbe always said 'pikuekh-nefesh' before she drank her tea on Yom Kippur?" I asked. Last Yom Kippur was the first time I had fasted the entire day. Before that, I broke my fast with Shloyme and Hannah at lunchtime.

"Yes, she was too weak to go without food all day. That is very good, Raizel." Papa smiled at me.

"Too bad Raizel cannot go to cheder instead of Lemmel." Mama frowned at Lemmel.

"Ouch!" I cried. "Lemmel hit me with a pine cone."

Mama grabbed Lemmel by his ear. "Stop hitting your sister! What are you, a wild Indian? Behave yourself or you are never going to America!"

Lemmel ducked his head to hide his tears. His ears must be really sore if Mama had made him cry. I almost felt sorry for him.

We were outside Jibatov now. Blond-haired farmers wearing tall leather boots worked in the fields among the beets and potatoes. Papa carried Baby Hannah on his shoulders.

"When will we be at Uncle Nahum's?" Shloyme asked. His face was red and sweaty.

"We are not going to Uncle Nahum's today." Mama took his hand. "Let's sit by the river where it will be cooler."

The thick darkness of the pine forest enveloped us as we turned into the woods. Springy layers of dry needles swallowed the sound of our feet and gave off the sharp smell of resin. On winter nights, Bobbe had told scary stories about wolves eating travelers in the forest.

"Look, there's a wolf print!" Lemmel cried. "I bet they're starving after the long winter."

I moved closer to Papa.

"Wolves do not hunt during the day," Papa assured me.

"Raizel's scared of her own shadow," Lemmel taunted.

"I am not!" I spotted the glimmer of the river through the trees and began to run. Shloyme pounded after me on his fat little legs.

The banks of the Polota were lined with willows. The spring grass grew high and soft as a feather bed. Lemmel and Shloyme rolled in the daisies and threw handfuls of grass at each other. Mama gave Hannah a drink of icy river water from a tin cup she carried in her pocket and set her down under a willow tree for a nap. We all took turns drinking from the cup until the water had quenched our thirst. The water was so cold it pierced my teeth like needles.

The river looked like a pane of black glass reflecting the overhanging trees. Lemmel skipped a rock along the flat surface. It sank to the bottom like a drowned man.

"Bet I could swim across the river," Lemmel said.

"Not now you couldn't, when it's swollen with melted snow." In the summer I swam with the women in the shallows near the laundry rocks. But I never swam to the middle. It was too deep. "Remember Devoraleh's third son?"

"He was only a baby. I can swim good. Nothing will happen to me, scaredy hen." Lemmel stuck his tongue out at me. I looked at the river and shuddered. A farmer had found little Mendel's body three days later.

"Is this the River Sambayton?" Shloyme cuddled against me and stuck his thumb in his mouth.

"No, it's the Polota."

"Does it flow all the way to 'Merica?"

"I don't think so." Where did the Polota flow? It flowed past Jibatov and past Uncle Nahum's house. Leah said it flowed all the way to Lubov. I had never been that far away from home. Maybe it joined up with other rivers and flowed all the way to the ocean. I wished I had a map so I could see what countries you had to cross to get to America. And how big the ocean was.

"Tell me a story," Shloyme begged. Lemmel threw a rock so hard the ripples touched the farther shore.

I glanced at Mama and Papa. They were sitting under the willow tree with Hannah curled up between them. All I could hear was the drone of bees humming in the clover.

"Once upon a time there was a poor shoemaker," I began. "He worked from morning to night fixing shoes but barely had enough money to feed his wife and children. One night he had a dream. He saw a great bridge spanning a river with a tall soldier standing guard. In his dream, the shoemaker dug under the bridge and discovered a treasure chest full of gold and jewels."

"Were there honey cakes in the chest?" Shloyme asked.

"Are you hungry already? No honey cakes, but enough money to buy all the honey cakes in the world." Shloyme smiled. "When the shoemaker woke up, he knew it was only a dream and was very disappointed. But the next night he dreamt the same dream. And again the next night. So he decided that the dream was a sign, and he would go and search for the treasure.

"He packed a loaf of bread, kissed his wife and children under the huge oak tree next to his house, and set off down the road. He walked for days and nights until he was so tired and hungry, he almost turned back. Then one morning as he approached the big city where the king lived, he saw it."

"The treasure?" Shloyme popped his thumb out of his mouth. Lemmel had stopped throwing rocks in the river.

"No, the bridge. Guarding it was the same tall soldier he had seen in his dream! The shoemaker ran up to the soldier and asked if he could dig under the bridge. 'Why do you want to dig under the king's bridge?' the soldier asked sternly. The shoemaker told him the story of his dreams and how he believed there was a treasure buried under the bridge. When he finished his story, the tall soldier began to laugh. 'What a fool you are to believe in dreams,' said the soldier. 'Why, I too had a dream like yours. For three nights in a row I dreamt I entered a tiny hut. There were brass candlesticks on a carved wooden table that was covered with a white cloth embroidered with red flowers. Buried under the table was a chest full of gold and jewels.'

"The shoemaker began to tremble. 'Was there a big oak tree growing outside the house?' he asked.

"The soldier nodded. 'Yes. Now see how foolish you are? I don't go running all over the countryside every time I have a dream. Go home and don't disturb me anymore.'

"The shoemaker hurried home, barely stopping at night to rest a few minutes. Without a word to his wife and children, he rushed past the big oak tree growing outside his house. He removed the brass candlesticks and white embroidered cloth from the old wooden table and began to dig. And what do you think he found?"

"The treasure!" Shloyme bounced up and down.

"Yes, the treasure in his dream was in his very own house!" That was one of my favorite stories. Bobbe had told it every time she heard someone was going to America.

"Do you think there is a treasure buried under the table in our house?" Shloyme asked.

"I think if you try to dig up the floor, your stomach will go empty until the next morning."

"Raizel, Lemmel, time to go home," Mama called. Baby Hannah was sitting in Papa's lap wearing a daisy chain on her curly brown hair.

"Did you finish discussing?" Lemmel asked.

Mama frowned at him.

"Tell them, Havaleh. It is hard for them to be patient."

Mama gestured for us to sit down. I picked a long blade of grass and nibbled on the tender white stem as she spoke. "We have decided the most important thing is for Lemmel to continue his studies. Who knows if Papa will find a good cheder in America? Studies are more important."

"It's not fair!" Lemmel punched the ground with his fist. "I'm the oldest and I should go with Papa. I promise I'll go to cheder every day. I promise I'll study hard. I . . . "

"Enough! We have made up our minds," Mama said sharply.

"But it's not fair for Shloyme to go. He's too little."

"Who said anything about Shloyme?" Mama patted Shloyme's hair. "Raizel will be the one to go. She can keep house for Papa. She can do the shopping and cook his food just the way he likes. Raizel is a big girl and she can help Papa in many ways."

Suddenly everyone was staring at me. Lemmel's eyes were knife slits. Papa smiled. Mama nodded her head calmly. I felt like a bolt of lightening had smashed a huge oak tree on my head.

"Will you send me candy from 'Merica, Raizel?" Shloyme asked.

I tried to say something, but the words caught in my throat.

"Why aren't you smiling, Raizel? Everyone says America is a wonderful place. And soon we will all come too." Mama's voice was as soft as a summer breeze.

I looked at the ring of happy faces around me. I had never spent a day away from Mama. Shloyme would cry for my stories. And Baby Hannah was so little. She would forget she had a big sister. Lemmel would have no one to whisper with at night.

How could I leave them? I loved them so much. And I loved Jibatov and the relatives and helping Mama with the little ones and swimming in the Polota and picking cherries in the orchards and . . .

What would I do in America? Papa would work all day and I would be all alone with no friends and no family and no one to love and protect me.

"What's the matter, Raizel?" Papa asked.

I shook my head. How could I go on a long journey to a strange country where we knew no one? What if I got lost? I didn't know how to get to America. I didn't even know where America was.

Suddenly it was cold in the forest. What if something happened to Papa? Who would take care of me? How would I ever get home to Jibatov again?

Home. This was my home. This was my family. I didn't want to go looking for treasure. My treasure was right here.

The voice that exploded from my mouth was so loud it frightened me.

"No, not me! I want to stay here." Tears erupted from my eyes. "I don't want to go to America!"

4:

Everyone Wants to Go to America

"Will you stop crying already? How can I sleep with you sniffling like a whiney puppy?" Lemmel grumbled as we lay in bed that night. "I wish I were going instead of you."

"That's because you don't want to go to cheder." I sat up in bed and rubbed my eyes with my sleeve. "I want to stay home with Mama and the little ones. I'll be all alone in America with no family and no friends."

"You'll be with Papa."

"He'll be at work all day."

Lemmel was silent a moment. "There are plenty of children in America. You'll find someone to play with."

"But I won't know any of them or have time to play with them. Anyway, it's a long journey. What if we get sick? What if we don't have enough money? What if I get lost?" The tears overflowed again.

"Why should you get lost? Yossel says you take a train and then a ship and then you're in America. He should know. His uncle lives there and sends them money twice a year. Anyway, you worry too much, Raizel. Move over, Shloyme. You're getting too fat."

"Wanna story 'bout 'Merica." Shloyme was half-asleep.

"I already told you a story," I said. "Go to sleep."

Everything seemed so simple to Lemmel. Maybe that was because he was a boy. Were boys ever frightened? I had never really wanted to be a boy before, but now I wanted to be one. If I were a boy, I wouldn't have to go to America. No, if I were a boy, I would love to study and Mama wouldn't be afraid to send me to America. I couldn't win.

Lemmel was snoring lightly. I lay back down and folded my hands over my stomach. "Please let Mama change her mind," I whispered. "Please let me stay home."

I didn't sleep much that night. I kept dreaming about a long train like a huge black snake. Papa was waving to me from a window and I was running after the train trying to catch it, but I could never run fast enough.

"Mama, why do I have to go to America?" I asked the next day as I helped Mama with the mending. Papa had left on his peddling rounds and Lemmel was at cheder. "I want to stay home and help you."

Mama bit the thread. "Because Papa needs your help. And besides, what would we do with the extra ticket? Such a waste."

I had to go to America because of an extra ticket? "But Mama, maybe we could sell it back. Please, Mama, I don't want to go. I'm frightened."

Mama sighed and smoothed a worn linen sheet. "In Jibatov there is nothing to be frightened of? Have you forgotten the pogroms? You are the one who is afraid of the vendors in the market, who hides behind me every time a peasant boy looks at you. Such a baby you are."

"But what if I get lost, or Papa gets sick, or the ship sinks, or . . . "

"Oy, what nonsense you have in your head. What's the use of a good head if the feet can't carry it? It comes from all those stories Bobbe told you."

"But, Mama . . . "

"Raizel, my ears are tired of listening! If you would sew more and talk less, we might have time to bake a noodle pudding for dinner. You must learn to cook for Papa now. Who knows what the food is like in America? And your Papa eats less than a butterfly."

The hole in Lemmel's best shirt blurred before my eyes. I plunged the needle into the white cloth and sewed the frayed edges tightly together.

No one could change Mama's mind. Not Papa. Not Uncle Nahum, her older brother. And not me.

"Raizel, wipe your eyes. Honestly, you would think going to America was a punishment. Why, everyone wants to go to America!"

Everyone but me.

The next few weeks were even busier than the week before the Passover holiday. I helped Mama cut and sew new shirts for Papa and alter some of my cousin's old clothes for me. I learned to cook chicken soup, potato kugel, barley, carrot tzimmis—all Papa's favorite dishes so they would taste just like Mama made. Mama was always fussing at him to eat more because he was too thin. Mama taught me how to bargain in the market and how to boil the sheets and pillow cases so every stain came out. And whenever I had a few moments to myself, there was Shloyme demanding a story as if he wanted to suck every last one out of me before I left.

I barely had time to think about the journey, at least during the day. The nights were different. Lemmel fell asleep so often to my crying that he no longer noticed, just like he never noticed the roosters crowing at dawn. Our tickets were for July. Two months, I kept telling myself, you have two whole months, but the days disappeared like a piece of cheese nibbled by a mouse.

"Today we go to market," Mama announced one Thursday morning after breakfast.

"Can't I stay home and watch Shloyme and Hannah?"

"No. They must come with us. You still have much to learn about bargaining with the vendors. They'll steal the crack of a whip if you don't watch out."

Shloyme squealed with delight when he heard we were going to market. Even Baby Hannah smiled. Everybody liked going to market but me.

A group of little girls was playing on the corner clapping hands with each other and singing:

"The dove flew all around the world
And saw a lovely land,
But the land was locked
And the key was broke.
One, two, three
Out you go!"

I had known the rhyme since I was a little girl, but suddenly I saw myself as that dove flying over the ocean until I found a piece of dry land. Noah's dove had plucked an olive branch. I must remember to tell Shloyme the story of Noah's ark that evening.

"Raizel, we have no time for games!" Mama called. I ran to catch up. "Honestly, I don't know why you hate the market," Mama said pulling Hannah by the hand as Shloyme toddled alongside me.

"It's noisy and dirty," I said. "And I don't like being in a crowd of people, especially farmers. They smell like chicken manure and rotten eggs."

"Too much singing and not enough noodles. Stop acting like a baby. You are almost twelve. Soon you will be married and have babies of your own."

Tears pricked my eyes. Why didn't Mama understand that I was afraid of the peasants, afraid of the pogroms?

"Here, take this." Mama thrust a clean handkerchief into my hand and picked up Hannah. For a moment her eyes met mine. Were those tears in her eyes? No, it must be a reflection from the sunlight.

I could smell the cow manure, rotten meat, and spoiled vegetables before we saw the market. I picked my way among the stalls, careful not to step on a mushy apple or a slimy rotten egg.

Mama loved touching the warm brown eggs and fingering the first summer cherries. She smiled and looked the vendors straight in the eye when she spoke to them. Mama's parents had been innkeepers and she knew how to handle the peasants.

The Ukrainian peasants were different from the Jews of Jibatov. The women had huge rough hands and wore brightly embroidered skirts and blouses, not like the plain dark clothes Mama wore. They tossed their thick yellow braids and yelled at me if I touched even a withered onion. The men were tall as trees with woolly black beards and broken teeth. Their voices boomed in Ukrainian, a language I barely understood. But I wasn't scared of them because of the way they looked. I was scared of them because of the pogroms.

I was little, maybe Shloyme's age, the first time I heard of a pogrom. One morning I woke up to find our house full of strange people. A man lay in Papa's bed with a bloody bandage wrapped around his head. A woman with a bruised face and huge stomach sat rocking two children back and forth. Mama was putting food on the table and feeding the woman's children. I remember crying because no one gave me my breakfast.

All day the man lay moaning on Papa's bed. In the evening the woman began to scream. The children slept with me in my bed and cried all night long. When I woke up in the morning, Papa's bed was empty and the woman was nursing a tiny baby and sobbing.

I don't remember how long they stayed with us or when Papa took me outside and explained that the family had fled a pogrom in a village not far from Jibatov. Papa said a peasant boy had been found dead in the woods outside their village. The village priest said the Jews had used his blood to bake the Passover matzohs. That same night a mob of angry peasants had raged through the Jewish quarter, bursting into houses, beating and killing people.

"But matzoh is made with flour and water," I said.

"That doesn't matter to the priest. He hates Jews." Papa's voice was tired.

"Am I a Jew, Papa?"

"We are all Jews, you and Mama and baby Lemmel."

"They hate even baby Lemmel?"

Papa nodded.

"Why do they hate us?"

"They say we killed their lord, Jesus."

"I didn't hurt him, Papa. I don't know anyone named Jesus."

"Of course not. It happened almost two thousand years ago in Jerusalem. And it was the Roman soldiers who killed him. But none of that matters to the priests and the peasants. They say we steal their money and take away their land and their work. It has been like this in every country in Europe ever since the fall of the Temple in Jerusalem and the exile of the Jewish people from the Land of Israel. Always they hate us. Always we must move to someplace else, someplace safer, like America."

"I don't understand, Papa. Why are they still mad at us for something that happened so long ago?"

Papa stroked my hair. "I do not know, meydele. That is a mystery to me and to all the Jews. But don't worry. We are safe in Jibatov. The priest here is a good man."

After that I looked at the peasants differently. They might smile and greet Mama at the market. They might pat me on the head and give me a fresh apricot, but I knew that overnight they could change into a horde of murderers rampaging through the streets, beating men and women with huge sticks and stealing the Sabbath candlesticks and wine cups. I dreamed of pogroms for years and years. I still dreamed of them.

Mama nudged my shoulder and picked up a brown speckled egg. "These don't look fresh to me."

"This morning they were inside the chicken," said the seller tossing her blond braids. "If you don't want them, I have other customers."

Mama reached into her pocket and counted out a few kopecks. "If we didn't have to eat, we'd be rich," she muttered. Her bag was already full of turnips and onions and carrots.

"Mama, don't we have enough eggs at home?" I asked.

"Your Papa needs extra eggs so he will have strength for the crossing." Mama had been trying to fatten Papa up the past two months, but he remained as thin as ever.

Next we went to the Jewish butcher shop. Mama never bought chickens in the market, because the meat we ate had to be slaughtered and salted according to Jewish law to make it kosher. The butcher shop was full of chickens in wire cages. Shloyme poked his finger in a cage.

"Ouch! She pecked me!" Shloyme sucked his wounded finger as Hannah squealed with laughter.

"He probably thought your finger was an ear of corn," I said. "Remember the little boy in the story who held out a chicken bone to the witch so she would think he was too thin to cook?"

"Raizel, stop talking nonsense and listen to me," Mama said. "First, be sure the chicken is plump and healthy. You can pinch the back to feel the fat. Here, try it. And always make sure the wings and legs aren't broken, or it won't be kosher."

"Yes, Mama. Do I have to watch while he kills and plucks it too?" Chickens tasted good, but watching the butcher kill them made me feel sick.

"Today you can take Hannah outside. But in America you must stay and watch so the butcher does not substitute a skinny chicken."

"So, Haveleh, when is Reb Binyumin leaving?" the butcher asked.

"Not for another week. There is so much to do, I barely shut my eyes at night."

Only one more week! I took a long breath of air outside the shop and tried to calm my galloping thoughts.

Where would I be in two weeks time? Would I ever see Jibatov again? I couldn't understand what was so bad about Jibatov that we had to leave. I had tried asking Papa, but he only shook his head and said I would know the answer when we got to America.

Somehow I didn't believe all the stories people told about golden streets and marble houses in America. They sounded just like that: stories. Why should we trade our life here for the unknown? Here in Jibatov people knew us and respected Papa. They called him Reb Binyumin as if he were a rabbi. We weren't rich but we had our house and yard and horse and wagon. And there were no pogroms in Jibatov. Why couldn't we just stay here?

"Pretty."

I woke up to the noise of the market. Hannah was holding a ripe red cherry. I grabbed her hand away. We had no money for cherries.

"If you don't buy, don't touch!" the seller snapped at me.

Just then a blond-haired boy approached the fruit stand. He waited until the seller turned his back. Suddenly he grabbed a handful of cherries and began to run. Quick as a blink, the peasant jumped from behind the stand and grabbed him by the shirt.

"Dirty thief!" He slammed the boy's head with his fist. The cherries scattered in the dirt. Before I could stop her, Hannah rushed to pick them up. The boy pushed her away and struggled to his feet. Blood dribbled from his nose, mixing with the dirt on his face. The seller spat in the dirt and went back to his stall.

"Here, your nose is bleeding." I handed the boy Mama's handkerchief.

The boy wiped his nose and crushed the handkerchief in the dirt under his bare foot. "Take your handkerchief, you filthy Jew-girl!"

"Raizel, why is Hannah crying?" Mama asked as she walked out of the shop.

She listened to my explanation and sighed. "Pick up the handkerchief. I have told you to stay away from those children."

"But I only wanted to help him, Mama. Why did he act like that?"

"Why does a crow have feathers? Why does a pig like mud? Peasants hate Jews, even the children. Come, the little ones are tired and we have much to do. Your Uncle Nahum and his family are coming for the Sabbath."

The thought of seeing my cousins made my feet dance all the way home. Uncle Nahum owned a lumber mill several kilometers outside of town. When we went to visit for the holidays, I would sleep with my cousin Leah, who was a year older than me, and we would whisper together until we fell asleep.

"Where will they sleep?" I asked. They couldn't ride home after the Sabbath began.

"There is always room for family," Mama said. "Nahum wants to give Papa advice about the journey. Imagine, he has been all the way to St. Petersburg! Now hurry. The house has to be extra clean. You know your Aunt Freida."

I made a face. A peasant woman did Aunt Freida's cooking and cleaning. She had nothing to do all day but embroider tablecloths for Sarah's dowry. Maybe that was why she was so fat. She reminded me of a plump chicken ready for the oven. She picked at things like a chicken, too.

"Raizel sweetie, let me look at you," Aunt Freida said the next afternoon. She was sipping tea from the samovar and nibbling the almond cookies Mama had made especially for the guests. "Hmmm. You are tall like your Mama. You shouldn't grow too tall. Men don't like tall wives."

Papa was short and he liked Mama. But I knew better than to argue with Aunt Freida.

"You have clear brown eyes and good teeth. That is important. Too bad you don't have your Mama's beauty. It's all that curly hair. Look how your braids are coming undone. My girls are lucky to have nice straight hair. What do you think, Sarah?"

"I read you can straighten your hair using a hot brick wrapped in flannel. That's what they do in Lubov." Sarah tossed her smooth braid over her shoulder. "Mama, may I go out for a walk? I want to say hello to Taibeleh."

"She wants to say hello to Moyshe, Taibeleh's big brother," Leah whispered to me. Sarah was sixteen. Her parents had already consulted a matchmaker to find her a husband. Uncle Nahum wanted his eldest daughter to marry a scholar and Moyshe worked in his parents' hat store. Uncle Nahum would never agree to the match and Sarah knew it. Papa had no money to support a Torah scholar as a husband for me. I would just have to accept what I could get. I hoped he would be young. Handsome would be nice, too.

Leah grabbed my hand and pulled me outside. "Come, let's go for a walk. I haven't seen you since Passover."

"I can't. I have to help Mama get dinner ready."

"Then let's sit here for a while. Aunt Haveleh won't miss you while my mama is telling her all the latest gossip."

I sat down on the front stoop where Mama could find me when she needed me. Leah sat down too, carefully smoothing her skirt so it wouldn't wrinkle.

"Come, I want to hear all about America! Aren't you excited? I'm so jealous. I wish we could all go to America, but Papa says that we aren't poor like you, so we don't have to go."

I bit my lip. I loved Leah, but she stepped on other people's feelings like you step on an ant. She chattered on about her new dresses and piano lessons and the gold earrings Uncle Nahum would give her for her birthday.

"Mama brought you my best old dress so you'll have something nice to wear in America," Leah continued. "Just think! My dresses will be in America while I'm stuck here in Jibatov! It's not fair."

"It's not fair that I have to leave Mama and the family and go to America," I said.

Leah stared. "I don't understand you. I would give anything to be going to America. They say everyone goes to the seaside for vacations. And they buy new clothes every week."

"I don't care about those things, even if they're true."

"Of course they're true. Everyone knows that." Leah tossed her head. "You can be so stubborn, Raizel Balaban. Maybe I won't give you the going-away present I brought you." She pulled a little package out of her skirt pocket and put it on my lap.

I smiled and unwrapped the paper carefully. Inside was a book, my very own book! I traced the letters on the cover with my finger: "Sh . . . l . . . m . . . A . . . l . . . ch . . . m."

"It's by Sholem Aleichem," Leah said. "I already read it."

"Thank you so much!" I threw my arms around Leah. "I never had my own book before! I just wish I could read it. Do you think girls can go to school in America?"

"I don't know, but I knew you wanted a book. Maybe your Papa will have time to teach you to read it on the boat. Just think! You'll sit in an easy chair in the sunshine watching the waves and reading your book like a baroness!"

I hugged the book. "It's the best present anyone ever gave me! Oh Leah, I'm going to miss you so much." Suddenly my eyes overflowed with tears.

"I'm going to miss you too. Maybe I'll marry a rich husband and we'll come to visit you."

We hugged each other tightly.

"Raizel, come help me set the table," Mama called.

At dinner the chicken was extra plump and the carrot tzimmis was studded with raisins. Everyone was laughing and eating and praising

Mama's cooking, even Aunt Freida. We had stuffed gefilte fish and horse-radish so hot it made my eyes water, just like on Passover. Everyone said Mama was the best cook in Jibatov. I tried to follow her instructions, but somehow her chicken soup tasted like liquid gold while mine tasted like hot sweat and her potato kugel melted in your mouth while mine sat in your stomach like a brick. Maybe I would marry a rich man too, and have a hired cook!

Uncle Nahum drank glass after glass of the wine he had brought while he told us about his travels to St. Petersburg. I was enjoying myself until they began telling stories of America.

"Did you hear this one?" asked Uncle Nahum nibbling the last morsels of meat from his drumstick. He was as fat as two Papas, but not as fat as Aunt Freida. "Two men who had met on the boat going to America meet again on the street in New York.

"'How's business?' asks the first.

"'All right,' answers the second.

"'In that case, can you lend me five dollars?'

"'Why should I lend you five dollars? I hardly know you,' says the second.

"'Now isn't that strange,' says the first man. 'In my town in Russia, people wouldn't lend me money because they knew me. In America they won't lend me money because they don't know me.'"

"Raizel, why aren't you laughing?" asked Leah, wiping the tears from her eyes. "Don't you think my papa's story is funny?"

I shook my head. How were we going to live in America? All Papa knew was peddling.

"I heard a good one just the other day," Papa said. "A poor man comes to New York and tries to get a job as the caretaker in a synagogue.

"'Can you read and write?' asks the head of the synagogue.

"'No,' says the man.

"'Then you can't have the job. In America even the caretaker must know how to read and write.'

"The man hangs his head and leaves. Finally he finds work. He saves his money and buys property. Soon he's a rich man. One day he goes to the bank to finance a big land deal. The president of the bank is happy to give him the loan.

"'Write your own check,' he says, handing the man a pen.

"'I don't know how to write,' says the man. 'I can only sign my name.'

"'That's amazing,' says the bank president. 'If you've become so rich without knowing how to write, just think what you would have been today if you had known how to write.'

"'Yes, yes,' says the man. 'I would have been caretaker of the synagogue!'"

When everyone had finished laughing but me, I helped Mama clear away the dinner plates.

"Tell them the story about the yeshiva students." Aunt Freida poked Uncle Nahum. "I split a seam laughing when you told it to me."

Uncle Nahum glanced at Papa and shook his head. "I don't remember it well enough."

"What nonsense! You told it only yesterday! I'd tell it myself, but I always ruin a story."

Uncle Nahum sighed. I wondered why he didn't want to tell this particular story. "The Czar's recruiters come to a yeshiva and draft all the yeshiva students into the army. While they're in training, the students amaze the officers with their excellent marksmanship on the rifle range. They never miss the target even once! So when war breaks out, the yeshiva students are put in the front line.

"When the first line of enemy soldiers appears, the commanding officer calls out: 'Ready . . . aim . . . fire.' Nothing happens. 'Fire, I said!'

yells the officer. 'Didn't you hear me?' Again nothing happens. 'What is the matter with you?' the angry officer shouts. 'Why don't you fire?'

"One of the students answers quietly, 'Can't you see? There are people in the way. Someone might get hurt.'"

This time I joined in the laughter with everyone else. But as I put the honey cake on the table, I noticed the strangest thing.

Everyone was laughing but Papa.

5

The Leaving

Suddenly it was the day before leaving. The mouse had nibbled my two months of cheese and left me only the tiniest crumb. And I couldn't even have that crumb to myself.

"Raizel, where are you going?" Mama called. "I told you to lay your clothes on the bed."

"Mama, I did that this morning."

Mama rubbed the pinched line on her forehead. "Then help me mend Papa's winter coat. The pocket is coming loose."

"Mama, please . . . " Every time I thought we were finished, Mama found something else to do. All week she had stayed up half the night mending clothes that didn't have a single hole. She cleaned and cooked until Papa shook his finger at her.

"That shawl you're mending will be your shroud if you keep working like this." Papa's voice was angry, but his hand squeezed her shoulder as he spoke. Mama kissed his hand. I turned my head away so as not to disturb their privacy.

This time it was just too much. "Mama, please," I touched her arm. "I want to say good-bye to Jibatov."

Mama looked away. Were those tears in her brown eyes? "Go. But only for a few minutes. We still have to bring in the bedding and fix the krupnik for dinner and . . ."

Before she could finish her sentence, I was out of the house, dodging Shloyme and Hannah.

"I'm coming too!" Shloyme called. Mama grabbed his hand before he could follow me. For once Mama understood I needed to be alone, and I was grateful. Shloyme had been such a devil today. He stuck his finger into the freshly churned butter and spilled his milk on Hannah. Mama had slapped his hand and sent him to bed where he cried until I told him a story. Everyone had his own way of reacting to our departure. Mama worked day and night. Shloyme demanded constant attention. Lemmel disappeared from the house for hours, and even Mama had no time to check if he went to cheder or not. Hannah sat in a corner sucking her thumb, and Papa ran all around town making arrangements and listening to advice. And me? During the day I tried hard to learn everything Mama taught me, and at night I cried into my feather pillow. Good thing geese go out in the rain!

I walked quickly past the low wooden houses, the synagogue, the market square. Soon I was in the orchards on the edge of Jibatov. We loved to walk here on the Sabbath. Lemmel would gather green apples to throw at Reb Yankel, while I sat with the little ones and told them stories.

Here was the tree Lemmel had climbed when he was six. He had fallen out and broken his arm. A woodcutter carried him home. Papa put Lemmel to bed and gave the woodcutter a schnapps to drink while Mama ran to the pharmacist for some powders. There was no doctor in Jibatov.

Here was the ancient oak tree with a trunk so wide it took ten people to encircle it. There was a hollow in the tree big enough for a small child.

And here was the wild cherry tree, its branches heavy with midsummer fruit. I bit into the firm red flesh and rolled the sweetness around my tongue. I would bring some to Shloyme.

"Hey you, stop stealing those cherries!"

My heart skipped. The boy from the market square stood in front of me, both hands planted on his hips.

"Jew girl, what do you think you're doing?" He thrust his face close to mine. His front teeth were broken and he smelled of garlic.

"Picking cherries." Was that my voice? It sounded like a kitten's whisper.

"Well, get out of here! That tree is mine!"

I wanted to tell him the tree was wild and didn't belong to anyone. I wanted to tell him that this was my last day in Jibatov and my last cherry. I wanted to ask why he hated me so.

Instead, I turned and walked quickly out of the woods, the spot between my shoulder blades tingling with fear. Please let me go. Please don't hurt me, I prayed silently, remembering another time years before.

I must have been about five. Mama had sent me out in the snow to bring a pot of soup to Mrs. Stein, who was sick. As I carefully carried the soup across the snow-packed street, a group of boys ran by throwing snowballs at each other. They shouted "Jew girl" and I felt a snowball hit the center of my back. Hard. Another hit my cheek and I dropped the soup tureen. The boys howled with laughter as I tried to pick up the onions, turnips and carrots that lay scattered in the snow.

I ran home to Mama, the soup pot empty, blood streaming down my cheek from the rock hidden in the snowball. Only when I was safely home did I begin to cry. Mama rocked me in her arms and sang my favorite song until my tears were gone:

> "Under little Judah's cradle
> Stands a pure white goat,
> The goat went off to market;
> That will be your calling
> Raisins and almonds
> Sleep, little Judah, sleep."

Now I hummed the song to myself as I walked out of the woods. This time I didn't run to Mama. I strode with my head high and my heart beating like a soldier's drum until I was back in town. Only then did I wipe away the tears tickling my cheeks.

My legs were still shaking when I got home.

"Raizel, where have you been?"

Mama was standing with an armful of Papa's shirts and a deep worry line in her forehead.

"I went to say goodbye, Mama. I went to the grove with the cherry tree and . . ."

"Did you bring me cherries?" Shloyme grabbed my skirt.

"Not this time," I said.

"Raizel is mean. I hate you!" He hit my arm and burst into tears.

"Don't mind him, meydele," Mama said. "He wanted to come with you to Lubov, but I told him it was too far away, so he got mad. You know how he is."

I followed Shloyme into the bedroom. He was huddled against the wall sobbing.

"I'm sorry I didn't bring you cherries," I said softly. "I'm sorry I'm going to America and won't be able to tell you any more stories."

Shloyme turned over and looked at me out of startled brown eyes. "Will I see you again, ever?"

"Of course. Papa will work hard and send Mama tickets for all of you."

"Then you can tell me a story when I come. Next week."

"No, Shloyme, it won't be next week. It will take months and months for Papa to earn enough money." Years. My friend Rivka and her family had been waiting over five years. Today Rivka had confided that she no longer remembered what her father looked like. I couldn't bear not seeing my family for so long!

"I won't let you go."

"I don't want to go, Shloyme, but I have to."

"No, you don't." He grabbed my hand. "You can stay here with me."

I had to smile. "Now Shloyme, what would happen if children didn't obey their parents and I didn't obey Mama and Papa? The world would be a terrible place, as bad as the house haunted by the goblin."

"What house? Tell me the story!" Shloyme demanded.

"I have to help Mama get ready."

Shloyme's lower lip swelled like a bee sting.

"I'll tell it quickly," I said. "Once upon a time in a certain house in a certain village, a goblin lived in the basement. Everything would have been fine if he had stayed in the basement, but he loved to come upstairs and bother the people who lived in the house. Do you know what he did?"

"What?" Shloyme held his breath.

"He tipped over the water barrel. He chased the chickens until they were too frightened to lay eggs. And he even put salt instead of sugar in the porridge."

"Did he stick his finger into the butter and lick it off?"

"I'm afraid so. Thank you for reminding me. Well, as you can imagine, the people who lived in that house didn't like the goblin one little bit. They hung charms in the windows and wrote holy names on the walls, but nothing stopped the goblin's mischief.

"One day a holy man came to spend the night. All night long he heard loud knocking on his window. The fire went out in his fireplace. Someone laughed in the closet. But the holy man ignored everything and kept on praying. Suddenly, the goblin blew out the holy man's candles so he couldn't read his prayer book.

"'Be gone, evil one!' cried the holy man, finally angry.

"The goblin just laughed. The holy man couldn't see him, but he could sense his presence. He picked up his prayer book and flung it at the goblin. When the holy words touched the goblin, all his evil power vanished. He flew right up the chimney and never ever came back."

Shloyme looked at the floor and rubbed his eyes with his fists. I put my arm around his shoulder. "Don't feel bad. Mama knows you won't lick the butter again. Or spill milk on Hannah. You must behave yourself when I'm gone and help Mama, just like I do."

"But I'll forget all your stories and Mama doesn't know any." Shloyme's shoulders heaved. I wiped his runny nose and gave him a hug. Suddenly I felt a strong hand squeeze my shoulder.

"I'm sorry, Mama. I didn't mean to make Shloyme cry."

"I know, meydele. I've packed all the clothes and Papa should be back from Uncle Nahum's any minute." Mama leaned against the wall. Her face was pale and there were dark circles under her eyes.

"Mama, who will help you when we're gone?"

"Nahum will help us until Papa can send some money. He'll sell the wagon and Bunchik too, if we have to. We don't need much."

"I hope we don't have to sell Bunchik. You know what Bobbe used to say: if you can't afford chicken, herring will do."

"You miss her, don't you?"

I nodded.

"I miss her, too. I wish she were still here to help me when you're gone."

"Lemmel can help."

"Lemmel? Help like his I don't need." She looked at me, her eyes filling with tears. "You're my big girl. I couldn't ask for better help."

"Mama . . . " Suddenly I was in her arms, hugging her like I had when I was no bigger than Shloyme. "Mama, I don't want to leave you and go far away to a strange place. Please, Mama . . . "

"Shhh, meydele. I know. But it's all arranged." Mama touched my chin and tilted my head to hers. "You must be brave and keep your feet on the ground. Promise me you'll stop filling your head with those stories. I need you to be practical and help Papa."

"I promise, Mama. I'll do everything I can to help so you can all come over soon." Even as I spoke I wondered how I could possibly keep my promise. Stories flew into my head without invitation. Before they had been welcome guests, but now . . . ? I would just have to shut the door. A promise is a promise.

The first neighbor arrived as we sat down to supper. It was Lyuba bringing a package of fresh baked cookies "for the journey." She was followed by Hirshel and Sholem and then by Yente and her children. Soon it seemed like half the Jews in Jibatov were crowded into our little house, all talking at once, all giving a last piece of advice.

"You should take plenty of feather bedding. I hear they don't have good quality feathers in America," said Hirshel, folding his arms over his fat stomach.

"Nonsense! In America they have everything, only better. But take plenty of lemons for the crossing. They keep your teeth white. The Americans like white teeth." Yente showed her own teeth, which were the color of bread crusts.

"Remember to go to Rivington Street when you get there. That's where my cousin Sollie lives. And you should tell him to write his wife once in a while!" Lyuba clucked like a worried hen.

"Here is the letter for Yossel, my ungrateful son," said Hayke. "I don't have his address, but you can ask his old neighbors. He wrote he was going to Fiddlefia, or something. That was nine months ago and I haven't heard a word from him since. Do you think they have man-eating Indians in Fiddlefia?"

Everyone had a relative in America. Everyone knew something about America. Everyone had an opinion about what kind of work to do in America. Everyone had an opinion about what to say to the Americans so they would let you into America. Two Jews, three opinions, as they say. Who knew what to believe? Soon my head was aching from all the noise. The supper plates were long gone, but still they sat talking.

"Raizel, could you put Hannah and Shloyme to bed?" Mama was leaning against Papa's shoulder.

Hannah fell asleep the moment I tucked the sheet around her. My little sister. I kissed her curly head and combed her silky ringlets with my fingers. We were the only ones with curly hair in the family. Would she remember her big sister the next time we met?

Shloyme was sitting in bed wide-awake and waiting for me. "Tell me a story," he demanded.

"I told you one before." Did my promise to Mama mean I couldn't tell stories to Shloyme anymore? He would never agree to go to sleep without a story.

"What do you want to hear?"

"About 'Merica!"

"Shloyme, I don't want to tell a story about 'Merica." I hadn't told him about America since the Friday evening we sat waiting for Papa. It seemed so long ago—before I knew I was leaving.

"You promised! I want to hear about 'Merica!"

I sighed. "All right." Shloyme always got his way. I guess I spoiled him like Bobbe spoiled me. Why is it called spoiling when you show someone how much you love them?

I told Shloyme about the wonderful houses, the wonderful trees, and the wonderful food in America. I listed every single thing he loved to eat. I told him once, and then I told him everything all over again, until his eyes closed and his breath rose in tiny sighs. I disentangled my hand from his and kissed him on the cheek. "Good-bye, my little brother. I love you so much."

"Are you crying again?" Lemmel asked. I hadn't seen Lemmel at dinner. I felt like I hadn't seen him for days. He undressed and joined

Shloyme under the covers. "Mama said we have to go to bed. And I have to go to cheder tomorrow even though you and Papa are leaving. I get punished and you get to go to America. It's not fair!"

"Nothing is fair."

Lemmel sat up in bed. "I don't understand you, Raizel. I would give anything to go to America. What's so terrible?"

Lemmel would never understand. For him, going to America was a big adventure. For me, it meant leaving everything I loved. "I'm tired. I don't want to talk about it anymore," I said. It was true. I was tired of hearing about America, tired of thinking about America. When Mama came to wake me in the morning, I would tell her I was just too tired to go. Papa couldn't carry me to America, could he?

"Lemmel?"

"What?"

"Are you still mad at me?"

"Yes. No. I don't know. I'd give anything to be going in your place."

"But it's not my fault."

"I know. But I can't help being mad."

"Lemmel?"

"What?"

"Please don't be mad. I'm going to miss you."

"Come on, Raizel, are you crying again?" Lemmel pulled the covers over his ears.

"G'night."

"G'night." I shut my eyes and tried to sleep.

The voices in the next room sank softer and softer until they sounded like a lullaby. But instead of singing about raisins and almonds, they sang: "America . . . America . . . America . . ."

6
Inside the Whale

"Raizel, time to get up," Mama whispered. I was walking down a street filled with marble houses and orange trees. All night I had been knocking on doors looking for my house, but no one could understand what I said. And now Mama was here to save me!

Mama shook my shoulder.

I pried open my eyes. It was still dark in the room, too dark to see Mama's face, too dark to think. "I'm tired. 'Wanna sleep."

"Shhh. Fishel will be here any minute. Get dressed and come into the kitchen."

A long chill passed through me like wind blowing down an endless corridor. It was morning.

I stumbled into my clothes. I was shaking so hard I couldn't button my dress. I stepped into the kitchen where the lamp glowed in the dim pre-dawn. Papa smiled at me over his bowl of barley porridge, but the smile didn't reach his eyes.

"Mama, my head hurts."

Mama put her hand on my forehead. "Cool as a snowflake. Drink some hot milk. I've put chicory in it just the way you like."

I picked up the cup of steaming milk and my stomach turned inside out.

"What's the matter? You have to eat something. You have a long day ahead of you." Mama pushed the cup back into my hands.

"Leave her, Haveleh. We will eat something in Lubov before we catch the train."

I looked at Papa gratefully.

"Aren't Lemmel and Shloyme going to say good bye?"

Mama's lips tightened. "That I do not need. I will have my hands full enough later."

"Haveleh . . ."

"I know. I know." Her hands fluttered like frightened doves. "I hear the horses. Oh Binyumin!"

I ran to the window. Fishel, the waggoner, was just turning the corner between the rows of sleeping houses. I turned around. Papa was holding Mama and rocking her gently.

"Shhh. It will be all right. You know I have to go. I have no choice. God will look after us. I will write you from Brody when we cross the border. I will work hard and we will be together again before Shloyme is old enough to start cheder. I promise."

Why did Papa have no choice? I stored the question away to ask when we had more time.

Mama shook herself and shivered. She seemed to grow taller. "Do you have the tickets? The passports?"

Papa patted a package inside his black coat.

"Raizel, get your shawl. It is chilly outside. You are in charge of the food baskets. You have enough cookies to last you a month!"

Papa picked up our two wooden suitcases and started for the door. My feet froze to the floor. For two months I had been telling myself that everything would be all right, that I still had time. And now it was now. Jibatov, Mama, Shloyme, Lemmel and Hannah were dissolving like a lump of sugar in hot tea. "Mama!"

Mama's arms were around me. She kissed my hair and rocked me back and forth. "My baby. My big girl. Be brave, my sweet one, be brave." For a moment I felt warm and safe and loved. If only the moment were forever and time ran backwards: the sugar returning to the spoon, the tears receding into my eyes. Then Mama tore herself away, and the cold rushed in as Papa opened the door.

"Come, Raizel," Papa called. "Fishel is waiting."

"About time," grumbled Fishel as Papa lifted me into the wagon. He flicked his whip over the bony back of his horse. "I have things to do, important things like buying the almonds and dried fruit for the wedding next week and mailing these letters for the butcher's wife and . . . "

"Not as important as going to America," Papa whispered in my ear. I smiled through my tears. Fishel was always complaining.

Papa handed me the two food baskets and joined Fishel. Mama ran out and tossed up my woolen shawl. She didn't look at me.

The wagon lurched forward.

Mama stood in the gateway clutching her shawl around her shoulders. Tears poured down her face.

The door opened and Lemmel burst out of the house in his nightshirt. "Papa, Raizel, good bye!" He ran after the wagon in his bare feet, his long side curls flapping like goat's ears.

"Lemmel, get back here! What will the neighbors think?" Mama took off after him, raising her long skirt so she could run better.

I laughed through my tears. Mama would paddle him good for going out in his nightshirt.

"Raizel, I'm not mad at you! Good-bye! Good-bye!" he shouted as the wagon picked up speed. I waved my hand and Lemmel waved back. The last I saw was Lemmel waving in the dust as Mama ran yelling after him.

The early morning chill dissolved as the sun climbed in the sky. Riding in a wagon was so much faster than walking. In the time it took me to walk to the well, we were out in the fields past Jibatov. Farmers came out of their huts, stretched, and strode to their fields of corn, beets, and barley. Barefooted children stared at us as we rode by.

"No rain for a long time," said Fishel. "It's not good for the harvest. The peasants will be hungry."

"How can they be hungry when there is so much barley?" I stood, holding on to Papa's shoulders and pointing at the golden fields.

"The barley belongs to the landowners," explained Papa. "The peasants work the land and only get a small portion of the harvest."

"Cholera!" Fishel spat in the road. "The rich get richer, and the poor starve. That's the way it is in Russia."

I wondered why he didn't leave for America. He had no wife and children. Fishel had been a soldier in the Russian army. When he got out he was already forty, too old to start a family. With the little money he had, he bought a horse and wagon. People in Jibatov paid him to carry packages to and from Lubov.

I sat back down on a bundle of turnips. Papa and Fishel talked on the driver's seat and the breeze blew me an occasional word—"America . . . Czar . . . border." The sun rose higher in the sky and I used my shawl as a shade. By the time the wagon clopped into Lubov, I was hungry and thirsty and covered with dust. And I had to admit I was excited. I had never been this far from Jibatov before, and even know-it-all Leah had never ridden on a train.

The wagon rode through the outskirts of town: the same run-down shacks, the same pigs wallowing in the mud and chicken droppings. Why, Lubov looked just like Jibatov! I half-expected to see the blond-haired boy with the broken teeth leering at me from a yard. But I had left him behind in Jibatov along with the insults and the ice balls and the pogroms. There were no pogroms in America, everyone said. I prayed they were right.

Double Crossing

In the center of town the houses were taller and built of stone. I caught a whiff of rotting cabbage and burnt chicken feathers as we passed through the market square and pulled up in front of a low yellow building.

"Down you go, little lady. You don't want to miss your train to America." Fishel's strong arms lifted me from the wagon. He handed down the suitcases and baskets to Papa. Papa held out a few rubles, but Fishel shook his head. "I was going to Lubov anyway. Let it be my mitzvah for the day, Reb Balaban."

I smiled up at Fishel. Papa was so tiny next to him. Years of study in the cheder and yeshiva had ruined Papa's eyes and curved his back. Both Papa and Fishel had thick black beards and curling side locks, but while Fishel wore the rough linen shirt and full pants of a peasant, Papa was dressed in a long black coat, black pants, and a white shirt. The fringes of his prayer shawl hung below his coat as he bent to help Fishel with the baggage. On his head he wore a heavy felt hat and beneath it a black skullcap which he never took off, because a man must always cover his head in the presence of God.

I looked at the people milling around the station. Papa was the only one dressed in black, except for an old man with a long white beard.

I had never thought about how Papa looked before. All the Jewish men in Jibatov dressed like Papa. In Jibatov you were either a Russian peasant or a religious Jew. And there were a few men like Fishel who belonged to neither world. I wondered how people dressed in America.

Tonight Fishel would be back in Jibatov. Where would I be?

"Raizel, stop dreaming and watch the luggage," Papa said.

I sat down on the suitcases while Papa joined the line of people at the ticket booth. The line crept forward like a spider inching toward its prey. Finally Papa came back counting his change and clutching two cardboard tickets. His face was screwed in a frown.

"What is it, Papa?"

"The tickets cost more than I thought. We have to watch our rubles or we will get no farther than Brody." Papa's mouth smiled, but his eyes were serious. I knew that look. Mama wore it when Papa handed her the money he had earned during the week.

"Don't worry, Papa. In America we'll be rich. We'll have as much money as Uncle Nahum. Even more!"

"Careful, Raizel. If you wait for challah, you lose the black bread."

"Papa, did you make that up?"

Papa winked at me and opened his prayer book.

"Could I have some of that black bread, Papa? I'm hungry."

Papa shut his book and slapped his cheek. "Oy, I forgot all about eating. It will be your job to remind me to sleep and eat, Raizeleh. Sometimes I'm so busy studying, I forget."

He cut me a thick slice of black bread and another for himself. Then he cut slivers of hard yellow cheese and laid them on the bread. Mama said Papa even read his prayer book while he was driving Bunchik, but Papa denied it. That was why she expected me to be the practical one and not cloud my head with stories.

Suddenly there was a terrifying shriek. I grabbed Papa's arm as the benches trembled and the station windows rattled.

"Hurry, the train is coming!" Papa grabbed the suitcases.

I stuffed the last crumbs of bread into my mouth and followed Papa to the edge of the platform. A violent wind engulfed me as the locomotive roared into the station. Ashes blew into my face. Dirty windows like a thousand eyes glared down. The train looked like a deep sea creature about to swallow us whole.

It came to a shuddering stop and we pulled our luggage up the steps and into the third-class compartment. Inside it smelled like an outhouse mixed with sweat and vodka. The passengers were squashed against one another on narrow wooden benches.

"Papa, where do we sit?"

"Here, on the suitcases."

People were sitting on their baggage up and down the aisle. Some were even sitting on the wooden floor, which was littered with dirty straw. I perched on the edge of my suitcase.

The train started with a jerk and Papa grabbed my shoulder before I could fall on the filthy floor. Ugh, I didn't want to dirty Leah's almost-new blue skirt and embroidered blouse the first day.

A conductor dressed in a dark brown uniform with shiny brass buttons examined our tickets and continued on, stepping over people and sacks of potatoes until he reached the next car.

"Papa, how long to our stop?"

"Seven or eight hours." Papa put on his wire-rimmed spectacles and began to read his prayer book.

Seven or eight hours! It would be night before we got there. Where would we sleep? If only I had a seat near the window so I could watch the scenery. All I could see were the dusty boots of a farmer and the worn leather shoes of a woman holding a basket of eggs on her lap.

If only Lemmel were here so that I had someone to talk to. Or Shloyme so I could tell him stories. That would pass the time.

Let's see, what story would I tell Shloyme? The Passover story! I would tell him about the Israelites escaping from slavery in Egypt, only Russia was Egypt, and we were the Israelites. And instead of the Red Sea, we had to cross the Atlantic Ocean.

The hours passed as I told stories in my head and watched the other passengers. At one stop a girl about my age got on with her mother and sat down on a box opposite me. She had fat cheeks and pale hair braided into stiff sausages. Her mother carried a basket, which wiggled and jerked. I tried to guess what was inside. A baby pig? A family of mice?

Just then a pair of black beady eyes peeked over the edge of the basket. "Buck, buck, buck!" complained a cross brown hen.

I smiled. The hen looked just like Aunt Freida in a bad mood. The girl giggled and smiled at me. Her mother swatted the basket with a rough hand and the hen disappeared. I kept my eyes on it. Sure enough, a few minutes later the hen poked her head out and clucked noisily. This time we both exploded with laughter. Papa glanced at us over his prayer book.

Suddenly the train shifted tracks with a jerk. The terrified hen flew out of the basket and over the heads of the startled passengers.

"Catch her, catch her!" cried the mother in Ukrainian, knocking over two suitcases and a basket of apples as she leaped to catch the flapping fowl. A woman screamed as the hen grazed her head and landed on a wooden rack above the window.

"Down! Get down you stupid old hen!" The woman threw an apple at the hen. She squawked into the air, knocking off the high felt hat of a soldier. The girl threw herself on the hen as she bumped to the floor. Half the passengers were yelling in anger while the other half laughed so hard they almost fell off their seats.

"Mama, I've got her!"

The mother grabbed the hen, tied her feet together, and thrust her head first into the basket, muttering curses to herself. A few minutes later the train pulled into another station and mother, daughter and hen got off the train. As she passed, the girl winked at me and nodded at the feet sticking out of the basket. I waved farewell. Maybe if their trip had been longer, we could have become friends. I never had a non-Jewish friend before.

The time seemed to pass even slower now. "Papa, how much longer?" It must be late afternoon already.

Papa closed his book and rubbed his forehead. "Reading on a train is not like reading in the synagogue."

"Papa, will you teach me how to read? I mean on the boat when we have time. Leah gave me a book for a going-away present. I can read the letters, but not the words."

Papa smiled. "Of course. If only Lemmel had the thirst like you do."

"The thirst?"

"The love of learning. The love of learning and the love of God make one a great scholar and a wise man. Plus a rich father-in-law helps." He smiled.

"Maybe there will be a school for girls in America," I said. "Then I can read the Bible and learn history and all about the world." Wouldn't it be wonderful?

Papa shook his head. "I need you to keep house. Who will do the shopping and cooking and cleaning if you sit all day in school? What am I, a rich man who can afford twenty servants?"

I bit my lip. "But maybe you'll find a good job and we'll have lots of money and . . ."

"And if Hirshel had wheels, he would be a wagon."

I giggled. Papa sounded like Mama.

"That reminds me of a story I heard last week," Papa said with a smile. "You know how the people of Chelm are such worriers? One day they called a meeting to do something about the problem of worrying. They decided that Yossel, the shoemaker, would receive one ruble a week to do all the worrying for the people in town.

"Everyone was about to vote on the idea when a wise man stood up and asked the fatal question: 'If Yossel earns one ruble a week, what will he have to worry about?'"

I burst out laughing and Papa joined me.

"I know a Chelm story, too," I said. There were many stories about the foolish people who lived in the town of Chelm. Papa looked at me expectantly.

"A man named Zelig had never been outside of Chelm. One day at the synagogue he met a rich merchant who told him all about the wonders of Warsaw. 'I must see Warsaw,' Zelig said. He packed a bag with bread and cheese and said goodbye to his wife and son. 'I'm going to Warsaw,' he announced.

"'But you have no money to ride there,' said his wife.

"'Then I'll walk.'

"'But you'll wear out your shoes.'

"'I'll carry them in my hands. Good bye!' said Zelig and began his journey.

"He walked a long time until he felt hungry. He sat down in the shade of a tree at a fork in the road. After he ate his bread and cheese he felt sleepy. 'I'll take a little nap before I continue to Warsaw,' he said. 'But I'm at a fork in the road. One road goes to Warsaw and one road goes to Chelm. How will I know which way to go when I wake up?'

"Suddenly he had an idea. He set his shoes in the road with the toes pointing in the direction of Warsaw. Then he lay down and fell asleep."

The train jerked and I looked up. Papa was watching me intently. I felt my cheeks grow hot. I had told stories to Shloyme and Hannah, but I had never told a story to Papa before. I always sat and listened hard when the grownups told stories, so I could remember them later. And then there was my promise to Mama.

"Please continue, Raizel. I have never heard this story before."

I took a deep breath. For a moment I couldn't remember where I was.

"Well, let's see. Yes, while Zelig was sleeping, a peasant passed and saw the shoes in the road. 'Good luck!' he thought. 'I'll take these shoes home with me.' But when he picked them up, he saw they were full of holes. 'Cholera! Who needs these?' He put them back in the road. Only now they were pointing to Chelm, instead of to Warsaw.

"When Zelig woke up, he picked up the shoes and began walking down the road. After a time he saw the first houses of a town.

"'How strange,' he said. 'Why the houses in Chelm look just like this. But I know I'm in Warsaw because the shoes were pointing in this direction.'

"As he walked along, he saw a man standing in the bathhouse doorway. The man waved and smiled at him.

"'How strange,' Zelig said. 'That man looks just like the bathhouse attendant in Chelm.'

"He came to a street and stopped in front of one of the houses.

"'How strange,' he said. 'That house looks exactly like my house in Chelm.'

Suddenly a woman came out of the house. 'Zelig, what are you standing there for? Dinner is ready.'

"'Why that woman looks just like my wife Rachel,' thought Zelig. He followed her into the house.

"'If I didn't know I was in Warsaw, I would think this was my own house,' thought Zelig. 'The soup even tastes too salty like my wife Rachel's.'

"Zelig thought and thought until he came up with an explanation. 'I know! Chelm is exactly like Warsaw. But that means there must be a man in Warsaw named Zelig who looks just like me. I wonder where he is and why he doesn't come home. I'll just pretend to be him until he arrives.'

"And to this day Zelig is waiting for the other Zelig to come home. And missing his own family back in Chelm."

Papa was silent a moment. "You tell a fine story, Raizel."

"Mama doesn't like my stories." I told Papa about the promise I had made.

"I think Mama does not like you telling stories when you should be working," Papa said with a frown.

"But I never do that! I only tell stories to Shloyme and Hannah to keep them quiet."

"So maybe you think about the stories when you are working?"

That was true. While my hands were peeling potatoes, my mind was far away. Mama could always tell when I was dreaming. She said even my hands dreamed.

"So don't ask me to tell any more stories, Papa. I have to keep my promise to Mama."

Papa smiled and patted my head. "Mama's good girl."

By now the smeared windows of the train were dark blue like a deep ocean. We were traveling through the night, as if inside some fantastic creature that had swallowed us whole. Why, that was what had happened to Jonah and the whale! Shloyme loved that story, but he always worried about Jonah having nothing but herring to eat. Mama wouldn't mind if I told the story in my head. After all, I wasn't peeling potatoes now.

When I looked up again, the people around us were rustling their baskets and pulling out hunks of sausage and thick brown bread.

"Papa, is it time for supper yet?"

Papa started. He must have fallen asleep. "Who turned off the sun?" He took out the gold-plated watch he kept on a chain in his pocket and opened the cover. "Seven o'clock. Train or not, it is supper time."

This time we ate apples and cookies. They were crisp and sweet with little bits of almonds inside.

"Will we get to the border tonight, Papa? Where will we sleep?"

"In the station. We must catch another train in the morning to reach the border."

The station? How could we sleep in a noisy station? "But there are no beds in a station!"

"For one night you can bear anything. Did you think you would sleep in a fine feather bed?"

I bit my lip. Nobody had told me I would sleep in a train station or sit on my suitcase all day. If only Lemmel had come instead. He wouldn't mind where he slept, as long as he didn't have to go to cheder.

"Does it take long to cross the border?"

Papa had traced our route on a map back in Jibatov. After Russia we crossed the border to Austria, then to Germany and then to Belgium, to the city of Antwerp, where the boat was waiting for us. On the map the borders were outlined in thick black lines, as if a stone wall surrounded them. Was the border a stone wall? No, Russia was too big to have a wall around it. Maybe there was just a line painted on the ground.

"Crossing borders is not something I do every day. They say sometimes the guards make trouble, especially when there is cholera or another disease in Russia. Then they will not let you cross."

"But there's no cholera now, is there, Papa?"

Papa shook his head. His forehead was wrinkled with worry. He took a piece of paper out of his pocket and read it hurriedly.

"Papa, is everything all right? You didn't forget the passports, did you?"

"No, meydele. Why should I forget them when we do not have passports?"

I felt the warmth drain from my body. "But Papa, you need a passport to cross the border! Everyone in Jibatov says so."

"Hush!" Papa looked around at the other passengers. They were nodding in sleep or eating onions and apples. "In Jibatov they do not know everything. You think there is only one way to cross a border?"

"But how . . . ?"

"Shhh! Not now!" Papa put his finger to his lips and tilted his head at the other passengers sitting near us. "Try to sleep a little."

Sleep? How could I possibly sleep?

What if the police caught us trying to cross the border? What if they threw us in jail? What if they threw Papa in jail and I had no money to get back to Mama in Jibatov?

Right now Mama would be cooking dinner. Lemmel would be skipping home from cheder. And Shloyme and Hannah? Were they hanging on to Mama's skirts or watching for Lemmel at the window? Were they missing me like I missed them? I sniffed and wiped my eyes on my sleeve. My head throbbed and my body ached with tiredness.

The train jolted through the night, rocking, rocking to America. Every minute it took me farther from home, like the whale carrying Jonah to the depths of the ocean. But the whale had no borders to cross and Jonah had no passport. Had Jonah been excited about his adventure like Lemmel?

I wasn't Jonah. The only place I wanted to go was back home to Mama, and Jibatov, and my very own bed.

7

The Squint-Eyed Giant

By the time we reached the station, I was so sleepy that Papa half carried me off the train. I barely noticed when he stretched me out on the suitcases and covered me with a blanket. I pulled it over my head, breathed in the lavender smell of home, and fell asleep.

The shriek of whistles and clatter of passengers rushing to catch their trains fragmented my sleep. When Papa shook me awake, I felt like I had barely closed my eyes. Dawn bathed the station in an underwater light. Papa handed me a steaming cup of tea he had bought from a man with a huge copper samovar hung over his back.

"Mmmm." The sweet hot tea rolled down my throat, filling me with warmth. "Have some, Papa."

Papa whispered a blessing and took a sip of tea. He looked rumpled from lack of sleep.

"Papa, the border, how . . . ?" The rumble of our approaching train swallowed my words.

The third-class compartment was still half-empty at this early hour, so we easily found seats on the wooden benches. When we had settled our luggage, I turned to Papa.

"Papa, how are we going to cross the border?"

"Shhh! Not now!" Papa tilted his head at the other passengers on the bench. They swayed back and forth, their eyes shut in sleep. "The Czar has ears throughout Russia."

I stared out the window at the tall trees that lined the tracks. A woman was pumping water in front of a small house. A cart piled with potatoes waited at a train crossing. At home Mama would be heating water for tea and stirring the porridge. I knew she was thinking of us. I rubbed the sleep out of my eyes and wondered where we would be by the end of the day. The not-knowing was so hard to bear.

"Here, eat something." Papa handed me a chunk of bread and cheese.

"I don't want any."

He put the bread carefully back into the basket. "You do not feel well, meydele?"

I shook my head. "I just don't understand how . . . ?"

"What, you no longer trust your papa? Everything will be fine."

I leaned my head against Papa's shoulder. I wanted to believe him so badly, but something kept whispering: was it possible Papa didn't know everything?

This morning Papa didn't read his prayer book. Each time we pulled into a station, he studied the names on the sign and glanced at the crumpled piece of paper in his hand.

After an hour or so, the train stopped and Papa stood up.

"Are we at the border?" I asked as I gathered up the food baskets.

"We are going to visit your aunt and uncle," Papa said loudly. "What, you have forgotten, foolish girl?"

My face burned as the other passengers looked at me. Why did Papa have to talk like that? Was he afraid someone from the Czar's secret service was listening?

Only a few other people got off the train. Papa hurried out of the station and examined the carriages waiting to pick up passengers. He strode purposefully to a wagon hitched to a thin gray horse with a red ribbon braided into its dusty mane. I followed, sniffing back my tears.

Papa spoke briefly to the driver and gave him a handful of rubles. The driver picked up our suitcases and lifted me up after them. Papa climbed into the seat beside the driver.

The wagon clopped down the main road of a town that looked no bigger than Jibatov. Soon we were passing fields and tiny farmhouses. Where were we going?

We turned off the main road into the woods. Huge pine trees spread long shadows over the wagon. The smell of resin and rotting mushrooms reminded me of the woods near Jibatov. The trees closed over us like a black wedding canopy. The wagon drove deeper and deeper into the woods until the sky was swallowed in the hungry clutch of branches.

I preferred the heat and dust of the main road to the darkness of the woods. Even with Lemmel's laughter and Shloyme's squeals of joy as he raced along the springy ground, the woods had always frightened me. On winter nights Bobbe had told stories of hungry wolves that ate travelers and little children who wandered far from home. Even the crackling fireplace couldn't warm me after those stories. There were demons in the woods, too. Everyone said so.

The rutted path disappeared. Just as I had decided we were lost, the wagon pulled into a clearing and stopped before a small wooden hut with heavy shutters. A tall peasant with a bushy black beard stepped out of the house. Without a word, the driver lifted me and the baggage out of the wagon. With a nod to the tall man, he flicked his whip and drove away.

"Papa, is this the border?" I asked. Papa was staring after the wagon. He took a deep breath and turned around.

The tall peasant planted his brown leather boots wide apart. His pants were splattered with dry mud and his shirt was filthy. Even his beard was laced with twigs and bits of leaf. It failed to hide the pockmarks that pitted his face. Under thick brows, one eye was half-shut in a squint. He looked like an evil giant glaring down at Papa.

"Ten rubles apiece and two for each suitcase." The giant beat his fist into the palm of his meaty hand.

"I was told fifteen rubles for two." Papa shook his head stubbornly.

"Either you pay or go back where you came from!" Squint-eye spat on the ground.

Papa bit his lip. It had been a mistake to let the wagon leave. Or perhaps the waggoner had left quickly on purpose. In any case, we were trapped. We couldn't carry our suitcases out of the woods and back into town, even if we could find the way.

"An extra five rubles and that's all. Everything had better get there in one piece," Papa said finally.

Squint-eye snorted and held out his hand. It was as big as a cabbage leaf. Papa counted out the money.

"Put the suitcases in there." Squint-eye nodded at the woodshed. "Keep food for the journey, and a bottle of water."

Papa dragged our things into the woodshed. A pile of boxes and suitcases lay on the sawdust-covered floor.

So we weren't alone. We took out some bread and cheese and a tin bottle of water and followed Squint-eye into the house.

"Get down there with the other rats." He lifted a trapdoor and pointed to a ladder.

The root cellar was a dark hole in the ground. A damp moldy smell wafted up. "Papa, I don't want to go down there." I hated rats with their sharp teeth and scratchy nails. Squint-eye glared at me.

"It is only until the evening." Papa patted my shoulder. "Just a few hours." He climbed down the ladder carefully.

Squint-eye narrowed his good eye. "Down!" he shouted and took a step toward me. I scrambled down the ladder after Papa. The trapdoor banged shut over our heads.

It took a minute for my eyes to adjust to the dimness. Candles were set on piles of potatoes, turnips, and onions. A few people huddled on the sacks or lay on the dirt floor. The cellar smelled of earth and rotting vegetables.

"More people. As if it weren't crowded enough down here already. Soon half of Russia will be here," said a woman with a small boy on her lap. A girl about Shloyme's age was leaning against her, sucking her thumb.

"Hush, Rivka. There's plenty of room down here." The man held out his hand to Papa. "My name is Yakov Schwartz. We're from Plotsk." I recognized the name of a town not far from Jibatov.

"I know it well," said Papa. "The caretaker at the synagogue is the son of my mother's cousin."

Papa sat down next to Yakov. It turned out that Yakov knew our neighbor Yankel. They were going to America too and began exchanging information about trains and boats. Two young men were sprawled on the floor asleep. I waited impatiently until Papa and Yakov fell silent.

"Papa?"

"Yes, meydele? Are you hungry? She ate no breakfast," he explained to the others.

"Better save your food. Who knows when that madman will let us out of here," Rivka said sourly.

"Rivka . . . " Yakov shook his head.

The little girl began to cry. "Mama, I'm hungry too. Can't I have something to eat?"

"Don't blame me if we all die of hunger. To think I could be back home in my nice clean kitchen."

Silently I agreed with her. Rivka groaned and got up, lifting her huge belly.

"Is it wise for a woman in her condition to be traveling?" Papa asked Yakov.

Yakov sighed. "We wanted to wait, but my brother sent us tickets and the steamship company refused to exchange them."

Papa shook his head in sympathy. He looked at me as if to say how fortunate we were to be strong and healthy.

"Papa, who is that big man?"

"His name is Ivan. A friend of Uncle Nahum's told me about him. He has taken many people across the border."

"But I thought everyone crossed with passports. Mama thought so, too."

"Most people do. Why should I worry your Mama? We can cross without them."

"You lied to Mama?" I couldn't believe it. Papa never lied. And to Mama!

"Why should I lie? I simply neglected to mention it. That is not a lie."

I wasn't so sure. Mama said a half-truth is a whole lie. Maybe if Mama had known, she wouldn't have let me go. And now it was too late.

"Passports are expensive," Papa continued. "And who can tell if the border guards will honor them? They might take our passports and send us back."

"Why would they do that, Papa?"

"Because . . . because Russia does not want the Jews to leave. That is, sometimes she lets them leave and sometimes she doesn't. Who can know ahead of time?"

That made sense. I knew that sometimes the Jews were allowed to live and work outside the Pale of Jewish Settlement and sometimes they weren't. Sometimes they were allowed to go to Christian schools and sometimes they weren't. Sometimes the peasants started a pogrom and attacked the Jews, and sometimes they were friendly. People said you could never depend on anything in Russia, except the winter. It was always cold.

"But how will we cross the border? How will we get out of this forest? What if they catch us?"

"Raizel, what good will come of all this worrying?"

"Papa, just one more thing. Yesterday morning, why did you say to Mama that you had no choice? Aren't we going to America to be rich? And safe from pogroms?"

Papa stared at me for a moment and stroked his beard. "Of course, why else would we be going?"

"Papa, please answer me. I want to know."

"Raizel, there are some things children do not need to know. Now stop with your questions and let me read my prayers."

Papa opened his prayer book and moved closer to the candle. It wasn't fair. I was old enough to go to America, but not old enough to know everything about the journey. What else hadn't Papa told me? I curled up on a sack of potatoes and tried to find a comfortable place for my bones among the hard lumps. I must have dozed off because suddenly the trap door was open and Squint-Eye was yelling at Rivka to climb out.

"Yakov, I don't understand." She grabbed her husband's hand. "Are we leaving? It isn't night yet."

Yakov put his arms around his wife. "You're traveling with the baggage. I paid Ivan extra so you wouldn't have to walk."

"But I can't leave you and the children!" Rivka's voice rose to a scream. "I won't go! Don't make me go!" She burst into tears and hugged the children to her.

"Come now. The wagon is here," Squint-eye barked hoarsely. I moved closer to Papa. The two young men sat up watching. The thinner one was coughing into a handkerchief.

"Rivka, you have to go. The crossing will be too hard for you. We have to walk at night through the forest. And there's a river . . . "

"But I can't swim, Yakov!"

"I know. That's why you have to ride in the wagon. We'll meet you in Brody. Here, take some money and meet us at the station." He put some coins into Rivka's pocket.

"No! I won't leave the children. They need me." The children were sobbing and clutching at her clothes.

"I'll carry Soyrele. Ivan will take Yossel." He pulled the children away from her. "Now hurry and go. We'll see you in a few hours."

Rivka shook so hard I thought she would come apart. "What if they catch you crossing the border? What if I never see you again? Oh, Yakov . . . " She swayed and fell into her husband's arms.

"Help me get her up the ladder." The two young men pushed Rivka from behind while Yakov pulled his wife up the ladder. She was sobbing quietly now. In a few moments Yakov was back, wiping his brow. The howling children threw themselves into his arms. The trap door shut with a bang and darkness enveloped us again.

I shook off my fear. Of course Yakov was right to send his wife with the wagon. It would be too difficult for her to walk through the forest at night in her condition. Still, I would rather walk through the forest with Papa then ride alone in the fanciest carriage.

"Thank you for your help," Yakov said to the two young men. "Ivan put her under a blanket with the luggage. I hope the wagon will not bounce too much." In the dim candlelight his face was pinched with worry.

"Do you have relatives in America?" Papa asked the older of the two men.

"We are brothers, yeshiva students. I am Moyshe and this is Nathan. Our parents don't have money to buy us out of the army. We have no relatives there, but I am certain we will find work in America." The younger brother coughed. The older patted him on his back.

"Better get rid of that cough fast," said Yakov. "They won't let you on the boat if you're sick."

"I'm not sick," said the younger one. "I've had this cough all winter."

"Even if they let you on the boat, they won't let you into America."

I looked at Yakov in surprise. Not let you into America? Why not?

"What have you heard?" Papa asked.

"My brother wrote me a long letter. They only let the first and second-class passengers straight into America. The third-class passengers they take to an island. There American doctors check you and give you tests."

"Tests? What kind of tests?" Papa looked worried.

"Not hard ones. Tests to see if you are crazy or dumb. If you're sick or fail their tests, they send you back."

"Just imagine making the whole long trip and being sent back," Papa whispered. "What a terrible tragedy!"

"Not to mention the money. We only have enough to get to America. How will we get home if they send us back?" asked the older brother. The younger began to cough again.

I watched him as he lay back down on the potato piles. Suddenly I had a horrible thought. What if they let Moyshe into America but didn't let Nathan? Would the older brother leave his younger brother behind? I would never leave Shloyme. Or Lemmel.

The air was heavy as a miller's grindstone. Finally Papa opened his prayer book. The older brother did the same.

"I want my Mama!" The little girl kept sobbing. "I want to go home!"

"Mama!" wailed little Yossel.

"Enough crying, Soyrele!" Yakov shook the little girl.

She pulled away and flung herself at the ladder. "Mama, wait for me!"

There was a sharp thump on the ceiling.

"Quiet!" Yakov hissed.

"Do you want me to tell you a story?" I asked the little girl. She cried and clung to the ladder. "Then I'll tell it to your brother. You can listen if you want."

I sat down next to Yossel. "A long time ago, there was a happy family with seven children. They lived in a house at the edge of the woods."

Soyrele let go of the ladder.

"One day, the papa went to synagogue and the mama went to gather blueberries in the forest. But before they went they said, 'Remember children, never ever let anyone into the house when we're gone.' The children promised.

"Not long after the mama and papa left, a great big bear came out of the forest and knocked on the door. 'Open up for your father, children,' he said in a gruff voice."

Soyrele squeezed herself between Yossel and me. She wasn't crying anymore.

"'You're not our father and we won't open the door!' shouted the children.

"A few minutes later there was another knock. 'Open up for your mother, children,' said a squeaky voice.

"'You're not our mother and we won't open the door!' shouted the children.

"'Open this door or I'll break the door down!' roared the bear.

"The children ran to hide as fast as they could. The first hid in the oven. The second hid in the pantry. The third hid behind the rain barrel. The fourth hid under a sack of potatoes. The fifth hid in the linen chest. The sixth hid in the washtub. The seventh was so frightened that he jumped into bed and pulled the covers over his head.

"There was a terrible noise as the bear crashed through the door. He ran through the house looking for the children and swallowing them whole. He found the first child in the oven and the second in the pantry and the third behind the rain barrel and the fourth under the potato sack and the fifth in the linen chest and the six in the washtub. He swallowed each down in a single gulp. But who didn't he find?"

Double Crossing

"The little boy in the bed!" cried Soyrele. She clapped her hands.

"Yes! When the mama and papa came home, they found the door smashed in and the seventh child hidden in bed. He told them about the bear that had swallowed his brothers and sisters.

"The mama didn't wait a single moment. She grabbed a jar of honey, six loaves of bread, a knife, a thread and needle and ran into the forest.

"'Bear, bear, come here,' she called. 'I have honey for you.'

"Now the greedy bear's stomach was nearly bursting. But he loved honey so much that he came out of his den and ate it all up. Then he fell fast asleep. As soon as he was asleep, the mama cut open his belly and out popped the six children, covered with honey. Quick as a wink, the mama put the six loaves of bread in the bear's stomach and sewed him back up again. Then she took the six children home, gave them a bath, and tucked them into their nice warm beds. And the papa built a door so strong that all the bears in the forest couldn't break it down ever again."

"I like that story," said Soyrele sucking her thumb.

"Mmmm," her brother agreed.

"Tell me another."

Suddenly I remembered I had broken my promise again by telling a story. But what could I do? It was wicked to disobey Mama, but wasn't it even more wicked to let two unhappy children cry? I knew Mama would understand.

"Please!" Soyrele pleaded.

"Yes, tell them some more," said Yakov. "They love stories."

Just like Shloyme and Hannah. How I missed them. I pulled the two children closer and closed my eyes. What would Shloyme like to hear? Of course, the story about the mischievous goblin! "Once upon a time a goblin lived in the cellar of a house," I began.

The stories flowed one after another, banishing the children's misery and quieting my fears of the terrors waiting for us outside in the deep dark forest.

8

Fleeing from Egypt

Squint-eye lifted the trap door. "Out! Everyone out!"

I stretched and followed Papa up the ladder. My hands shook as I climbed the wooden rungs. What would happen now?

Firelight sent tall shadows dancing around the room. A woman with a face like a dried apple was serving cups of hot stew.

It smelled like garlic and new potatoes. Chunks of browned meat floated among the carrots and sent a delicious aroma to my nose. I sat down at the table and picked up my spoon.

"No, Raizel." Papa touched my elbow. "We don't eat tref."

"But Papa, I'm hungry." The spicy smell was making my mouth water.

"Have some bread and cheese." Papa cut off a hunk of bread. I sighed. I was getting tired of bread and cheese.

The two yeshiva students stared at their plates. "Eat," said Yakov. "It will give you strength."

"But it is forbidden," said Nathan, the younger brother. "At home we only eat meat slaughtered by the kosher butcher."

"My Rivka keeps a kosher home, too," said Yakov. "But we're not at home now."

"All the world is God's house," said Papa. "We must follow His laws no matter where we are."

Yakov glared at Papa. "They need hot food for the journey. If they don't eat, they'll be sick."

"Pikuekh-nefesh," Moyshe said and picked up a spoon. His younger brother followed his example.

I watched them longingly. "Papa . . . ?"

Papa shook his head firmly. "You know pikuekh-nefesh means you may break a law to save a life," he said. "We're not in danger. We have plenty of food. Now eat, child."

The old woman put cups of hot apple kvass in front of us. What could be unkosher about apple kvass? "Papa . . . ?"

"No, Raizel. The cup could have been used for milk. It is forbidden to mix milk and meat at the same meal."

"Fanatic," Yakov muttered under his breath. He took a noisy slurp and licked his lips.

I chewed the bread slowly, trying to pretend it was a plump potato. Of course Papa was right. Why, everyone in Jibatov thought he knew as much Jewish law as a rabbi and called him "Reb" Balaban. But I still envied Soyrele and Yossel spooning hot rabbit stew into their mouths while I gnawed on bread and cheese.

"Time to go," said Squint-eye. "I'll carry the lantern. Keep quiet and don't lose the light. If you get lost, the soldiers will find you. You go first." He pointed at Yakov.

"Then you." Papa and me.

"Then you two." The yeshiva students.

"Put the little one in here." He pointed to a burlap sack attached to his back. Yakov tucked Yossel into the sack. He whimpered and then stuck his thumb into his mouth and closed his eyes. Yakov hoisted Soyrele onto his shoulders. I took a last look at the blazing fire and followed Papa into the darkness outside.

There was no moon that night. We walked slowly, keeping to a path between the trees. I was wearing my old shoes from last winter. After a while my toes began to hurt. Soon every step I took felt like knives sticking in my feet.

"Raizel, hurry up," Papa whispered. "The yeshiva boys have passed us."

I walked faster. "Papa, my feet hurt. These shoes are too small."

Papa sighed. "There's nothing we can do. You want to walk barefoot?"

I stumbled over a tree root and fell, bumping my knee.

"What now, Raizel?"

I rubbed my bruised knee. "Papa, I can't go so fast."

Papa took my hand and pulled me along. After a few minutes he stopped, out of breath.

"Why are we stopping?" All I could hear was Papa's harsh breathing. Twigs crackled around us. Were there bears in this forest?

"Can you see the light?" he asked.

I peered around me. The forest was too dense to let starlight trickle down. I could barely see Papa standing next to me. "I can't see anything. Are we . . . lost?" My teeth began to chatter.

"Shhh. I hear something."

There was a loud crash in the underbrush.

"Papa!" I flung myself into Papa's arms waiting for the bear to lunge at us.

Squint-eye strode toward us carrying the lantern! I was so glad to see him I almost hugged him.

"Hurry up!" he barked. "Everyone is waiting. Either keep up or I will leave you for the soldiers, you lazy Jew."

The others were resting in a clearing when we approached.

"Move on," Squint-eye ordered. Nathan began coughing. "Quiet!"

I hurried after Squint-eye, ignoring the knives in my feet. I didn't care how much they hurt, as long as he didn't abandon us in the forest. I knew he would leave us. He had taken our money and he hated Jews. Yet when he returned for us, he had reminded me of someone. Someone in the

Bible. Moses! Squint-eye was leading us out of Russia just like Moses had led the Israelite slaves out of Egypt.

In my imagination, I joined a long line of slaves trudging through the desert. It had taken the Israelites forty years to reach the Land of Israel, a land flowing with milk and honey. Shloyme would have liked it there! It would take us only a few weeks to reach America. If the Israelites could walk for forty years, I could walk for one night.

We rested more frequently as the night wore on. Soyrele and Yossel were so quiet I knew they must have fallen asleep. I envied them. I was too big for Papa to carry. And Papa was too little.

"Drink some water, Raizel." Papa passed me the cup.

"How much further is it?"

"Not too far, I hope."

"Do your feet hurt too, Papa?"

"A little. But never mind. Soon we will be across the border in Brody."

"Will we have a place to sleep there?" It had been two nights without sleeping in a bed.

"You have seen gold coins growing in my beard? We will sleep on the train."

I sighed. I was so tired even the train sounded good to me.

"Everybody up," Squint-eye ordered. "And be quiet. We are coming to the border. There may be patrols around."

Papa got to his feet with a sigh and pulled me up. After walking a little ways, I heard a sound like the hum of a beehive. The noise grew louder and louder until it became a roar.

"What's that noise, Papa?"

"It sounds like water."

"Everyone wait here." Squint-eye disappeared with the lantern as we sank onto the forest floor. In a few moments he was back. "The river is too high to cross in the dark. We will wait for dawn. Everyone go to sleep."

Here? On the cold damp ground? Until last night I had never slept any-place but a bed.

"Lie down, Raizel. Use my lap for a pillow."

I put my head in Papa's lap. "How will we cross the river? Is there a boat?"

"Shhh. Go to sleep and stop worrying. Everything will be just fine."

I closed my eyes and heard Papa murmur, "Yea, though I walk through the valley of the shadow of death, I will fear no evil; for Thou art with me; Thy rod and Thy staff, they comfort me . . . ."

I knew the psalm. The words spread over me like a warm blanket. I listened to Papa's prayer and the roar of the river faded into sleep.

Papa shook me awake. I was cold, stiff, and soaked with dew. I would have given anything for a cup of hot tea. I rubbed my eyes. The night had faded into a chilly gray dawn. I got up and stumbled still half-asleep after Papa.

Then I saw it.

"We can't cross that!" cried Yakov.

The river was twice as wide as the stream that flowed past Jibatov. The water was dark and foamy in the half-light. Dead branches beckoned from the shores like the arms of a drowning man.

"The current is too strong." Papa crossed his arms.

I pressed against him and shivered. The Polata bubbled and sang like a happy friend. There was a shallow shady hole where the women swam after finishing their laundry. I couldn't swim across a river like this.

"It rained too much last week," Squint-eye said.

"Isn't there a bridge?" Yakov asked

"Soldiers guard the bridge. Do not worry. We can cross. I have a rope."

Squint-eye tied the rope to a tree stump, wrapped the slack around his waist, and waded into the river. The water rushed around his boots, creeping up to his knees. As he approached the middle, the water rose to his waist.

"It's not too deep, is it Papa?" Then I remembered that Squint-eye was so tall that Papa barely reached his chest.

Squint-eye was out of the water now, tying the rope to a tree. Without wasting a moment, he plunged back into the current.

Soyrele began to cry. "Papa, I can't swim. I want Mama." Little Yossel held on to his father's leg.

Yakov hugged the children. "I should have sent you with the wagon," he said, watching Squint-eye with a worried frown. "Rivka will never forgive me if something happens to you."

Papa nodded. "Perhaps it is better to go by the bridge then lose a child?"

"They'll put me in jail," said Yakov miserably. "Then what will Rivka do?"

Squint-eye shook the water out of his boots and glared at us. "See? Just hold tight to the rope and everything will be fine."

"But what am I going to do with the children?" Yakov sounded like he was about to cry. I felt sorry for him.

"Put the baby into the sack on my back. I will tie the girl on your back."

"But if I fall into the water, we'll both drown. No, she'll ride on my shoulders." Yakov was almost as tall as Squint-eye.

Squint-eye gave his orders. "You, after me," he said to Yakov.

"Then the girl, then you." Papa and me.

"Then the sick one and then you," he finished, pointing to the brothers. Moyshe patted Nathan on the shoulder and nodded encouragingly.

"P-papa . . . ?" I was shaking so hard I could barely speak. What would Mama say if she saw us? I hoped she was praying for us right now.

"Give me your shoes." Papa put them in the food sack tied to his back. "Just hold tight to the rope. I'll be right behind you. Don't let go for anything."

Squint-eye and Yakov were already in the water. I stuck my bare foot in. The water was freezing!

"Go, Raizel," Papa ordered.

Sharp stones stabbed my feet. The freezing water seemed to race up my body, turning my limbs to ice. I held onto the rough rope with all my strength, carefully inching my hands forward, never letting go completely. I concentrated on finding a place for each foot as I edged slowly into the current.

"Good girl. Keep going," Papa's voice sounded in my ear and gave me courage.

The water was up to my waist now. It pushed against me as I tried to find a firm place for my feet. In the growing light I could see trees on the opposite bank. Why were they still so far away?

My feet slid out from under me as the water reached my chest.

"Hold on tight, Raizel!"

I struggled against the current until I felt my feet touch solid rock. A boulder jutted out of the middle of the stream. I paused a moment to catch my breath. Squint-eye was climbing onto the bank and untying Yossel from the sack

Yakov was just ahead of me. He stepped carefully off the boulder and suddenly sank into deep water.

"Papa!"

Soyrele shrieked as she lost her grip on Yakov's neck and fell backwards into the water.

I threw myself forward and pushed her back up as my feet flew out from under me. Papa grabbed my blouse, but it ripped in his hands. I struggled to stop myself as the river carried me downstream.

I hit a tree trunk and grabbed onto a dead branch.

"Hold on, Raizel!" I heard Papa scream.

The branch broke in my hands as the river tore me away. My mouth filled up with water. Air. All I wanted was air. Pain seared my lungs like hot coals. I pushed the water aside with all my strength, pushing, pushing toward the light. Then everything went black.

I opened my eyes and saw darkness. Was I dead?

"Thou anointest my head with oil, my cup runneth over. Surely goodness and mercy shall follow me all the days of my life; and I will dwell in the house of the Lord for ever." That was Papa's voice!

I was hanging over a log. Someone pounded my back. Hard. Water gushed out of my mouth as I vomited. Then Papa's arms were around me and I was sobbing onto his shoulder.

"Make a fire, you good-for-nothing Jews!" Squint-eye ordered. "The little girl will die of cold." He was sitting next to me on the ground, his black beard dripping mud and water. Had he . . . ?

"P-p-papa, is Soyrele all right?"

"She is fine," Yakov said. "You saved her life."

Soon we were all huddled around the fire. Gradually I stopped shaking. Papa wrapped me in his coat and dried my clothes over the fire.

"Papa, who pulled me out of the water?"

"Ivan, God bless him." Yakov and the yeshiva boys murmured "Amen."

"How?" Everything was a blur. All I could remember was the burning in my lungs and the overwhelming need to breathe.

"My Soyrele slipped. You saved her and fell in the water," Yakov said.

"I tried to hold you, but the current was too strong," Papa continued. "We thought you were lost. But Ivan ran along the bank until he could grab you. He saved your life."

I looked at Ivan. He was sitting in his wet clothes smoking a pipe and staring at the other side of the river. I wanted to thank him, but suddenly he got to his feet.

"Put out the fire. The wagon is waiting for us. Hurry." He plunged into the forest. Papa put his arm around my shoulders and helped me walk. My body felt like it belonged to someone else. Only my mind was still my own, full of darkness, rushing water, and fear.

The wagon was waiting with our baggage and Rivka on a road not far from the river. The children screamed when they saw their mother and clung to her sobbing. Yakov told Rivka what had happened and she cried and kissed me. Everyone was smiling and laughing and crying at the same time. We had made it across the border. We were out of Russia forever!

Ivan put the children, the sick brother, and me in the wagon. I must have fallen asleep because the next thing I knew we were in the middle of a city street, and Ivan was handing down the luggage.

The yeshiva students picked up their bags and hurried into the train station. As Ivan swung me down, I looked into his eyes.

"Thank you for saving my life," I said. "You have led us into the promised land."

Ivan set me on the ground with a thump as if he hadn't heard. I caught hold of the wagon to steady myself. My head ached and my legs felt like water.

"May God bless you," Papa said.

Yakov pressed some rubles into Ivan's huge hand. He pocketed them without a word and mounted the wagon next to the driver. He hadn't even smiled.

I watched as the wagon clopped down the cobbled street. I had never met anyone like Ivan before. What kind of man was he? He took too much money and called us filthy Jews, yet he carried Yossel through the forest and risked his own life to save me.

How could one man be so bad and so good at the same time?

9
Strangers' Hospitality

Men and women hurried in and out of the pale gray train station carrying parcels and leather cases. There were no peasant women carrying chickens, but otherwise it looked like Russia. Yet we were no longer in Russia, I reminded myself. We had crossed the border into Brody. We were in Austro-Hungary. What an adventure I would have to tell Shloyme when next we met! Even Lemmel would be impressed.

"Sit here, meydele, while I go for tickets." Papa led me to a bench.

I sat down with a shudder and wrapped my shawl around my shoulders. An elderly man moved over to give me more room. He stared at my muddy clothes, but I ignored him. My head felt like a flock of chickens was running around inside.

"You are catching the train?" Yakov asked Papa.

"Yes," Papa answered. "You do not continue?"

"I have a cousin in Brody. We will stay with him for a few days so Rivka can rest."

Papa looked at me and sighed. I held my spinning head in my hands. Despite the midday heat, I was freezing.

"I only wish we had relatives here," Papa said. "Raizel needs to rest also."

"A man from my town was helped by people in Brody," Yakov continued. "His money and tickets were stolen crossing the border. These Austrian Jews are richer than we are in Russia."

"Charity I do not need," Papa said.

The man sitting next to me cleared his throat as if he wanted to say something. He was wearing a long black coat and felt hat just like Papa's.

"But the little girl may have a high fever." Rivka touched my forehead. "Burning. What did I tell you?"

Rivka's hand on my forehead felt like Mama's kiss. I wanted Mama so badly. And my own bed in Jibatov.

"I wish we could take you in," Yakov said. "But my cousin has eight children . . . "

"Thank you for your kind thoughts. We will manage," Papa said. "May God grant you a safe journey."

They shook hands and Yakov helped Rivka into a carriage waiting by the station.

Soyrele and Yossel waved to me from the window as they pulled away. I wanted to raise my arm to wave back, but it was too heavy to lift.

"Come, Raizel, you can rest on the train." Papa began pulling our suitcases into the station.

I got up to follow and the street whirled under my feet. I sat back down on the bench with a thud.

"The little girl is ill?" The man on the bench spoke in Yiddish with an accent that made him sound foreign. His faded blue eyes peered out over his white beard.

"She will rest on the train," Papa said.

"She will rest better in a nice warm bed. My name is Hirshel." He held out his hand to Papa.

Papa took his hand briefly. "Excuse me, but I must see to the train."

"No wait, please! Your friend was right about the Jews of Brody. I sit here every morning just in case."

"Just in case what?" Papa was already picking up a suitcase.

"Just in case there comes a Jew in need. Many times their money is stolen while crossing the border. I take them to the charity office and we arrange a loan."

"I look like I need charity?" Papa stood straight as a new board in Uncle Nahum's lumber mill.

"You look like your little girl needs a soft bed and not a train bench." Hirshel blocked Papa's way. "Let me take you to Frau Buchthal's house. She is the widow of Reb Buchthal, may he rest in peace. She will be happy to take you in for the night."

"Please Papa," I said. "My head hurts and my bones ache so. I want to go to bed."

Papa glanced at me. I must have looked like a drowned cat, because the anger was gone from his face when he turned to Hirshel. "We have very little money to pay her."

"Money? Who said anything about money?" Hirshel brushed away an imaginary fly. "It is a mitzvah to help a fellow Jew. You will be doing Frau Buchthal a good deed. Now take your suitcases and follow me!"

I let out a sigh of relief as Papa picked up the luggage. My legs felt as heavy as a blacksmith's anvil. I dragged them down the street while Hirshel carried my food basket. Luckily the house was only a few blocks from the station.

We stopped in front of an elegant gray stone house with white painted shutters. It was two stories high and had a well-kept flower garden in front.

"Papa, are we going to stay here?" Even Uncle Nahum's house was built of wood.

"Reb Buchthal was a successful leather merchant for many years, in addition to being very pious," Hirshel said. He banged on the shiny brass door knocker.

A plump woman wearing a white apron and streaks of flour on her rosy cheeks opened the door. She stared at my muddy clothes for a moment. Then she turned around and called, "Frau Buchthal! Another mitzvah on your doorstep."

It felt like hours until I heard the thump of a cane. A tall elderly woman appeared wearing a black dress with a silver brooch on her lace collar. Her lined face lit up with a smile when she saw Hirshel. "What have you brought me today? Come in, come in! Why is Helga keeping you outside on the doorstep? Ach, a lovely child! Such fine skin," she said, her words fading farther and farther away like a departing train. Papa caught me as my legs turned into air.

I woke up in a deep soft bed. Water was roaring in my ears but my mouth was dry and my head ached. "Mama?"

"Drink some tea, meydele." Papa leaned over to help me sit up.

The room was filled with a pink glow. The coverlet felt silky under my hands and smelled of lavender. "Where's Mama? Am I in heaven, Papa?"

Papa laughed. "You're in Brody at Frau Buchthal's house. Now go back to sleep."

I fell into a dream of water and darkness. The current tossed me back and forth, swirling around rocks and under fallen branches. I sank down, down into the darkness. Suddenly Moses with a long white beard seized me from the water.

"Where are we going?" I asked, clinging to his broad back.

"To the Promised Land, of course." Moses swung his heavy staff as we strode through a pine forest.

"Wait! Let me take Shloyme," I begged him. "And Hannah and Mama."

And suddenly there was Mama waiting for me, dressed in a green silk dress and holding a bowl of steaming soup.

I blinked. The woman sitting on the bed next to me was older than Mama. Where had I seen her before?

"Open your mouth, child." I was propped up in bed. Frau Buchthal sat next to me spooning soup in my mouth. "Her fever has gone down," she said to Papa who was peering over her shoulder at me.

This time my sleep was dreamless and deep. When I opened my eyes again, the room was full of sunlight. My body felt light and fragile as an autumn leaf.

"Hungry?" Frau Buchthal was sitting in a rocking chair crocheting white lace. Her face crinkled into a smile when she saw me sitting up in bed.

"Yes, very." My stomach felt like it had forgotten what food was. "Where's my Papa?"

"Gone to synagogue. It's Friday afternoon."

Friday! We had left Jibatov on Sunday and crossed the river on Tuesday. Where had Wednesday and Thursday gone?

My confusion must have shown on my face for Frau Buchthal burst out laughing. "Come, meydele. We will brave Helga's wrath and see what she is hiding in the kitchen."

I slipped a shawl around my nightgown and followed her down a flight of polished wooden steps to the kitchen. The woman in the apron was stirring a huge pot of soup on an iron stove. Chicken soup! It smelled just like Mama's.

"What can we give this young lady to eat, Helga?" Frau Buchthal asked.

Helga frowned and wiped the sweat from her broad red face. "The soup isn't ready yet." She opened the pantry door. "All we have is bread and cold meat. That will have to do. I have the Sabbath dinner to finish." She pulled out dish after dish, setting them on the table with a bang.

Frau Buchthal winked at me. She cut slices of fresh challah and spread them with yellow mustard and thick slices of cold beef. Then she poured me a tall glass of apple kvass.

The challah melted in my mouth and the meat was so tender I barely had to chew it. "Mmmm," I said with my mouth full. "This is very good, thank you." Helga looked a little less cross.

"Save room for dinner," Frau Buchthal said as I finished my second sandwich. "Come, we will heat some water for a bath."

Frau Buchthal had a tin bathtub long enough to lie down in rather than the round washtub we used at home. She poured hot water over my hair and lathered it with soap that smelled like lemons. I felt like a princess as I lay among the bubbles dreaming of castles among the clouds. I enjoyed the bath almost as much as I enjoyed the food. When the water turned cold, Frau Buchthal wrapped me in a thick white towel and combed the knots out of my hair.

"Ouch!" I shut my mouth tightly.

"What a tangle!" She sighed like Mama. "Your braids came undone while you were asleep."

"I wish I had straight hair," I said.

"You have very nice hair, so thick and curly. It goes perfectly with your delicate face." She took my chin in her hand. "You are a very pretty girl, Raizel. Not that it's important. A good heart is the most important thing, and from what your Papa tells me, you have that, too."

My face burned. No one had ever told me I was pretty before. They always said I had my mama's nose and my papa's eyes and wasn't it a shame I didn't have straight hair like Leah. Pretty? Not even Bobbe had said that.

After Frau Buchthal finished combing my hair, she braided it into a single braid and left me to dress. I studied my face in the large mirror over the dressing table. The mirror we had at home was small and cracked. You could only see one eye or part of your mouth. The face that stared back at me from the mirror was too thin, especially with the long wet hair. The forehead was high, the eyes a plain mud brown under black brows. I studied my nose. It was straight like Mama's. That made me feel good. It was like having a part of her with me. The mouth troubled me. It wasn't wide like Papa's or capped with little points like Mama's. Where had I seen it before? Then I smiled. Yes! It was like Bobbe's with the curling corners. I was made up of pieces of my family, a walking scrapbook, like the velvet-covered book where Leah saved pictures and dried flowers.

The door opened downstairs and I heard the bustle of people. I hurried to put on my clean blue skirt and the blouse with the embroidered corn-flowers. Someone had washed and pressed my clothes to make them smooth as silk. The braid made me look almost grown up, better than with those two pigtails sticking out like elephants' ears. Soon Mama would let me pile my hair up on top of my head like my cousin Sarah. A pain stabbed my stomach. Mama was in Jibatov. Who would show me how to pin the braid smoothly around my head when the time came?

"Raizel, are you coming?" Frau Buchthal called.

I hurried down the stairs and paused a moment in the doorway. There were so many people in the room. Suddenly I felt as shy as Hannah. Papa smiled at me and patted the empty chair next to him.

"Welcome back from the land of dreams." Papa squeezed my hand and kissed me on the forehead.

With my head bowed, I glanced around the room. The long mahogany table was covered with a fine white cloth. China dishes gleamed at each place and the silverware was so bright and shiny you could see your face in it. An enormous china soup tureen in the shape of a hen sat in the middle of the table and spiced the air with a salty Sabbath aroma.

Frau Buchthal covered her head with a veil and recited the prayer over the Sabbath candles. A man with a dark black beard and flashing eyes recited the blessing over the wine. Everyone took a sip. It wasn't sweet like our raisin wine at home. It warmed my mouth and made my stomach tingle.

"Herr Balaban, will you do us the honor of reciting the blessing over the challah?" asked Frau Buchthal.

Papa rose and recited the blessing. Then he broke off bits of the huge braided loaves and gave them to the assembled guests. I studied them as we began to eat the stuffed fish. Hirshel was sitting back in his chair and sipping the wine. He waved to me across the table. Next to him sat a thin young man with a scraggly beard who looked like a yeshiva student, then an elderly couple dressed in fine clothes, and next to them a man whose clothes were worn and dusty. He kept his eyes on the table and ate everything that was put on his plate. The yeshiva student, too, seemed to have an enormous appetite. Frau Buchthal had to give him two helpings of chicken soup and several portions of roast chicken and potatoes before he sighed, patted his stomach and leaned back from the table.

I guessed he was lucky to be invited to Frau Buchthal's house for Friday dinner. He probably went hungry most of the week. That was one of the reasons Lemmel didn't want to go to yeshiva in Lublin. He complained that he would be farmed out for meals to charitable people in the city and never get enough to eat.

"Your tsimmes is as good as my wife's," said Papa spooning the sweet carrots and raisins into his mouth. "And my Hava is an excellent cook."

"How are things in Russia these days?" asked the man with the black beard, whose name was Yisroel. "We had quite a stream of travelers after the pogroms last spring."

"Praised be His Name, in Jibatov everything is quiet," Papa said. "But you never know what will happen. And then there is the war in Siberia."

"And why are you going to America, Herr Balaban?" asked Hirshel.

Papa hesitated a moment. "Things in Russia are very uncertain. I can barely make ends meet and feed my family."

"Surely you don't believe the streets of America are paved with gold?" Yisroel forked a chunk of potato into his mouth. He had bushy eyebrows which made him look like an owl.

Everyone laughed. I clenched my fists. Did he think Papa was a fool?

"Of course not," Papa answered. "But if I work hard, I will have the opportunity to get ahead in the world. In Russia, I have no chance. The law keeps us pinned in the Pale of Jewish Settlement and no one can make a good living. How about the Jews of Brody? They do not want to go to America?"

"Oh no!" Hirshel looked shocked. "Here in Austro-Hungary and Germany, we don't have the problems you have in Russia. There are no pogroms. We can live where we please. And the laws protect us."

"That reminds me of a story," said Yisroel, wiping his mouth on his napkin. Everyone looked at him expectantly. I was relieved he had decided to tell a story instead of needling Papa. "Two brothers lived in the city. One day they decided to visit the countryside where they had never been. As they walked along the road, they saw a farmer plowing.

"'What is he doing?' asked the first brother. 'He took a nice smooth field and turned the earth over.'

"The brothers watched. The farmer took sacks of grain and sowed them in the field.

"'He's crazy,' said the first brother. 'He's throwing good grain into the dirt. I'm going home. Only crazy people live in the country.'

"The second brother was more patient. He stayed in the country and watched as the field began to sprout green shoots and the wheat grew taller. 'What a beautiful field,' he said. 'Now I understand what the farmer was doing.'

"Time passed and the wheat grew golden. The brother watched as the farmer cut down the wheat with his scythe. 'Why is he doing that?

He worked so hard to grow the wheat and now he's cutting it down? Maybe he is crazy after all.'

"The patient brother kept watching. He saw how the farmer gathered the wheat. He saw him separate the wheat from the chaff. He was filled with wonder as he saw that the farmer now had a hundred times more seed than he had before. 'Now I understand the mystery of God's ways,' he said."

Yisroel paused and looked at Papa from under his bushy brows. I waited for him to continue the story, but instead he took a sip of wine and another portion of chicken. I glanced around the table. Everyone was smiling and nodding their heads except Papa. He was studying his fingernails. "I don't understand, Papa," I whispered. "What does the story mean?"

Yisroel glared at me. I felt my face go hot with embarrassment.

"It is a parable, Raizel. The story tells us that man cannot always understand the ways of God, because the logic is hidden from him."

"It tells us that we must have faith." Yisroel's voice was sharp.

"I have faith," Papa said.

"Then why do you run away to America?"

"Because in America there is freedom," Papa continued in his soft voice. "And that freedom is protected by law, even if you are a Jew."

"Freedom!" Drops of spittle caught on Yisroel's beard. His face grew red as he glared at Papa from his owl eyes.

I put my hand on Papa's arm. Why was he so mad at Papa? He was mean and vicious and I hated him. Bobbe told better stories than Yisroel even though he was a learned man!

"Because of that freedom, Jews forget they are Jews," Yisroel continued. "They go to work even on the Sabbath. They eat tref and pretend it is kosher." He banged the table with his fist. "America is a godless place, full of heretics and sinners!"

Double Crossing

"Herr Wasserman!" Frau Buchthal's soft voice cut him off like a knife slicing butter. "Such behavior on the Sabbath! Herr Balaban is a guest in my house. I'll thank you to speak politely." She clapped her hands briskly and Helga stepped out of the kitchen. "Please bring out the tea, Helga. I think we are ready for dessert."

"That's all right, Frau Buchthal." Papa spoke firmly. "That won't happen to me."

I smiled at Papa. I was so proud of him. Herr Wasserman was a horrible man and he told horrible stories. What right did he have to accuse Papa of lacking faith? I wanted to tell him that Papa was a learned man. He could have been a famous rabbi like his grandfather, if he didn't have to support our family. My anger was bubbling like a pot of soup, but I clenched my teeth and kept my mouth tightly shut. Papa would be furious if I tried to defend him. Children shouldn't speak in front of their elders, Mama always said, for silence is the fence around wisdom. If I spoke, everyone would think my parents had given me a poor education. I would shame them. Better to stay quiet like Papa.

I looked around the table. Yisroel and Hirshel were sipping tea. The yeshiva boy was licking poppy cake crumbs from his fingers. Frau Buchthal smiled at me and passed me a slice of cake. The storm was over.

As they began to sing Shabbas songs, a huge bubble of homesicknesses swelled inside me. If we were home, we would be sitting around the table singing just like this. Mama would be leaning back in her chair with a loving smile on her face. Shloyme would be clapping his hands and bouncing up and down to the music. Hannah would be sucking her thumb and resting her head against my arm as her eyes began to close.

The Shabbas candles blurred in front of my eyes.

"Please excuse me," I said.

"Where are you going, Raizel?" Papa asked as I pushed back the chair.

"Let her go." Frau Buchthal's kind voice followed me up the stairs. "She's tired, poor little thing, after all she's been through."

I threw myself on the bed as the bubble burst and tears engulfed me. I missed Mama and Lemmel and Shloyme and Hannah so much I felt like I would drown in my tears. It was the first Shabbas I had ever been away from home.

How many Sabbaths would pass before we were all together again?

10

Crossing the Map

"Ach, I wish you could stay longer," said Frau Buchthal on Sunday morning. She was helping Helga pack our food baskets. "Put in another jar of your famous plum preserves, Helga. Ja, and those mandelbrot cookies you keep hidden on the top shelf, you thought I didn't know?"

I gripped a lump of sugar between my teeth as I sipped my tea, and silently agreed with her. After resting all day Saturday, I felt like a newborn calf ready to go out to the meadow for the first time, but I was sorry to leave Frau Buchthal. She was so kind to us. If only Jews were allowed to stay in Austro-Hungary where it was safe.

"You have been very good to us," Papa said. "We will thank you in our prayers."

"Helping unfortunate people is a mitzvah. But in your case it was more than a mitzvah. Seeing the apples come back to Raizel's cheeks has given me great happiness." She pressed her hands to my face.

"Thank you very much, Frau Buchthal." I kissed her powdery cheek. She smelled like lilacs.

"Ach, what a sweet child you are." Frau Buchthal hugged me and smoothed my hair, which she had braided herself this morning. "You take care and don't fall into any more rivers!"

I laughed and brushed away a sudden tear.

Frau Buchthal insisted we take a carriage to the station. Hirshel was sitting on his bench in the morning sunlight. Papa shook hands with him and thanked him for his help.

"What a nice lady Frau Buchthal is," I said to Papa as we sat on our suitcases waiting for the train. Our food baskets were stuffed with cold chicken, fresh bread, and Helga's special plum preserves. It looked like enough food to last a week at least. How far was it to Antwerp?

"There are good people everywhere," Papa said.

"Was Ivan a good person?"

"Of course. He saved your life and took us safely over the border." Papa looked at his watch.

"But Papa," I lowered my voice to a whisper so the other people on the platform wouldn't hear. "He hates Jews."

"He hates Jews, but he loves his fellow man."

"I don't understand." How could someone hate us and love us at the same time. Weren't we people just like everyone else?

"He has been taught lies. Taught that the Jews killed his savior Jesus. Taught that Jews kill little children to bake matzos."

I shuddered. Always that same lie, the lie the priests told to start the pogroms. "So he hates us."

"Yes—and no."

"Papa! I still don't understand."

"Neither do I, meydele." Papa sighed. "I guess people are a mixture of good and bad. Sometimes the bad comes out, sometimes the good." He took out a handkerchief and wiped his glasses. "Think of it as wearing a pair of dirty glasses. When you look through them, the world is smeared and distorted. That is how Ivan sees the Jews. When you take them off, the world is clean and bright. Unfortunately, too many people walk around with dirty glasses. But in any case, no one is perfectly good or perfectly bad."

"Mama is perfectly good."

Papa laughed. "Your mama is a very good woman, but not perfect. Only God is perfect."

"But man was created in His image. The Bible says so. So man must be perfect."

"Yes, but do not forget, man was created out of earth and clay. Man can never be as perfect as God." Papa patted my hair. "What a fine mind you have. Too bad Lemmel does not have your head. It is wasted on a girl."

I jerked away from Papa as if he had slapped me! Why could I never have a conversation with him without being reminded that I was just a girl? It wasn't my fault I couldn't go to school like Lemmel. I didn't want to waste my mind.

Before I could reply, the train roared into the station. Papa grabbed the suitcases and I stomped after him with the food baskets. This train was divided into small compartments with benches facing each other. I plopped into the window seat and pressed my burning face to the glass as the train pulled out of Brody. How would I ever convince Papa to let me go to school?

If only I knew more about America. How much did it cost to go to school? Were there schools for girls in New York? No one in Jibatov ever talked about school in America. All those stories they told . . . how much truth did they contain? Maybe they were just trying to put a face to the unknown, as Mama would say. I shivered and tightened the shawl around my shoulders. We were so far from America and so far from home at one and the same time.

In Brody I had felt safe. Now we were traveling once again into the unknown, like stepping out from a cliff into a vast chasm. Lemmel called it an adventure, but to me it was like falling through empty space, not knowing where you would fall, what you might hit, or the kind of people you would meet on the way.

Thoughts about Ivan kept crawling around in my mind like a persistent spider. What would happen if I met him during a pogrom? Would he try to kill me even after he had saved my life? Would the bad part win out, or the good part?

"Papa, why did God create evil?" I asked.

Papa put down his prayer book. "Such questions you have today! The rabbis say man chose evil when he disobeyed God's commandment not to eat of the tree of the knowledge of good and evil in the Garden of Eden."

"But Papa, it was the snake who tempted Eve. And God made the snake."

"Oy, meydele! Today you have questions our learned men have been trying to answer for thousands of years."

"You mean there are no answers?" I couldn't believe it. I was sure the wise rabbis knew everything. Why, they spent their whole lives studying!

Papa closed his book. "Let me tell you a little story. One day the Evil One came to God wailing and tearing his clothes. 'Almighty God, I am so unhappy. I have no work and am bored to tears. All day there is nothing for me to do.'

"'That's your own fault,' God replied. 'Your job is to lead people into sin. Why don't you do your job?'

"'You don't understand.' The Evil One cried even harder. 'Why, before I get a chance to tempt someone into evil, he's already gone and sinned!'"

I laughed. "Papa, that's a silly story."

"True, but it has a serious moral. God gives man the freedom to choose. Man makes his own choice."

That made sense. But it still didn't explain why Ivan could make one choice to save me and another choice to hate Jews.

"Papa . . . ?"

"More questions? You are like a dry well."

"I was just going to say it's time for lunch, Papa." My stomach was grumbling almost as loudly as the train wheels.

"Mmmm." Papa bit into a cold chicken leg. "That Helga knows how to cook almost as well as your mama!"

I took a deep breath for courage. "Papa, sometimes I do feel like a dry well. There are so many things I want to know." I forced myself to look Papa straight in the eyes. "May I go to school in America, Papa? That is, if there is a school near where we live. I will clean the house and cook for you after school. I promise, Papa."

"And when will you have time to go to market? And mend the clothes? And bake bread? And prepare for the Sabbath? No, Raizel, what do you think your mama does all day, sit around drinking cold lemonade with her feet up?"

The idea of Mama having time to sit fanning herself and drinking lemonade almost made me smile. "But Mama has Shloyme and Hannah and Lemmel and me to take care of. In America there will be just the two of us."

"Raizel, who has been putting these ideas in your head? Your mama never went to school and neither did Bobbe or your Aunt Freida. They are good pious women. You should be proud to be like them."

I turned my head to the window so Papa wouldn't see the tears sprouting in my eyes. I felt like Papa had stabbed me with a bread knife. Of course I wanted to be a good wife and mother like Mama. But I also wanted to read books and learn about the world. Why wasn't it possible to do both?

"Never mind, meydele." Papa's voice was softer now. "You think I do not know what it is like when you want to learn? It is like a thirst that can never be quenched. If we have time on the boat, I will teach you to read. But you must never forget that the important thing is for all of us to be together again as a family. We have no money to spend on luxuries like school."

I felt ashamed. How could I be so selfish and think only of myself? "Yes, you're right, Papa." In my mind I saw myself wrapping my dreams in brown paper and tucking them away in the back of the cupboard. Perhaps someday I would unwrap the package, blow away the cobwebs and the dust, and wear my dream again. For now there were more important things to worry about.

And worry I did as I stared out the window at the fields and towns of Austro-Hungary. Where would we sleep? Would our food last the journey? How were Mama and the children getting along back home? My mind gnawed at my worries until the sun set. Darkness came and we slept, waking each time the train stopped at a station and people got on and off. Sometimes the train stopped for a few minutes and a man came down the aisle selling hot tea. After a day or two, the fresh food Frau Buchthal had given us was gone, except for some hard loaves of bread and the plum jam. I wished Papa would buy food in the station like the other passengers, but I knew he wouldn't. It wasn't kosher.

One exciting day we passed through Berlin. It was late afternoon when we reached the outskirts of the city. I had never seen such tall buildings or so many people in the streets at one time. The central railway station had high ceilings like an enormous cave, filled with noise and smoke. I stayed close to Papa as we changed trains. If I lost him, how would I ever find him again in this crowd?

When we pulled out of the station, it was already dark. The streetlights streaked past like fireflies on a summer night. Berlin was so big that a thousand Jibatovs could fit inside and still leave room for more. I fell asleep that night with streamers of light twirling through my dreams.

I lost track of the days. Every morning I asked the same question: "Papa, how much further?"

Papa cleaned his glasses on his soiled handkerchief. "Not much. Only a few more days."

A few more days! The worst part was having to sit still most of the time. When the train wasn't too crowded, I wandered up and down the aisles. I never got out on the platform like the other passengers when the train stopped. What if it pulled out suddenly and left me behind?

No, the worst part was having no other children to talk to. Papa and I told Chelm stories to each other and made up riddles. I tried to remember every train story I had ever heard. In my head I held long conversations with Lemmel and Leah. I told Shloyme and Hannah bedtime stories and wiped my eyes with my handkerchief thinking how they must be missing me.

My favorite story was about America. I lived in a fine stone house, bigger than Frau Buchthal's and filled with thick Persian rugs and carved wooden furniture. Leah visited me and we took tea like two grown-up ladies.

"How brave you are, Raizel," Leah said as she sipped her tea from a delicate porcelain cup with blue forget-me-nots around the rim. "Weren't you scared when you fell in the river?"

"Oh no," I said, passing her a heaping plate of crisp almond cookies. "A handsome prince was passing by and he rescued me."

"And did he pick you up on his white stallion and carry you away?" Leah smoothed her green silk dress. My dress was red velvet with lace at the cuffs. My long hair was silky-smooth and I wore gold earrings.

"Yes, he took me to his castle. He was a Russian nobleman, but he was secretly Jewish."

"How romantic!" Leah clapped her hands. "Perhaps your Papa will let you marry him someday."

"Shall I tell you a secret?"

Leah leaned forward eagerly.

"Raizel, we have arrived. Get your things."

I opened my eyes. "Are we in America?"

"No, foolish one. We are in Antwerp and it is time to get off the train."

We dragged our suitcases off the train. We were in an enormous glass-roofed room, with lacy glass windows like the palaces of my stories. I caught my breath.

"Papa, what is this beautiful place?"

"The central railroad station of Antwerp. You thought you were in the Czar's palace? Stop gaping, Raizel, and come along. We must find the steamship office."

We carried our luggage down a gigantic winding staircase. The marble walls and intricate decoration made me feel like an arriving princess. But Papa dragged our suitcases along and didn't seem to notice.

After all those days on the train, the solid ground felt strange under my feet. There was no more rumbling and quaking. I moved through space slowly and deliberately, like a fly swimming in honey. I wanted to run and skip down the street, but I clutched the almost-empty food baskets and followed Papa out of the station.

Luckily the steamship office was just across the street. It was empty except for a bored-looking clerk smoking a cigarette and reading a newspaper. He glanced at us and examined the tickets Papa handed him.

"The Manitou. Yah." He spoke to Papa in a German that I understood because it sounded like Yiddish. "She is scheduled to leave in two weeks. Come any morning at ten o'clock for the doctor's examination."

"Two weeks? How can that be? Our tickets are for the day after next. See, it says right here." Papa pointed at the ticket.

The clerk shrugged his shoulders. "Two weeks. Maybe ten days." He went back to reading his paper.

"Papa, where are we going to stay until the boat leaves?" I tugged at Papa's sleeve as we left the office. I had an awful vision of sleeping in the train station.

Papa shook his head. He sat down on a suitcase and shook his head again.

"Do we have enough money for a hotel?" Before I finished the question, I knew the answer.

Papa took out his leather money pouch and counted slowly. Then he shook his head still again. I looked up and down the street, half expecting to see Hirshel coming to our rescue. Men walked by dressed in short gray coats and striped pants. Women in fine blue and green silk dresses strolled along wearing hats with gorgeous purple plumes fluttering in the salt breeze. No one looked at us. No one looked like Papa.

It was hot in the sun and I was thirsty. Perhaps we could find a synagogue and sleep there. Maybe some nice people in the synagogue would invite us home with them as Papa invited strangers in Jibatov to share our Sabbath dinner.

"No more charity," Papa said when I told him my idea. "I did not leave Jibatov to live on other people's charity. I have the money I was saving for our first days in America, until I find a job. Wait here."

Papa walked back into the shipping office. Around me people were pouring out of tall buildings. Everybody seemed in a hurry, gesturing with his or her hands and talking in a language I couldn't understand. Horse-drawn carriages bumped along the cobbled streets as people whistled and waved to them. Sitting on my suitcase, I felt like a tiny island in a raging river of people. As more and more people poured into the street, the current rose higher and higher, threatening to engulf me in the flood.

I had never felt so far from home in my life.

11

Antwerp Temptations

"Papa, where are we going?" I asked as he left the office and waved for a carriage.

"The clerk told me about an inn where Jews stay."

"Do we have enough money to stay at an inn?"

Papa didn't answer. He stared straight ahead, pressing his lips together as his mind calculated how much money we would have left to begin our lives in America. It must not have been enough, because Papa took off his glasses and pinched the bridge of his nose as if his head hurt.

I might have enjoyed the ride if I hadn't been so worried. After the railroad station, the rest of the buildings in Antwerp looked like the leftover bread from a wedding feast. When we reached an area of older crowded houses, I saw a synagogue and knew we were in the Jewish quarter.

Papa paid the driver and pulled our suitcases into a four-story building whose plaster was cracked and stained. A man with a long black beard and skullcap on his head came out of an office. His black coat was shiny with grease and his teeth were stained brown from tobacco. His mouth turned down at the corner like a question mark when he looked at us.

"You have a room for us?" Papa asked in Yiddish.

The man said something about francs. What was a franc?

Papa closed his eyes and whispered some numbers in rubles. Franc must be the Belgium ruble. Then he shook his head. "You have something cheaper?"

"The attic room." Again he mentioned francs. "Three kosher meals a day. Pay by the week. In advance."

"I have only rubles."

"You have a watch?"

Papa nodded. His gold watch had been a present from Uncle Nahum when he married Mama. Papa loved his watch.

"Then give me your watch for security and pay later. Dinner is at six." Papa pulled his gold watch out of his pocket. For just a second he hesitated. Then he put it into the man's hand and took a heavy iron key in return. Without a word, the man went back into his office. What an unfriendly person. I didn't like him, even if he was Jewish.

I helped Papa drag our suitcases up the narrow wooden stairs. We pulled and tugged until Papa had to sit down and rest. He wiped the sweat from his forehead as he tried to catch his breath. Just then a boy with curly brown hair came bounding up the stairs.

"Do you need some help?" he asked in Yiddish that sounded like ours. Without waiting for an answer, he grabbed the biggest suitcase. Papa and I followed with the rest of our luggage up to the top floor. We stopped before a narrow wooden door.

"Thank you," Papa called to the boy as he ran down the stairs again.

Our room was tiny and smelled like someone had forgotten dirty wet socks in a corner. Mold and damp patterned the crumbling plaster walls like black frost. The roof was so low even Papa had to stoop. I opened the tiny window and peered out at gray rooftops as I caught a breath of fresh air. I didn't care what the room looked like as long as I could sleep in a real bed again! I plopped down on the narrow bed and almost bumped the floor as the springs gave way. Still, it was better than a hard bench in the train station.

"Papa, do we have enough money? What if the boat is delayed even more?"

Papa took out his money pouch and counted carefully. "We have enough. I can sell my watch if need be. Now stop worrying." Papa was still breathing hard from climbing the stairs.

"Papa . . . ?"

"Not now, meydele. I want to rest a while."

Papa was used to carrying heavy loads. I hoped he wasn't feeling sick. I pushed the thought away as I unpacked the suitcases and arranged our clothes in the lopsided wooden closet, Papa's clothes on one shelf and mine on the other. Now everything felt more homelike. Mama would be proud of me. I turned to Papa, but he was asleep with his prayer book open on his chest.

Not wanting to stay in the tiny room, I quietly opened the door and walked downstairs. About twenty people were sitting in a large dining room on the ground floor talking or playing cards. Several children ran about shouting and trying to catch each other. They reminded me of Shloyme and Hannah and I missed them terribly. A woman wearing a brown silk dress with white lace at the cuffs and collar frowned and put a finger to her lips. She was reading to a girl with long golden ringlets.

"Shah!" Her handsome face looked stern.

The children stared at her and went back to their game. A woman wearing a faded gray dress and nursing a baby glared at the elegant woman. She muttered something in a language I couldn't understand, and then called out in Yiddish, "At the bathhouse, everyone is equal."

The elegant woman sniffed and adjusted her feathered hat. She bent her head and continued reading to the girl sitting next to her. I couldn't stop staring at the girl's hair, which fell in smooth curls like strands of honey. Why, she had the hair of a princess in one of my stories. Suddenly, the girl turned around and looked at me. She seemed about my age.

"Mother, I'm tired of reading. May I go outside?"

"Yes, but don't go far away." When the woman looked at her daughter, her face was soft and loving. "We'll be having dinner soon."

The girl pouted. "Can't I just eat some ice cream? I'm tired of potatoes."

"So am I. Well, we'll see." The woman gathered her skirts and walked slowly up the stairs. As she passed I caught a whiff of roses.

"What's your name?" The blond-haired girl planted herself in front of me. "My name is Susan."

"I'm Raizel Balaban. What kind of name is Susan?"

"An American name. Everyone knows that! In St. Petersburg they called me Soyrele, but Papa says in America my name will be Susan. And my brother Reuben's name will be Robert. What will they call you?"

"Why do I have to change my name?" Raizel had been my great-grandmother's name.

"So you won't be a greenborn. How old are you?"

I had no idea what a greenborn was, but I didn't feel like giving Susan the satisfaction of asking. "Eleven. Going on twelve. How old are you?"

"Ten." Susan pouted like I had won the game. "I lived in a big house with servants in St. Petersburg. Where did you live?"

"Jibatov."

Susan smirked. "I never heard of Jibatov. What ship are you traveling on?"

"The Manitou."

"So am I! How nice! Now I can have a friend almost my own age. I'm tired of Reuben—I mean Robert—bossing me around all the time. Do you have any brothers?"

"Two. And a sister. They're all younger than me. I miss them." My throat closed.

"I miss my Papa. He went to America three years ago. Reuben is fourteen and thinks he knows everything. Oh, there goes the dinner bell. I have to call Mother. The food here is awful. Sometimes she lets me get an ice cream for dinner. Want to come?"

Without waiting for an answer, Susan skipped up the stairs. I went to wake Papa, wondering what ice cream was.

At dinner we sat at a long table across from Susan and her mother and brother, the same boy who had helped carry our luggage. He didn't wear long side curls like the other men and boys I knew. I couldn't tell if he was wearing a skullcap. Suddenly I saw him watching me and ducked my eyes. Papa said the blessing over the food and Reuben joined him.

Susan refused to eat anything, but I thought the lentil soup and potatoes were delicious. It was wonderful to eat hot food after long days of stale bread and jam. There was even fruit compote for desert. Susan and her mother argued about the food all through dinner. Reuben ignored them and finished everything on his plate.

The next morning Papa went to synagogue and I ate breakfast with Susan and Reuben.

"We're going for a walk. Want to come?" Susan asked, putting down her bowl of coffee and milk. I noticed she had eaten even more bread and butter than Reuben.

I hesitated. Would Papa permit me to go out alone?

"Come on," Reuben said. "Don't be shy. We'll show you Antwerp."

"My papa won't know where I am."

"Why don't you leave him a note?" asked Susan.

I fixed my eyes on Susan's high-buttoned shoes. Should I tell them? What if Susan thought I was dumb and didn't want to be my friend? But I wanted to see the city with them. "I don't know how to write," I said finally in a low voice.

"You don't know how to write?" Susan snorted. "Everyone knows how to write! Don't they teach you anything in school in Bibatok?"

"Jibatov. In Jibatov we don't have a school for girls. Mama taught me to read a few prayers, but she never had time to teach me to write." I wished I could sink into the floorboards. I never should have told them.

"I'll write your papa a note, Raizel." Reuben took a small notebook from his pocket and tore out a page. He wrote a few words with a pencil. "Raizel has gone for a walk with Susan and Reuben. Back before lunch."

"Thank you." I took the note and ran upstairs. When I came down, Reuben was scolding Susan.

"But she must be stupid not to know how to write." Susan stamped her foot. "And she doesn't know anything about America, either."

"Stop acting like a spoiled brat," Reuben said. He saw me and smiled. "Come on, let's go. Are you coming, Susan?"

Susan turned her back.

"I don't care if you stay here all morning," Reuben said. "I'm going out with Raizel." He opened the front door for me and waited while I stepped outside. Lemmel always ran out in front of me. Maybe that's how they did things in St. Petersburg.

Once we were outside, I wondered if I had done the right thing. Walking with a strange boy without a chaperone felt wrong. Mama wouldn't approve. When Susan caught up with us a minute later, I let out a sigh of relief.

"Let's take Raizel to the park," she suggested, and smiled at me as if nothing had happened. Susan's moods passed as quickly as the wispy clouds overhead.

It was a warm sunny day. The park was lined with tall chestnut trees shading the paths. Strange exotic flowers in shades of scarlet and gold grew in neat flowerbeds. Men strolled along wearing white suits and tall hats. The women wore long pastel summer dresses and tilted silk parasols over their heads. They were so beautiful. No one dressed like that in Jibatov, even on holidays when people wore their best clothes to synagogue. For the first time I felt like I was in a foreign country. I wondered what they thought of my plain dark clothes and clumsy shoes. Or maybe they didn't even notice me.

We walked until we came to a grove of pine trees in the center of the park.

"Let's play hide and seek!" Susan shouted. Reuben covered his eyes and began to count. Susan grabbed my hand and we ran to the center of the grove. We crawled under the low hanging branches of an ancient pine tree that seemed to have escaped from a Russian forest.

"This is just like a cave, all dark and secret," I whispered. Outside sounds were muffled like a rainy day.

"It's too dark here." Susan huddled closer to me. "I don't like it. Let's find someplace else to hide."

"Shhh. I can see fine. I love the pine smell, don't you?" I was listening for Reuben's footsteps. "Hey, where are you going?"

Susan pushed my hand aside and rushed out of the hiding place. I ran after her and bumped into Reuben.

"Caught you!" He tapped my arm.

"Susan ran away."

Reuben dashed out of the grove. Susan was sitting on a bench hugging herself and rocking back and forth. Her face was streaked with tears.

"Susan, what happened?" I asked. "Are you sick?"

She curled into a ball and shook her head.

"She's just frightened." Reuben patted his sister's back. "She doesn't like the dark."

"But it wasn't dark under the tree. Not really."

"I'll get you something to drink," Reuben said to his sister. "Stay here with Raizel and try to calm down."

I put my arm around Susan. What had scared her so badly? I had been right there and nothing had frightened me. Maybe the pine grove reminded her of the dark Russian forests with their giant trees and wild wolves. I shuddered remembering my own fears of the forest. Maybe later I would tell her how we crossed the Russian border at night and how brave I had been. How silly to be frightened of a pine grove in the middle of Antwerp!

"I know a story about a beautiful garden. Want to hear it?"

"Stories are for babies." Susan blew her nose in her lace handkerchief.

"Not this one. My Bobbe only told it when we had grown-up visitors." Susan didn't answer, so I continued. "Once there was a young man. He took care of his elderly parents until they died and then went out into the world to seek his fortune. At nightfall, he found himself in a deep dark forest." Susan began to cry harder. I patted her back. "As the last light of day faded, he saw a tall golden gate. He knocked and a gatekeeper appeared.

"'You may enter this kingdom only if you can restore the lost name.'

"'But I don't know the name,' said the young man.

"The gatekeeper turned away. The young man peered through the golden bars. Dead and dying trees lined the stone paths. The earth was dry and hard around the marble statues. But outside in the forest, everything was fresh and green. Unable to enter the garden, the young man took shelter in the roots of an old oak tree and tried to sleep, even though he was hungry and thirsty and afraid of wild animals.

"He must have dozed off because he awoke to the sound of the most beautiful music he had ever heard. He followed the melody and found that he was no longer hungry or thirsty or afraid. All night he listened to the beautiful strains of music and, as the sun rose, he saw a fine wooden instrument hidden in the hollow of the oak tree. He took it in his hands and began to stroke the silken strings. Although he didn't know how to play, out came lovely notes and harmonies! He walked along playing the instrument until he came to the golden gate. As he approached, the gate opened by itself and the young man wandered into the garden. He sat down by the dry fountain. As he continued to play, water gushed forth and filled the fountain to overflowing. The trees raised their branches and leaves burst forth. Grass spread over the dry lawns and spring crocuses and daffodils popped out of the rocky nooks. The young man played on until the garden was green and growing.

"A beautiful princess appeared before him with tears in her eyes. 'Thank you for finding the lost name of our kingdom,' she said.

"'But I don't know the name,' the young man answered. Then he looked at the fine wooden instrument he was holding and smiled. The princess took his hand and led him into the castle at the far end of the garden. He married the princess, became king, and together they ruled wisely and well."

"But what was the name of the kingdom?" Susan wasn't crying anymore.

"Guess."

"I don't know. What do you think, Reuben?"

I swung around. Reuben was holding a glass of lemonade and looking at me. My face burned like hot coals. How long had he been listening? Did he think I was a baby for telling stories?

"Why the Kingdom of Music, of course." He smiled at me. "It's a pretty story."

Reuben handed the lemonade to Susan who gulped it down. Her eyes were dry now, but her face was streaked and red. "Come, let's go wash your face."

We found a water fountain. After Susan splashed water on her face, she seemed fine, just as chatty as ever.

"I love parks," she said.

"Do you think New York has parks like this?" I asked.

Reuben looked doubtful. "Father never wrote about a park."

"We're going to live in a big house with a flower garden, just like in St. Petersburg," Susan said.

"Susan, we won't have a house at first." Reuben corrected her. "We'll live in an apartment on the Lower East Side."

"My papa sells furs, only now he's working as a cutter until he has enough money to open his own store. What does your papa do?"

"He sells pots and pans and things to the peasants."

"He's a peddler?" Susan's mouth twisted downwards.

"He used to be a scholar, but he had to leave the yeshiva to support his family. My great grandfather was a famous rabbi, Rev Balaban."

"Never heard of him." Susan tossed her curls. "We're modern Jews, aren't we, Reuben?"

I was about to ask what a modern Jew was when Susan said, "Let's go buy some ice cream before lunch. Mama gave me five centimes."

I followed them out of the park. Now I would learn what ice cream was. We stopped in front of a shop window piled high with silver platters full of chocolates. When we walked in, the smell was so rich and thick I could taste the chocolate in my mouth.

Susan marched up to a woman dressed in a spotless white apron. "Deux glace," she ordered. She turned to me. "Do you have any money?"

I shook my head.

"Mama only gave me enough money for two, but you can share with us," Susan said. Reuben nodded approvingly.

The woman handed her two cone-shaped cakes wrapped in white paper. A shiny brown mound stuck out on top.

"Chocolate is my favorite. What's yours?" Susan took a huge bite of the brown stuff.

"I don't know."

"You mean you've never eaten ice cream before? Raizel, you're such a greenborn!"

"You mean greenhorn," Reuben said. "That's what they call newcomers to America. When we get there, we'll all be greenhorns."

"Not me!" Susan held out her cone to me.

I took a tentative lick. "Mmmm. It's delicious, so creamy and cold."

"Here, have some of mine." Reuben offered me his cone. By the time we were back at the inn, the ice cream had disappeared.

"See you at lunch!" Susan called as she ran up the stairs. "I have to do my lessons. Mama doesn't want me to fall behind. Come on, Reuben."

They entered their room on the second floor and I continued up to the attic. Papa was sitting on a rickety wooden chair reading his prayer book.

"Did you have a nice walk, meydele?" He looked up. "What's that on your chin? Mud?"

I licked my lips. "It's ice cream, Papa. Susan and Reuben let me share their ice cream cones. You should see how pretty the park is. The ladies all wear fine dresses and some of them even have funny little dogs on long chains."

"What is this ice cream?" Papa's face was stern. "Where did you get it?"

"In a shop. It was clean and full of chocolate. It smelled heavenly. I wish I could send some to Lemmel and Shloyme and Hannah. And Mama, of course."

"Who served you?" Papa paused between each word.

"A woman in a white apron, Papa." Why did Papa seem angry? What had I done wrong?

"Was she a Jew? Was the shop kosher?"

"I don't know, Papa." Susan had spoken French not Yiddish. "I don't think so."

"Oy, Raizel! What is the matter with your head? You go out for a walk in a strange city and forget everything your mama and I taught you? You know it is forbidden to eat tref! Your mama would hide her face in shame if she found out. She has never eaten tref in her life and neither have I." Papa's voice shook.

"I'm sorry, Papa. I didn't think." Tears poured from my eyes. Papa had never been angry with me like this before, only with Lemmel.

How could I have been so careless? I had broken one of the most important Jewish laws. Papa never broke the kosher laws, even when he was far from home and there were no Jewish families to give him food. And I had eaten tref when I wasn't even hungry! "Are you going to whip me, Papa?"

"No. You are whipping yourself enough." Papa opened his prayer book and turned his back to me.

It would have been better to take a whipping. My stomach felt like Papa had slit me open. Suddenly I had a syrupy metallic taste in my mouth. I dashed down the stairs and vomited sweet brown liquid onto the cobblestones. I spit out every last drop. People in the street made a wide circle around me. When I was sure there was nothing left in my stomach, I went back inside and up the stairs.

"Raizel, aren't you coming to lunch?" Susan called from the doorway of her room.

"I don't feel well."

Papa wasn't in the room when I got there. I lay down on the bed and pulled the blanket over my head. I didn't eat lunch that day or supper either. And I never ate ice cream again, as long as we were in Antwerp.

12

Setting Sail

Papa swayed back and forth with his prayer shawl over his head. I tapped my foot and began edging to the door. The Feinsteins were waiting for us. Why hadn't Papa begun his morning prayers earlier?

Finally Papa finished and picked up our suitcases. I carried the food baskets packed with toast, hard cheese, dried herring, and apples. Luckily the boat had arrived after a week, so we still had money left to pay our room and board and purchase food for the journey. The food on the Manitou wasn't kosher, so we were taking enough for two weeks. What would we do if the journey lasted longer? I pushed the thought to the back of my mind. I was too frightened of the ocean to think about anything else right now.

"Here you are!" Susan tossed her freshly curled hair. "Mama is so nervous."

There were dark circles under Mrs. Feinstein's eyes. She clasped and unclasped her hands as she looked out the door into the gray light of early morning. "It's raining. I knew we should have sold the house and made the crossing in summer. Who knows what storms we'll hit at sea?"

"Mother, it's only September. The weather will clear up," Reuben said. He set our wooden suitcases atop the pile of fine leather luggage belonging to the Feinsteins. They had invited us to share space on the wagon they had hired. Reuben was big for his age, and strong. His school had athletic classes and he told me how he enjoyed hiking, and even skiing! Lemmel would have liked Reuben's school.

We joined the Feinsteins in a carriage and followed the baggage wagon, clopping slowly through the rain-swept streets.

I could smell rotting fish even before we reached the harbor. We drove past wooden fishing boats bobbing in the rain until we reached the Manitou. It was enormous! I craned my neck to see the upper deck. It was bigger than the train station in Brody, bigger than the train station in Antwerp! I never knew a boat could be as large as a small town.

Many boats were anchored in a wide bay of dark oily water. I craned my neck to see further.

"Where's the ocean?" I asked.

"Antwerp is an inland port," Reuben explained. "We have to travel down the river for a few hours to the North Sea."

A long line of passengers stood in the rain waiting to board the ship. Mrs. Feinstein called for a porter to carry their luggage aboard. Susan had told me all about going second class. They would have their own cabin and private bathroom. She promised that I could visit them. I wondered how many people would share our third-class cabin. I covered my head with my shawl to keep off the rain as we joined the line of third-class passengers.

The rain faded into a drizzle. I studied the black hull of the Manitou. Paint was peeling off it, exposing the rust below.

"Papa, this boat looks very old."

"You were expecting a luxury liner?" Papa coughed and pulled his coat around his neck.

"Papa, try not to cough when we give them our tickets," I whispered. Papa had caught a cold when the rain began last week. Luckily it was after the health inspection at the steamship office.

At the hotel, everyone talked constantly about the health inspections. They told stories of families who had to leave a grandparent—or even a child behind—because they had some contagious eye disease or sores on their head. America wouldn't let you in if you were sick, and the steamship company would have to pay your fare back to Europe. The doctor in the steamship office examined me quickly, but he took more time with Papa, listening to his lungs and peering into his eyes. "You are too thin. You should eat more," he said finally, stamping our certificates. "Americans like fat people."

Now Papa smiled at me. "It will be all right, meydele. We passed the health inspection already."

"But there may be another one on the boat."

Papa shook his head. "I asked. Anyway, I am not sick. I just have a sniffle. It will clear up in a day or two."

I chewed my lip. If we were home, Mama would put Papa to bed with a hot cloth on his chest and give him herb teas to drink. But there were no herbs growing on the streets of Antwerp and Papa had refused to see a doctor for "just a cold."

But instead of getting better, Papa's cold seemed to be getting worse. He had coughed all night. Not that I could have slept. I kept thinking about the crossing. Tonight we would be out in the ocean. Europe would be behind us. Somehow, as long as we were in Europe, I felt like we could still turn around, retrace our steps, and find ourselves back in Jibatov. Imagine the look on everyone's face when we returned! Mama would hug and kiss us. Shloyme and Hannah would grab hold of my skirts and not let go. Even Lemmel would be nice to me when he heard about the dangerous river crossing and how I had almost drowned. None of my friends had ever been so far away from Jibatov, not even Leah. I had enough stories to tell them for the rest of my life. If only we could go home!

"Come, Raizel." Papa handed our tickets to the steamship steward. I watched as he checked off our names on the passenger list. He motioned for us to follow the crowd of people pushing down the narrow metal stairs.

We were shoved and elbowed along until we reached a windowless room. Beds lined the room, built one on top of the other in a way I had never seen before. Men, women, and children were yelling and shoving to reach the lower beds.

"Quick Papa, there's an empty bunk over there!"

Papa pushed his way to the end of the room and threw our things onto a lower berth. The planks were covered with a thin mattress. Even thinner blankets were folded at the end of the bunk.

A steward came down the narrow aisle shouting orders.

"Put your baggage on your bunk!" he called. "Nothing must clog the aisles. The children will sleep with you," he said to the woman on the bed next to us who had two little children.

"But I paid for two berths," she said.

"No room, no room," said the man. "We're oversold as is." The woman looked like she was about to cry.

I sat down on the bed, careful not to bump my head. Lucky we were both so thin. So this was third class. People yelled and called to each other in languages I didn't understand. Women sobbed. Babies wailed. There must have been over fifty people in the room, all talking at once. My head felt like a beehive. I would have to sleep with these noisy strangers for the next two weeks. I envied Susan her second-class cabin.

"Papa, I'm going to look for Susan." Papa lay back on the bunk with his eyes closed. He opened his eyes for a moment as if he wanted to say something, then nodded and waved me to leave. He had gotten used to my coming and going with Susan while we were at the inn.

Outside the cabin the air smelled fresher. I climbed the narrow metal stairs to the second deck. Suddenly I heard familiar voices.

"But I paid for a second-class compartment! How dare you put me in third class!" Mrs. Feinstein's voice squeaked like a broken violin. "If my husband were here, you wouldn't do this. You're just taking advantage of a poor woman traveling alone. Well, you'll see. I'll write to the company president. You can't do this to me!"

Mrs. Feinstein, Susan and Reuben stood with their luggage facing a bearded man wearing the ship's uniform. He was holding a stack of papers and shaking his head.

"Oh, Raizel!" Susan's face was tear-streaked. Even the usually calm Reuben looked angry.

"What happened?"

"They don't have a cabin for us. We paid for a second-class cabin and they're putting us in third!"

"How can they do that?"

"They can do anything they want." Reuben's voice was bitter. "And if we refuse to sail on the boat, they won't even refund our money."

The steward carried their baggage down the stairs. In the third-class cabin all the bunks were taken except a few on the second tier.

"I can't sleep on that!" cried Mrs. Feinstein. "Oh, if only my husband were here."

"My mother requires a bottom berth," said Reuben to the steward. His voice was calm with authority. "You have taken away her cabin, so you must give her a bottom bunk."

He handed the steward a few centimes.

The steward looked around the room until he found a lower bunk with two children on it. He chased them into an upper berth and set the Feinstein's luggage on the bed. Reuben put most of it on his bunk in the second tier. Mrs. Feinstein looked around, covered her face with her hands, and collapsed in tears on the bed.

"Don't cry, Mama." Reuben patted her shoulder. "We have a place to sleep. It won't be so bad. It's only for two weeks."

Mrs. Feinstein sobbed more loudly.

Reuben sighed. "Come on, Susan. Let's go exploring."

"I'll stay with mother." Susan curled up next to her mother and stroked her back.

"I'll come." I had to get out of that stuffy noisy room.

Outside the rain had stopped, but the wooden deck was wet and slick. Iron benches were bolted down at intervals for passengers to sit on. We peeked over the locked gate separating the first-class passengers from the rest of us. Men in long woolen coats strolled around the deck smoking their pipes. A few women stood near them wearing white gloves and elegant hats. Fresh flowers were pinned to their coats. I tried to imagine what a first-class cabin looked like, but all I saw was the narrow bed in steerage where I would sleep the next few weeks.

"Will your mother be all right?" I asked.

"I hope so. At home we had a big house and servants, but when she was little she had six brothers and sisters so she knows what it's like to be poor. She'll cheer up soon—I hope."

"Why are you leaving Russia if your father was so wealthy?"

Reuben clutched the ship railing. When he spoke his voice was rough with anger. "The Czar passed a law outlawing Jewish management of estates outside the Pale of Settlement. My father managed an estate along with a non-Jewish partner, so he thought he was safe. But the partner turned on him. He said he would report my father to the secret police."

"How awful!"

"Yes. Father sold his share in the estate for a third of what it was worth. He decided the same day to leave for America. Mother was against it, but here we are. And I'm glad. Father says the Jews have no future in Russia, and I think he's right."

We leaned over the railing, watching the porters scurry around the dock loading boxes and parcels. A whistle hooted. The boat shifted suddenly under our feet. I grasped the rail so hard my knuckles turned white. "Have you ever been on a ship before?" I asked Reuben.

"No. Isn't it exciting?" Reuben smiled. "I think we're going to set sail."

"Do you think the Manitou is s-s-strong enough to carry us all the way across the ocean to America?" My voice quivered like an autumn leaf.

"The Manitou has been back and forth so many times it can probably steer itself like an old horse," he said. "There's nothing to be scared of."

"I'm not frightened," I lied. The whistle shrieked in my ears and the motor started with a horrible roar. The vibrations sent splinters through my bones. "I think I'll go see how Papa is feeling."

Reuben gave me an amused glance as I made my way unsteadily to the staircase. I hated him knowing I was scared, but I couldn't help myself. I knew what drowning felt like. When I fell in the river, I had choked on the water. Instead of air, the water crammed my mouth and nose and eyes like a wall of solid darkness pulling me deeper and deeper into death.

I paused on the stairwell to suck air into my lungs. My heart was beating like the hooves of a runaway horse. Calm down, I told myself. The Manitou is strong. It has lifeboats. Nothing will happen. People cross the ocean every day and you will too. Why, some people even do it for fun! Maybe I could stay in the cabin the whole trip. Then I wouldn't have to look at the ocean.

I was glad to be back in the cabin. Everyone had calmed down except the children racing up and down the aisles. And the babies. Did babies ever stop crying? Mama said that Hannah and Shloyme were good babies and only cried when they were hungry. I hoped these were good babies.

Papa was asleep with his prayer book on his chest, so I went to find Susan. She sat with her hands clasped staring straight ahead. In her fine velvet dress and neatly curled hair she looked like a princess lost in the third-class cabin.

"Are we starting?" she asked.

I nodded and sat down beside her.

"Good. The sooner we begin, the faster we'll get there."

I stared at her. "Aren't you afraid?"

"Of what?"

"Of the ocean. It's so big and deep and sometimes there are terrible storms and the ship might sink and . . . "

Susan put her hands over her mouth and giggled. "Oh Raizel, you are so funny. I think you have too much imagination."

I had to smile. "You may be right."

"So why don't you use it to tell me a story? It's too dark in here to read and I don't want to leave mother." Mrs. Feinstein had fallen asleep, still curled in her fur coat.

"I thought my stories were for babies," I teased.

"Rai-za-al!"

"All right, just let me think a moment." I settled myself against a suitcase until a story stepped into my head. "Once there was a poor man who always had bad luck. He was a woodcutter, but he could never find enough wood to support his family. Bad things were always happening to him. One day while he was out cutting wood, a huge black raven alighted on a branch and watched him while he worked. The raven followed him all day long until the man was sure the raven was the Angel of Death following him on his last day of life."

"Raizel, what a scary story!" Susan covered her ears. "I don't want to hear anymore."

A group of children had stopped open-mouthed to listen. I motioned to them to sit on the floor.

"Don't be scared. It has a happy ending. Finally the man felt a surge of courage and turned to the black bird: 'Who are you and why are you following me?'

"'I am your misfortune,' said the bird. 'I take different forms, but I will follow you all your life.'

"'How can I get rid of you?' asked the woodcutter.

"'If you leave your house tonight and never return, not even for a moment, you will leave me behind,' said the bird, and flew away.

"The woodcutter ran home and told his wife what the bird had said. Quickly they packed all their things on a wagon, and as the moon rose, they left their tiny hut in the forest. Before they had gone even a mile, however, their little son complained he was thirsty and wanted a drink. They discovered they had left the water jug behind. The wife nagged him to go back for it. At first the woodcutter refused, but his son cried so pitifully that in the end they turned back."

"Oh no! Something terrible is going to happen!" This time Susan hid her face in her hands. The other children nudged each other and stared at her.

"Sure enough, as soon as the woodcutter picked up the water jug, he heard a terrible voice say: 'Here we are again. Now you will never get rid of me as long as you live!'

"The woodcutter threw down the jug and ran out of the house, but there was the jug already sitting in the wagon. The wife took the jug and threw it into the woods, but in an instant, it reappeared back in the wagon. So they knew that nothing could be done, and misfortune had returned. Still they continued on their way, for they had no reason to remain in the forest. As they were crossing a deep river, the wife had an idea. Quickly she filled the jug with heavy stones, and threw it in the water. This time the jug sank to the bottom, and didn't return.

"After a few days, the woodcutter and his family settled by a lake. He became a fisherman and always caught more fish than anyone else. Finally he had enough money to feed his family. One day he caught a beautiful white fish. He decided to share it with his family rather than sell it. When his wife cut the fish open, she found a glowing stone inside. They put the stone on the windowsill. That very night, a tree grew up beside the window in the light of the magic stone. It flourished and bore delicious carob fruit that tasted like the Garden of Eden. Every day they sold the fruit for a great deal of money. The woodcutter was able to study Torah, and spend the rest of his days in peace and comfort."

"What a lovely story!" Susan hugged Raizel. "It makes me feel happy."

"Tell us another," demanded a little girl.

"Later." I felt better, too. "I hope we leave our troubles behind just like the woodcutter."

"Me too." Susan shuddered and turned her head away. "In America we won't have any troubles."

I wasn't so sure. In stories there were magic lands, magic stones that granted wishes, even magic animals that spoke. But I had never seen magic in Jibatov. And I had never met someone who had actually seen magic, except perhaps Aunt Freida who claimed she had seen a ghost walking by a dead man's house one night.

"I'm hungry," Susan said. "I'm going to find Reuben. The steward said we can eat in the second-class dining room, even if we have to sleep down below with all the, uh, other people."

I was hungry too, but I was afraid to waste our food. Before we went to sleep that night, Papa and I shared a hard roll and some cheese. The other passengers lined up to receive food cooked in the ship's third-class kitchen. The smell of meat and potatoes filled the room. There was no third-class dining room, so everyone sat on their bunks, spooning up stew out of metal pots. The odor of garlic and onions permeated the sweaty stuffy cabin.

People talked to each other and walked up and down the aisles. Babies cried and children called for their mothers. I was tired. The ship was still chugging slowly down the river towards the sea as I lay down to sleep. I pulled the blanket over my head, but it was too thin to shut out the noise.

"Papa, when will they be quiet? I can't sleep."

"Good night, meydele," Papa said as he covered himself with a blanket. "Sleep will come. Now that we are finally on the ship, our troubles are behind us."

"Papa, don't open your mouth to the devil," I whispered. Mama used to spit three times to avoid bad luck, but Papa said that was superstitious nonsense and wouldn't allow it.

When I was a little girl I collected pretty stones and wished on them secretly. I told Bobbe they were magic wishing stones. She laughed and said, "Raizeleh, don't you know you must make your own magic?" What would Bobbe say if she could see us now on the boat? Were we running away from our misfortune, or were we bringing it with us?

Life was a lot more complicated than stories.

13

Sea Sickness

I woke to the noise of loud groans. The dark cabin was pitching and bucking like a wild stallion.

"Papa, what's happening?" I clutched the mattress to keep from falling out of bed. "Is the boat sinking?"

"No, meydele. Go back to sleep. We are out on the ocean waves now." Papa turned over.

Go back to sleep? With all this noise and rocking? I tried to sit up and bumped my head on the upper bunk as the boat shot upward. My stomach heaved with it and suddenly I had to get to the bathroom. I reached for my shoes, but before I could put them on, my stomach threw up my supper onto the floor. Ugh, disgusting! I lay back on the bed tasting sour metal. My head whirled around and around. I had never felt so sick in my life.

"Papa . . . ?"

Papa leaned over the edge of the bed and retched. Above us someone vomited and the drops splattered on my bare arm. I pulled myself in as far as possible. Papa lay back down and groaned.

"Papa, what is it? Why are we all sick?"

"Sea sickness. They say it passes in a few days."

A few days? I closed my eyes and put my hands over my ears to shut out the groaning and crying. But I couldn't shut out the horrible disgusting smell. It was worse than a manure pile, worse than an outhouse, worse than a heap of decomposing chicken parts.

All through the night I vomited again and again as my head spun and my stomach heaved along with the waves.

"Raizel, do you want some water?"

I must have fallen asleep. Reuben was standing by the bed in the dim cabin light holding a tin cup.

I shook my head. I just wanted to sleep. I just wanted this awful rocking to go away.

"Have some. You'll feel better."

I propped myself on my elbow and took a few sips. I hadn't realized how dry my mouth was. "Thank you. Where are Susan and your mother?"

"They're sick too. I was sick all night, but now I feel better. Give your papa some water, too."

"Papa, drink some water." Papa pushed away the cup and curled into a ball.

"Come up on deck with me," Reuben said. "The smell in here is awful."

I tried to sit up. The room spun around me and I fell back like a splattered cherry. "I can't. But thanks for the water."

"I'll bring you more later."

Reuben disappeared, and the world went dark. I lost track of time, sleeping and waking, always with my head spinning and my stomach turned inside out. Sometimes I dreamed of Mama. Her cool hand stroked my forehead as she crooned my favorite lullabies. Then Reuben was there giving me water. I didn't know if it was night or day. I had fallen into a nightmare, and there was no way to wake up.

Sometimes I managed to stumble to the bathroom, holding on to the beds as I trekked along. But the bathrooms were so filthy with vomit that I couldn't stand going in. We had only two small bathrooms, one for the men and one for the women: three wooden toilets lined up in a row opposite three tin sinks. Six toilets for 50 people!

It was better to stay in bed, even with the rocking and the tossing. Papa slept most of the time, refusing the water that Reuben brought, and moaning and coughing when he was awake. I wanted to help him, but I couldn't even help myself. I missed Mama so bad I thought I would burst. Even when I had scarlet fever and my body burned like an oven, I hadn't felt this awful.

"Let me die, just let me die so I can be out of this misery," groaned a woman in the bunk near me. Silently I agreed with her. Would it never stop? I couldn't stand it anymore, but the misery went on and on and on.

Then one morning I woke up and it was gone. The ship rocked as gently as a baby's cradle. When I sat up, my head stayed firmly on my shoulders. My stomach felt like a shrunken raisin, but the nausea was gone. I wobbled to the bathroom and washed my hands and face in the cold salt water. I even scrubbed my hair with a cake of yellow soap. The washroom was filthy. The cabin was filthy. I wrung out my hair as best I could and pulled it into a braid. I had to get out of here, someplace where the air at least was clean.

As I climbed the metal stairs, every step required thought and energy. My body felt like a fragile shell. I had no idea what time it was or even what day it was. When I stepped on deck, the sea air rushed over me like a cool bath. For a moment I was blinded by sunlight. I blinked until my eyes adjusted to the brightness and made my way to the railing.

The ocean!

It stretched around the ship like an endless waltz of green and white waves dancing in the sunlight. The waves broke against the boat in scoops of white foam. Sunlight skipped on the dark surface. The boat plowed through the sea, leaving furrows of snowy froth in our wake.

"Beautiful, isn't it?" Reuben stood beside me. "How do you feel?"

"Fine now. How many days have we been sailing?"

"Five. If the weather holds, we should reach America in about ten days."

Five days! I felt like years had passed since we boarded the boat. "How are Susan and your mother?"

"They're feeling better. And your papa?"

"He's still sick. He was asleep when I got up." I noticed how dirty my clothes were. They must stink. "I'm going down to see how he's feeling."

"It's almost lunch time. We eat with the second-class passengers. Maybe you can come with us."

I shook my head. "Papa won't let me eat the food on the boat. It's tref. We brought food with us."

Suddenly I realized how hungry I was. Our dry toast and cheese seemed as inviting as Mama's Sabbath dinner.

As I entered the cabin, the smell hit me again. I tried to pretend it wasn't there as I searched through our baskets for something to eat. Papa was sound asleep. I found the dry bread, but where were the apples? And where was the cheese? I took everything out and looked under the blankets. Had Papa moved the food into the suitcases? No. Tears pricked my eyes. Half our food was gone. How could anyone be so mean as to steal our food?

I nibbled on a piece of toast. It was so dry I had to drink some water to moisten it. Finally I broke off tiny bits of bread and dipped them in the water until they were soft enough to eat. When my stomach felt a little less empty, I took clean clothes to the bathroom and washed myself as best I could in the sink. How lovely it would be to bathe in the laundry tub at home. Mama would pour hot water over me and soap my hair until it shone. But there was nowhere to bathe in the third-class cabin.

"Raizel! I'm so glad you're feeling better!" Susan skipped up as I came on deck. "Now I'll have someone to play with again."

"How are you, Raizel? And how is your father?" Mrs. Feinstein looked pale, but her elegant clothes were clean and neat. Her dark hair was piled in waves on top of her head. She didn't wear a scarf over her hair like Mama and the other women in Jibatov.

"Papa's still sick. I'm feeling better, but . . . " I swiped at the tears that were dribbling down my cheeks.

"What's the matter, child?"

"Someone stole our food. All we have is bread and water."

"Oh, you poor thing! But they serve food on the boat. Third-class passengers get soup and bread and meat."

"Papa won't let me eat the food. It isn't kosher."

"I have an idea!" Mrs. Feinstein pulled an apple from her bag. "An apple is an apple. It can't be tref. We get as many as we want at every meal. We'll bring them to you."

I bit into the crisp red fruit. The juice flooded my mouth with sweetness. After ice cream, I had never tasted anything so delicious.

Mrs. Feinstein kept her word. She brought me apples or oranges from every meal. She even brought me rolls, which she explained were baked from flour, water, and yeast so they were kosher too. I missed having warm cooked food, but at least my stomach was full. Day by day, everyone in the third-class cabin got better. People washed, changed their clothes, and began talking with each other. The cabin and bathrooms were cleaned and the sharp acrid smell almost disappeared, although it never entirely went away.

Only Papa didn't get better. He lay on his bunk coughing and moaning. I brought him water, but he wouldn't eat anything. When I tried to talk to him, he would close his eyes and go back to sleep. Mrs. Feinstein shook her head and said to give him a few days. The combination of seasickness and his cold had left him weak. But I worried that it might be more serious. If only Mama were here, she would know what to do. Finally Papa was so weak that he couldn't even sit up.

"Mama, Raizel's crying." Susan ran to get her mother.

"What is it, child? Is your Papa worse?" Mrs. Feinstein approached our bunk.

"I think he doesn't know me anymore." I wiped away my tears. "I'm afraid he's going to . . . "

"Hush, child. Let's call the ship's doctor. I didn't want to go to him before because it may hurt your papa in the health inspection. But it really would be the best thing."

A doctor? No one went to a doctor in Jibatov unless they were rich or dying. "How much will it cost?" I hoped we had enough money.

"The doctor is paid by the ship company. Do you want me to go with you?" Mrs. Feinstein asked.

"No, that's all right." I pulled the covers around Papa's neck. I hadn't left him alone for several days.

The door to the doctor's office was closed. I knocked once and then again more loudly. Finally I opened the door and peaked inside. A man wearing a black coat and pointed beard looked up from a book and frowned at me. He said something I couldn't understand.

"Office hours at ten. Come back tomorrow." He spoke Russian with a German accent.

"My papa is very sick. He needs a doctor."

"Many people are sick. Your papa is throwing up?"

"And coughing. And he has a high fever." I rushed the words out, but the doctor didn't answer. He poured pink liquid into a small bottle.

"Give him ten drops of this medicine in a glass of water every three hours."

"But . . . "

The doctor tapped his long fingers on the table. "Little girl, I am a busy man. Sea sickness will pass." He waved me toward the door like he was brushing away a fly.

I took a deep breath. I knew it was wrong to talk back to grownups, and especially an important man like a doctor, but I had to make him understand. "But Papa is more than seasick. Please, he is very very sick."

"I am the doctor, not you!" He banged the table with his fist. "You third-class passengers have no manners. Did you grow up in a cow barn? Children do not talk back to their betters."

I grabbed the bottle and fled. When I closed the door behind me, my legs were shaking and I was breathing hard. Of course I knew I wasn't supposed to talk back to a grownup. But this was an emergency! I waited for the tears to come, but instead of tears, my anger smoldered like hot coals.

All day and night, I measured out ten drops as best I could and gave them to Papa with a little water. Sometimes he kept them down and sometimes he threw them up. The medicine made him sleep more, but he tossed and turned with fever until I could barely sleep at night. Icy thoughts pricked my body as I lay there in the dark, listening to Papa cough and gasp for breath. What if Papa died? How would I tell Mama? Who would take care of me? How would I get back home? Please, please don't let Papa die.

Susan brought me a roll after breakfast. "Raizel, what a lovely time you missed last night. Someone was playing the harmonica and the ladies were dancing!"

"Susan, go and get your school books," Mrs. Feinstein ordered. "How is your papa today, Raizel?"

"Worse. His fever is up and he doesn't know me at all." I was so tired my hand shook as I measured out his medicine.

"That does it! What kind of doctor gives sea-sickness medicine to a sick man?" asked Mrs. Feinstein. "I'm going to the ship's doctor myself."

I followed Mrs. Feinstein to the infirmary and waited with her until the doctor had seen all the people ahead of us.

"You again?" He glared at me. His pointy face looked sharp as a fox. "You are giving your papa medicine like I told you?"

"Raizel is an excellent nurse," said Mrs. Feinstein. "But Mr. Balaban has a cough and a high fever. He needs a doctor."

"I will give him some pills." He turned his back.

"No!" I cried. "He'll just throw them up. He hasn't eaten for a week and he's out of his head with fever."

The doctor frowned. "Bring him to me. I will look at him."

Mrs. Feinstein shook her head. "He's too weak to get up. I insist you come to him."

The doctor pursed his lips. With a sour look he put on his coat and followed us down the steps. As he entered our cabin he took out a white handkerchief and covered his nose. I clenched my fists until the nails dug into my flesh. We had to live with the smell all the time and he couldn't come in for a minute without covering his nose. He acted like we were animals!

But when the doctor saw Papa his face grew serious. He put the handkerchief away and listened to Papa's chest. He looked at me. "Your papa is very sick. You should have come to me sooner."

Mrs. Feinstein put her finger to her lips and shook her head at me over the doctor's head. I bit my lip. Perhaps I should have come sooner, but so should he. With Reuben's help, we got Papa up the stairs to the infirmary. The doctor put him to bed and gave him medicine. Just seeing Papa lying in a clean bed with white sheets made me feel better.

"Please let Papa get well," I prayed.

He had to get well.

14

America Nears

"How's your papa this morning?" Mrs. Feinstein asked the next day.

"His fever's gone down, but he's still coughing." The doctor wouldn't let me stay with Papa. I was allowed to visit him twice a day for ten minutes.

"Were you scared to sleep all alone in your bunk?" Susan asked after I finished the orange Mrs. Feinstein had given me for breakfast. We were sitting in our secret cave, under the tarpaulin cover of a lifeboat. Sunlight filtered through the holes and we could peek out at the passing people without them seeing us.

I laughed. "Susan, there are over fifty people in that room. I was hardly alone."

Susan bit her lip. "But it's dark."

I remembered what happened in the pine grove. "Why are you so afraid of the dark?"

Susan looked up. "I've never told anyone about it," she said in a low voice. "I'm afraid someone will put the evil eye on me."

"I swear I won't tell anyone." I recited the chant Mama always said to avoid the evil eye: "Three women sit on stone. One says, 'The child has an evil eye.' The other says, 'No!' The third says, 'Whence it came, it will go! Phew! Phew! Phew!' I spat three times.

Susan seemed satisfied. "It happened when we were visiting my grandparents. We only visited them once a year. For Passover.

"We had to take a long train ride because they lived in a town far from St. Petersburg. It was the first time I was on a train and I was all excited. Just imagine! Five years old and I had never been on a train!"

My first train ride had been last month, and I was almost twelve. But I didn't say anything.

"At first I loved being in the country. I played with the kittens and fed the chickens and helped my grandmother make haroses for the Passover Seder out of wine and walnuts. When we sat down for the Seder, everything was perfect. The table was covered with a white linen cloth and wine filled the silver cups. All my cousins and aunts and uncles were smiling and laughing."

"That's how it is in my house, too." I missed my family so much it hurt. It was a hunger no amount of food could satisfy.

Susan went on as if she hadn't heard me. "Suddenly it all changed. We heard noises outside. Someone ran in shouting, 'The Cossacks are coming!' Everyone began screaming and running out the door. Oh, Raizel, it was so awful!"

Susan had been in a pogrom! I took her hands and squeezed them. "What did you do?"

"They hid Reuben and me in a big wooden box. They covered us with blankets until we could hardly breathe. It was so dark." Susan began to cry softly. "Ever since then I've been afraid of the dark."

"Did they find you?" I held my breath.

"No. My grandparents put out all the lights, locked the door, and hid in a wardrobe with my parents. The Cossacks never came into the house. But I could hear them on the street. They were yelling 'Death to the Jews!' and 'Death to the Christ killers!'

"And then what happened?"

"I fell asleep. When they came to take us out, both of us were asleep. We left the next day for St. Petersburg. It was only later I found out they killed my Aunt Esther. She was going to have a baby and couldn't run fast enough. They caught her and cut open her stomach!"

"No!" I hugged myself.

"They killed her and her baby and one of my cousins who tried to help her. She was my mother's sister." Susan rocked back and forth.

"Why do they hate us like that?" My mouth was so dry I could barely speak.

"I don't know. I never did anything to them. That's why I'm glad we're going to America. I don't care if I have to leave my dolls and my nanny and my friends. I don't care if I have to live in a tiny little room with no windows like Papa wrote. I just want to live in America where there are no pogroms! And I never want to go back to Russia, ever, ever again!"

We sat together in silence for a long time. I thought about Mama, Lemmel, and the little ones. If only they had come with us. If only I could be sure they were safe. Why did people hate us so? Why couldn't we be secure like the Jews in Austro-Hungary and Germany? For the first time I was certain how right Papa had been to leave Russia. In America we would be safe.

The next day Papa's fever went down. His cough no longer kept him up at night. After we had been sailing for ten days, the doctor released him from the infirmary.

"You must sit in the sun with a blanket over you for at least two hours every morning," he said. "And take this medicine three times a day, with meals." He handed Papa a big brown bottle.

"But Papa doesn't eat the food on the boat," I said.

The doctor sighed and shook his head. "You are far too thin. You must eat. Otherwise you will not get well."

"I will eat the food we brought with us," Papa said. He was so weak he had to lean on me as we climbed on deck.

"But Papa . . . " I hadn't told him about our stolen food.

"Mr. Balaban! How nice to see you up on deck!" Mrs. Feinstein smiled and reached in her pocket. "Luckily, I took two oranges today, so you shall have one too."

Papa shook his head. "We have our own food. We do not need charity."

Mrs. Feinstein pursed her lips. "My mother, may she rest in peace, used to say, 'A wise man eats to live; a fool lives to eat.'"

"You are calling me a fool?" Papa sat down heavily on the iron bench.

"I am saying you should at least let the child eat. You have no food left, and fruit cannot be tref."

"Raizel, what she says is true?"

"Yes, Papa. Someone stole our food, and I ate all the toast while you were sick."

Papa sighed. "I apologize, Mrs. Feinstein. I did not know we had no food. Under the circumstances, we have no choice but to accept your charity."

"Humph. That you call an apology?" Mrs. Feinstein gave me the two oranges and turned away.

"Papa, why were you so cross? Mrs. Feinstein helped me when you were sick. She persuaded the doctor to come and see you."

Papa took my hand. His face was as shrunken as last year's apples, but his brown eyes were bright and clear. "The taste of charity is bitter. All my life I have worked and provided for my family. Even when times were hard, did I ever ask your Uncle Nahum for anything?"

"But Uncle Nahum paid for our tickets, didn't he?"

"Yes, but that was different. I will pay him back as soon as we get to America."

I was about to ask why that was different when Susan came running up and grabbed my hand. "Raizel, come and play!"

Papa leaned back and closed his eyes. I put the orange in his lap and followed Susan.

"Have you finished your school work?" I asked. Even on board ship, Mrs. Feinstein made Susan and Reuben study.

Susan made a face. "Yes. The English teacher Mama found is so boring. "A – pal, Ta – ball, Pull –eez." What a funny language English is."

I wished I could learn English. Reuben seemed to like his lessons and spent all his time practicing. I had barely seen him for days, and I missed him. "So what shall we do today?"

"Let's go see if the lady will throw us candy like she did yesterday." Susan spun around on one leg.

"Susan, your mother will be furious." The first-class passengers some-times threw candy to the children in third class. I wouldn't eat it because it was tref, but Susan went running to show her mother. "Shame!" cried Mrs. Feinstein and threw the candy overboard. "They think we are animals." She hid her face in her hands and forbade Susan to take any more candy.

"I know." Susan pouted. "But I love sweet things and I miss them. I wish I could have a lick of chocolate ice cream or a slice of our cook's honey cake."

"Let's play cat's cradle so you won't think about sweets."

"All right," Susan said without enthusiasm. "But you always win." She took a piece of string out of her pocket and laced it around her fingers. I slid my fingers carefully into the holes of the intricate pattern and trans-ferred it to my hands.

We played for a while, but no matter how hard I tried, Susan always lost.

"I'm tired of this game." Susan tossed her curls and put the string back in her pocket. "I wish we could have a tea party like Mama had back in St. Petersburg."

"We could have a pretend party. I used to have a pretend Seder with Shloyme and Hannah."

"But we don't have any cups or saucers. Or tea or cakes."

"That's why it's pretend, silly."

"I'm no good at imagining." Susan stamped her foot. "I wish I had a real slice of sweet crunchy poppy cake. If we're going to play imagining, you can tell me a story."

"Why don't you read to us?"

"I don't see why you like my books. They're so boring, all about history and things. And books are always the same. You never run out of stories."

"All right, let me think." We stood at the rail staring at the ocean while I tried to think of a story I hadn't told Susan. I had grown used to the motion of the boat, the sweep and sway as we forged through the waves, but I never tired of looking at the water. The green depths changed from clear glass on a sunny day to blank lead windows when the sky was cloudy. Sometimes the waves danced like seagulls and sometimes they exploded like angry fists against the hull. Reuben said we were lucky to have such fine weather, that the ocean could be terrifying when there was a storm. Which reminded me of a story.

"I have one! It's a little scary. Sure you want to hear it?" I asked.

"Of course. I'm not a baby." Susan pulled me over to an empty bench.

"Once there was a rich man who lived in Jerusalem. He had one son whom he loved very much. When the man died, he left his son an inheritance.

"'I'm tired of studying in the yeshiva all day,' said the son. 'I want to see the world.' He took his inheritance and boarded a ship. The ship landed in the great city of Istanbul."

"I know where that is. It's in Italy!" said Susan.

"It's in Turkey," said a deep voice behind me.

I looked up. Reuben was standing next to us.

"Mind if I listen?" he asked. "My English lesson is over for today."

I gulped and nodded. Reuben made me nervous. "Th-the son walked all through the great city admiring the palaces and mosques. When he got to the Sultan's palace he saw a strange sight—an iron coffin hanging from a pole in front of the palace, with a guard standing next to it.

"'Who is in that coffin and why are you guarding it?' he asked.

"'The man in the coffin used to be the Sultan's favorite advisor,' answered the guard. 'He was a Jew. The Sultan's other advisors were jealous of the Jew's influence and told the Sultan he had stolen a great sum of money from the Sultan's treasury. The Sultan had the Jew put to death. He vowed to leave him hanging in this coffin until the money was paid back. I am here to see the Jews don't try to steal the coffin and bury it.'

"The young man felt very sad for the great man who lay unburied in his coffin. 'How much money does the Sultan want?' he asked the guard.

"'A thousand pieces of gold.'

"'Why, that is exactly the inheritance I have from my father,' thought the young man. 'Take me to the Sultan,' he ordered.

"When he stood before the Sultan in his enormous golden room, the young man bowed and pulled out a leather pouch. 'I have come to pay the thousand gold pieces so my fellow Jew can be buried,' he said. The Sultan accepted the gold and the next day the young man said the Kaddish prayer at the dead man's funeral.

"Not long after, he set sail for home. A terrible storm swept the sea and mountainous waves pounded the wooden vessel. Giant waves washed over the ship until it sank to the bottom of the sea. All the passengers were drowned except the young man. He tried to swim in the tormented sea, but his strength gave out. Just then an enormous white eagle swooped down and landed in the water. The young man climbed on the eagle's back. Together they flew high above the storm clouds, straight to the city of Jerusalem. The eagle set the young man down in his very own house. Grateful to be home, the young man turned to thank the eagle, but he was gone. In the dim light he saw a man dressed in a white burial shroud!"

"Mamaleh! I don't like this story!" Susan put her hands over her ears.

"I do! Go on, Raizel," Reuben said.

"It's almost finished," I assured her. 'Who are you?' asked the young man, trembling with fear.

"'I am the man you saved from a fate worse than death. I am the innocent man the Sultan killed for a crime I did not commit. You have saved my honor. In return, I have saved you from certain death. May you have a long happy life until we meet in the paradise of the world to come.' With these words the ghost disappeared.

"Everything he said came about, and the young man lived happily for the rest of his life."

"Ugh, I didn't like that story." Susan hugged herself and shivered. "Have you ever seen a ghost, Raizel?"

"No. But my Aunt Freida says she saw one late at night when she walked past a dead man's house . . . "

"I don't want to hear about it!" Susan got up from the bench. "I don't want to play with you anymore. I think you're horrible!"

"But you asked me to tell you a story!" I called after her. I knew Susan would soon be back. Her moods never lasted long.

"It was a very good story," Reuben said, sitting down next to me. "I liked it, but Susan's only a little girl."

"She's just a year younger than I am."

"But you seem older. Susan's never had to take care of anybody, not even herself."

"I always took care of my younger brother and sister and helped Mama around the house. I never had time to play." Or learn to read.

"Neither did I. After Father went to America, I had to help my mother. I was in charge of paying our bills and made the arrangements to sell our house. We had no relatives in St. Petersburg, and Mother isn't good at things like that."

I thought of Lemmel. Was he helping Mama now that Papa was gone?

"What are you thinking about?" Reuben asked.

"My family. When I left, my brother Lemmel was mad at me. He wanted to come to America with Papa instead of me."

"I think you're brave to travel alone with your Papa."

Me? Brave? "I didn't want to come. I wanted to stay home with Mama and the little ones."

"But you took care of your Papa when he was sick. And crossed the border at night. We just rode across on a train."

"And don't forget the river." I grinned at him. I had told Susan and Reuben about the river crossing.

"And the way you tell stories. You become . . . a different person."

I looked at my hands. "What do you mean?"

"Like now. You're acting shy and embarrassed. There, your cheeks are turning red! But when you tell a story, you forget to be shy. Your face lights up and you're really pretty."

My hands flew to my burning face. I wanted to hide under the bench, but I forced myself to look at Reuben. "Me? Pretty?"

"Well, of course. You have those big brown eyes and smooth skin. If you don't believe me, ask my mother."

I shut my mouth, which I suddenly realized was hanging open. Reuben stood up.

"Well, I guess I'll be going. It's almost lunch time and mother will be looking for me."

I put my hand on his arm. "Thank you. No one ever told me I was pretty before. I think you're the nicest boy I know!"

Reuben smiled. "How many boys do you know?"

I laughed. "Well, all the boys in Jibatov, but you're nicer than all of them, especially my brother Lemmel."

The next few days passed quickly. Papa grew stronger until he was able to stroll around the deck by himself. He ate the fruit Mrs. Feinstein brought us, but he wouldn't touch the bread. He read his prayer book in the sun or talked to the other men.

One morning Reuben ran up to us pointing at a seagull.

"So what?" Susan said. "There were plenty of seagulls in Antwerp."

"No, dummy. This is an American seagull, not a European seagull. It means we're close to land!"

I felt the deck sink under my feet.

Susan clapped her hands. "I'm going to tell mother right now!" She skipped away.

"What's the matter, Raizel? You don't look happy."

"When will we get there? To America, I mean." Suddenly all my fears of what would happen to us in America came flooding back.

"The steward said we might see land by this afternoon or tomorrow morning by the latest."

"Oh." I shivered in the light salt breeze. The sea looked dark as a moonless night.

"Are you afraid?" Reuben leaned over the railing next to me.

I nodded. "We hardly know anyone in America. We have to find a place to live and Papa has to find work. What if he gets sick again, and there's no one to help us?"

"My mother says he'll be fine as soon as he gets off the boat and starts eating. Don't you have relatives in America?"

"Just a distant cousin of my mother's. I don't know him."

"But there must be people you know from Jibatov."

"There's Shmuel the tailor and Yente the widow. Papa has their addresses."

"See, there's nothing to worry about. They'll help you. Jews always help one another."

"But what if they've moved? No one in Jibatov has heard from them for a long time."

"And what if America sinks into the ocean tomorrow morning? I've never seen anyone worry as much as you do. Maybe you enjoy it?" Reuben raised an eyebrow.

"Enjoy it? Of course not."

"Then stop. Worrying never helped anyone. It's no use worrying about things you can't do anything about, anyway."

"You're right." I shook my braids to shake the worries away. This might be the last time I was alone with Reuben. I didn't want to spend it worrying. "What are you going to do in America?"

"Why, go to school, of course, just like you."

"I'm not going to school," I said.

"You're not? Don't you want to go to school and learn to read and write?"

"More than anything in the world! But Papa says I have to take care of the house for him and cook his food. That's why I came to America instead of Lemmel."

Reuben frowned. "But all the children in America go to school. Even the girls."

"Are you sure?" I held my breath.

"Well, I think so. Father wrote that it's the law. They even send a policeman after you if you don't go to school."

"Then Papa would have to let me go!" I hoped Reuben was right.

Talking to Reuben made me feel so grownup. He told me how he wanted to be a doctor, but his father wanted him to work in the fur business. We talked for hours. When Susan returned we went on talking, our eyes fixed on the horizon. Everyone on board seemed to be hanging over the railing that day. Only Papa stayed in his bunk, tired from his morning stroll.

"Maybe you can live next door to us in America and I'll have someone to play with every day," Susan said.

Reuben shook his head. "New York City is a big place, bigger than St. Petersburg. There isn't much chance Raizel will live next door to us."

"So she'll come to visit," Susan said firmly.

"How will I know where you live?"

"I'll give you our address," Reuben said.

I felt warm all over. I would see Reuben again!

"Oh, the sun's going down. Now we won't get to see the lady." Susan stamped her foot like a child whose cake was taken away.

We watched the dull red ball slip beneath the waves.

"What's so important about a statue, anyway?" I asked. Susan had been talking about the statue for days. "There were plenty of statues in the park in Antwerp."

Susan burst out laughing. "Raizel, you're such a greenborn—I mean greenhorn. She isn't just a statue. She's the Statue of Liberty. They say she's the tallest statue ever built. You can see her torchlight all the way to Europe."

"Then how come we can't see it now?" I hated when Susan called me a greenhorn.

"Maybe there's a cloud in front of it."

"I don't believe you can see a light all the way across the ocean."

"So don't believe it. See if I care." Susan tossed her blond curls.

"Hey, stop fighting, you two." Reuben sounded amused. "The steward says we're going to wait outside the harbor and enter when it's light. That way we'll be able to see the Statue of Liberty."

"But why is she so special?" I asked.

"Because she is the symbol of America welcoming immigrants to her shores. Father sent me a copy of a beautiful poem about the statue written by a Jewish lady. He read it in a Yiddish newspaper."

"I don't like poetry," Susan said.

"You'll like this one. It's about us." Reuben's voice was deep with emotion as he recited:

"Give me your tired, your poor.

Your huddled masses yearning to breathe free.

The wretched refuse of your teeming shore.

Send these, the homeless, tempest-tossed to me:

I lift my lamp beside the golden door."

I felt a chill sweep through my body. "What a beautiful poem. Maybe someday I can read it in English. 'I lift my lamp beside the golden door.'" The words tasted like fresh warm bread in my mouth.

"I don't like the part about 'wretched refuse.'" Susan wrinkled her nose "We're not garbage. And now I'm going to bed so I can wake up early and be the first to see her! Good-night."

"Sometimes I think Susan wants to see the statue more than she does our father," Reuben said. "She barely remembers him."

"Three years is a long time. I hope it doesn't take Papa three years to earn the money for Mama's ticket!"

We stood in silence, watching the stars pop out like fireflies on a summer's night in Jibatov.

"Remember what we were talking about yesterday?" Reuben asked suddenly. "About being scared? Well, I'm scared too."

"You?" I couldn't believe it. Reuben always seemed so sure of himself.

"Yes, me. I haven't seen my father for so long, I'm afraid he won't like me. He's used to being the boss in the family. I'm afraid he'll treat me like a little kid, like Susan."

I looked at Reuben. His legs were planted firmly apart and his strong arms gripped the rail. He was like a young oak tree, giving his strength and shade to anyone who passed by.

"He'll like you," I said softly. I wanted to say more, but the words stuck in my throat.

Reuben put his hand over mine. His hand was warm and dry. The waves whispered in the dark and my thoughts whispered with them as I tried to hold the moment for as long as I could.

Double Crossing

15

The Golden Door

The green-robed statue rose gleaming in the morning sun out of the green waters of the harbor.

"See?" Susan pointed as if she had made the statue herself. "I told you the lady was beautiful!"

I had to agree with her. The statue's head was crowned with clouds as she guarded the sun-lit harbor with her raised torch.

"I lift my lamp beside the golden door," I murmured. Not only did America welcome us, but the welcomer was a lady!

Susan grabbed my hand and smiled at me. All the passengers in third class were dressed in their best clothes. Since dawn, the tiny bathroom had been full of women talking and trying to clean themselves in the cold salt water. Susan was wearing her best blue-velvet dress. Mrs. Feinstein had fussed over Susan's hair so "Papa will see how pretty you've grown."

Then she had braided my hair into a long thick braid and wrapped it around my head so I would look grown-up, as Papa watched with an amused smile. I would have loved a beautiful dress like Susan's, but at least I wore a clean blouse with fine red embroidery that Leah had given me. I had saved it through the whole journey so I would have something pretty to wear when we landed in America.

If only Papa looked better. His long black coat appeared several sizes too big for his shrunken frame. His cheeks were pale and drawn under his black beard, and his eyes looked like gray puddles. Still, he stood on the deck watching the Statue of Liberty with a huge smile on his face, just like the rest of the passengers.

"This is a great day, Raizel," Papa said. "Soon we will have a place to live. I will find a job and save money and the whole family will be together again."

I nodded. Fear and excitement choked my throat. If only Mama and the little ones were here with us!

"Do you know where you're going to live?" Reuben asked. He was standing next to me looking very grown-up in his checked suit and cap.

"No. We're going to look for our cousin. He works in a clothing factory. Papa hopes he can help him find a job."

"I'm sure he will." We had passed the statue now and were approaching the dock. Tall buildings, taller than those in Antwerp, lined the dock. Reuben strained to identify his father in the crowd of people milling around. There were hundreds of people there, all waving and shouting. If only someone were waiting for us.

"Here, Raizel." Susan thrust a hard red candy into my hand.

"Where did you get this?"

"The sailors are giving them out to all the children." Susan popped the red sweet into her mouth. "Mmmm. If you don't want yours I'll take it."

I glanced at Papa. He was staring over the railing as if he were eating up America with hungry eyes. Should I ask him if I could eat the candy? I already knew the answer.

"You can have it," I said. Susan stuffed it into her mouth without even a thank you.

"First- and second-class passengers line up on the lower deck," the steward called through a loud speaker.

"Reuben, that's us. Where's Mama?" Susan cried.

"Over there with the luggage."

Susan ran to her mother.

I stared after her. It was just like Susan to run away without a word of good-bye.

"Don't mind her. She's overexcited." Reuben handed me a folded piece of paper. "This is our address. When you get settled, you can come to visit. Or write us a letter and we'll visit you."

I tucked the paper safely in my skirt pocket. "Reuben, your father is going to be very proud of you," I said. I ducked my eyes in embarrassment.

"In America they shake hands when they say hello and good-bye." Reuben encircled my hand with his and squeezed it. "Good-bye, Raizel. Save me some stories for the next time we meet."

I nodded and smiled. I didn't trust my voice.

"Reuben! Hurry up!" Mrs. Feinstein called. She waved to me and said something to Susan. Susan turned around and blew me a kiss. Then they disappeared down the stairway to the lower deck. My eyes filled with tears. It was almost like parting from family.

"Papa, why can't we all get off the boat together?" I sat down on the bench next to Papa.

"The third-class passengers have to go for inspection."

"Yes, I know. On the island." Everyone had been talking about the island for days, but I hadn't known it was only for the third-class passengers. Why could first-class passengers just walk off the ship while we had to go through yet another inspection? It wasn't fair. "I hope it's the island with the statue. I'd like to see the lady close up."

Papa shrugged and leaned back against the wall. I returned to the railing. The dock was a jumble of people pushing and shouting and shoving and carrying suitcases and boxes to the line of carriages waiting at the far end of the dock. I couldn't see the Feinsteins anywhere.

Beyond the harbor rose tall buildings. Even taller buildings loomed behind them, like mountains in a morning mist. What was it like to live so high up? Would the air be too thin to breathe? And imagine carrying food up all those stairs! I hoped we could find an apartment close to the ground.

Suddenly I saw Mrs. Feinstein and Susan running to a tall man with a handlebar mustache. Mrs. Feinstein flung herself into his arms. He picked Susan up and whirled her around. Where was Reuben? I spotted him guarding the luggage. Mr. Feinstein walked up to him and put out his hand. Reuben shook it and smiled. Then Mr. Feinstein enfolded him in his arms, and I knew everything was going to be all right.

"Come, Raizel. It is time to get off." The crowd on deck was pushing down the staircase. "Stay near me. You must not get lost," Papa said. He picked up the suitcases and I followed with the baskets.

I tried to stay close to Papa as we crossed the deck and climbed down the wide gangplank. There were so many people. Someone shoved me from behind and I almost fell. A brown-coated official grabbed my arm. The sailors lined the dock and herded us toward a small wooden boat.

"Papa, where are you?"

"Behind you, Raizel. Wait for me."

Filled with people, the boat chugged away from the shore. I inched closer to Papa as another boat took its place. This time we were rammed on board, packed so tightly that we could barely turn around. The motor started with a shudder and the boat bobbed out to sea again. I wiggled my way to the side.

Sunlight danced on the water like gold coins. The Statue of Liberty gleamed against the blue sky, almost piercing the clouds with her torch. I felt a bubble of happiness swell inside me. The crossing was behind us. We were finally in America. Now Papa would get a job and the cousin would help us find a place to live. I would learn to bargain like Mama and save every penny. Soon, very soon, we would have enough money to bring over Mama, Lemmel, Shloyme and baby Hannah. It had to be!

The boat bumped against the dock and the crowd pushed us down the gangplank. I looked around. A long path surrounded by green grass led through a park toward an enormous building. "Where are we, Papa?" I asked as we walked toward the building. "This is the wrong island. There's no lady here."

"Hush, child. The statue is not important." Papa dragged our suitcases slowly along the ground. I transferred the baskets to one arm and helped him pull.

The crowd surged up the stairs into a huge brick building. I blinked in the sudden dimness of the vast hall. The smell of disinfectant mixed with the odor of people who hadn't bathed in weeks.

"Leave your luggage here. Leave your luggage here," a man dressed in a blue uniform called in Yiddish, Russian, and other languages I didn't understand.

"What if someone steals our things?" I set the baskets on our battered suitcases. What a strange pile! I spotted a carved wooden chair and a beautiful silver samovar. There were thick feather quilts and even a birdcage with a yellow canary huddled in a corner.

"Who would want our suitcases?" Papa looked at the crowd heading up the steep flight of stairs. "If we get separated for any reason, meet me here by the luggage."

Separated from Papa? I clung to his hand as we climbed the stairs. Halfway up, he stumbled and grabbed the railing.

"Papa, are you all right?"

"Yes. Just a little dizzy. I am fine."

I noticed another man in a blue uniform. Was he watching Papa or was it my imagination? Quickly I took Papa's arm to steady him and we continued up the stairs more slowly.

At the top of the stairs was a gigantic room filled with long lines of people. We joined a line and waited our turn. Finally a man wearing a white coat nodded at us. He motioned for me to raise my arms. Then he looked in my face and hair and had me turn around. He nodded and pointed to another line. The entire examination had taken just seconds.

He took more time with Papa. He made him turn around, touch the ground, and stand first on one foot and then the other. Then he looked in Papa's mouth and made him cough into a piece of white paper. Why was it taking so long? Finally he took a piece of chalk and wrote something right on Papa's black coat!

"What does that mean?" I asked Papa, pointing to the chalk marks.

"I should know?" Papa asked. His face was creased with worry. "I passed the examination in Antwerp."

I hated the eye exam. The doctor pinched my eyelids with a metal hook and turned them inside out. It hurt! The doctor frowned at me when I burst into tears, but I couldn't help it. The woman next to me was crying, too, but the doctor paid no attention. Grab and pull, grab and pull, the way Mama plucked a chicken. I rubbed my eyes to make them stop hurting and thought of Susan. She was lucky she didn't have to take an American eye exam.

"Papa, where do we go now?" I asked when Papa was done.

A guard looked at the mark on Papa's coat and directed us to a door off the main hall. We sat on a wooden bench to wait our turn. Papa leaned back and closed his eyes. I was tired too, but I was even more hungry. I had eaten an apple for breakfast, but that was hours and hours ago. The room smelled of sweat and garlic. People took bread and cheese out of their baskets, but no one offered us anything. I looked away. I had learned it was better not to think of food if you couldn't have any.

Finally the door opened and a woman in white motioned Papa in.

"Wait here for me," Papa said before the door closed.

I leaned against the doorway where I could see the main hall. It was huge, almost as big as the train station in Antwerp. There were red tiles on the floor, while the walls and ceiling were covered with white tiles. Light poured in from tall windows on either side of the hall. The center was filled with people waiting in long lines or sitting on the wooden benches. The lines moved so slowly! The hall never seemed to empty. So many people coming from the ends of the earth. And so much noise! My head was beginning to ache from the din.

At the far end of the hall was a huge flag with red and white stripes and a blue square. Was it the American flag? Reuben would know. He knew everything.

The door opened and Papa came out of the room with a smile on his face. "They said I am not sick! I could have told them that." He laughed.

"But what about the mark? Why didn't they take it off?" I asked.

"Maybe they forgot. Come, we go to the next examination."

Again we joined a long long line. Papa swayed from side to side as he stood. Once he rested his hand on my shoulder to steady himself. Even though he wasn't sick, he was still weak from the illness, the trip, and not eating properly. My legs were tired, but I stood as tall as possible to help Papa. Finally we reached the front of the line. A bald man with glasses asked Papa a question. He looked annoyed when Papa didn't answer and asked more loudly. Then he called to a woman standing at another table.

"You speak Yiddish?" she asked. She was plump as a pigeon, and just as gray.

"Yah." Papa looked relieved.

"I will translate for you. Answer the questions truthfully."

The bald inspector asked if we had family in Russia.

"I have a wife and three children. This is my oldest girl," Papa answered.

"What do you do?"

"I am a merchant," Papa said. "I sell things."

"Do you have a profession? Are you a tailor? A watchmaker? A baker?"

Papa shook his head.

"Did someone promise you a job?"

Papa hesitated. People said you were not allowed to enter America if someone promised you a job. "No, but my wife's sister's husband's brother works in a shirt factory. He will help me get a job," Papa answered.

"But you are not a tailor," the man said. The man stared at Papa and wrote something on a piece of paper. The pigeon lady frowned. She cooed at the inspector in a soft pleading voice. The inspector answered curtly and waved us away. Cold fear crept up my back.

"That is all?" Papa asked the woman. "Where do we go now?"

"Now you go to the detention room."

"What is this detention room?"

"You have to wait there," the woman said. She sounded tired. She looked down at the floor. "You didn't pass the inspection."

"Yes, I did," Papa said. "The doctor said I have no communicable diseases."

The woman studied the piece of paper. "The inspector says you're not fit to work," she said.

"N-no, there must be some mistake." Papa's voice shook. "I am a hard worker. Tell them, please. I work all day, every day!"

"I'm sorry, Mr. Balaban. I am only the translator. There's nothing I can do. The inspector is finished. You see, if you can't work, the American government will have to support you. That's what those letters mean: "LPC" – liable to become a public charge."

"NO!" Papa rubbed at the chalk letters. "It's a mistake. There's been a mistake." He was shaking all over. He swayed suddenly. The pigeon lady put out her arm to steady him.

I clenched my fists so hard that pains shot up my arms. This couldn't be happening! Not after all we had been through.

"Don't worry, you'll be taken care of," the lady said. "And they will pay your way back."

"Back? I can't go back!"

"There is no choice. When you are not allowed into America, you must go back where you came from." The pigeon lady sighed. "But I will try to find someone from HIAS to help you."

"What is this HIAS?" Papa asked.

"The Hebrew Immigrant Aid Society. They help immigrants for no charge."

She took Papa's arm and led us to a small room lined with benches. "Wait here and don't make any trouble. It will only be worse."

Papa sat down on the bench like a crumpled paper bag.

"I'm sorry," said the lady. She patted Papa's shoulder. "You'll see, everything will be all right in the end."

I plopped down beside Papa. My head was whirling and a thousand questions struggled for breath.

"What did she mean, Papa? Why won't they let you work? Why do they think you're sick? When will we leave? How will we get back? Do we have enough money? I don't understand."

Papa stared straight ahead. His shoulders slumped liked an old man. "It means they don't want me in America," he said in a hoarse whisper. "It means we have to go back to Russia."

I thought of the parting from our family. The river crossing. The endless hours on the trains. The sea sickness and Papa's illness. All to reach America. And now they were sending us back?

I was shaking all over. I wanted to run into the huge hall and shout at the inspectors that they had made a mistake. My papa was the hardest worker in Russia, the hardest worker in the world. Just give him a chance! Just let us in!

All I could think about was they had made a mistake. Papa was healthy. The doctor had released him from the infirmary and he had taken all his medicine. Papa could work. Why, in Russia he had worked all day, every day but the Sabbath. We hadn't been rich, but there was always bread and herring, barley and potatoes to eat. Mama always had a few zlotys to give to the poor beggars who wandered from house to house. And everyone in Jibatov respected Papa. They knew he could have been a scholar if he didn't have to support his family.

"Papa, go talk to them!" I pulled at Papa's sleeve. "Tell them you'll work hard."

Papa shook his head. "What can I do, meydele? There is nothing I can do." He glanced at the guard standing at the door.

I hadn't noticed the guard before. Were we in prison? I looked around the room at the other people. An old woman with straggly gray hair rocked back and forth and mumbled to herself in a strange language. A younger woman, maybe Mama's age, but with a huge belly, sat with her arms around two small children. Her face was red and swollen with tears. The children were crying, too, but the mother made no attempt to comfort them.

So many tears. It was an island of tears.

The door opened and a tall thin woman walked in carrying a sheaf of papers. Her black hair was pulled into such a tight bun that not a single strand of hair escaped. I wondered if her scalp hurt.

She walked up to the rocking lady and touched her on the shoulder. The woman's face contorted with anger and she spewed a string of words at the tall lady. The lady took a step back and said something to the guard, who moved closer. The angry woman cowered away from him as if afraid of a beating. The tight-haired lady glanced at a piece of paper and turned to Papa.

"Mr. Balaban?"

Papa looked up.

"Come." She gestured for us to follow. We walked down a long hallway and several flights of stairs. Our footsteps echoed like falling stones on the marble floors. Finally the lady opened a door to a large dining hall, noisy with the click of plates and cups and people talking in different languages as they sat at long wooden tables spooning food into their mouths. Suddenly I remembered how hungry I was.

We found two empty chairs. A woman dressed in white set bowls of soup in front of us. The fragrant steam tickled my nose. I was so hungry I almost thrust my head into the bowl. When was the last time I had eaten hot food? In Antwerp in the hotel. It seemed like years away.

"Please, Papa, I'm hungry. Can I eat it?"

"Is this kosher?" Papa asked the lady in white. She shrugged her shoulders and walked away. Papa turned to the man sitting next to him, who had mashed potatoes stuck in his brown mustache. "Is the food here kosher?"

The man shook his head and kept eating. "Italiano," he said.

"It's not kosher," said a man sitting across from us in Yiddish. "But you'll be here for several days. If you don't eat, you'll starve."

"Days? I don't understand."

The man put down his spoon and looked at Papa. His eyes were red as raw meat.

"They're going to send you back, right? So until the ship leaves, you live on Ellis Island. They feed you and even give you medicine. But you can't get off the island. A real paradise, no?"

"Papa?" The soup was getting cold.

"All right, Raizel, you can eat it. We have no other food and I can't let you starve."

Before Papa could finish I had the first spoonful in my mouth. It was delicious, full of potatoes and lentils. I tried to make each spoonful last as long as I could. "Papa, why don't you eat your soup? You can't starve."

"Hungry I am not. But I will eat a piece of bread, so you should not worry."

I knew Papa was afraid the soup contained meat. "Can I have your soup, Papa?" I finished it off while Papa chewed on a piece of bread.

"How long have you been here?" Papa asked the red-eyed man.

"Over a week. They weren't sure about my eyes. They were fine when I got on the ship. So they brought a specialist. Imagine! An important American eye doctor came all the way to Ellis Island just to examine Joseph Plotsky's eyes and say he can't cure me. So much for the golden medinah!" The man spit on the floor.

The woman in white screamed something at him, but he just laughed. "Stupid sow," he muttered and looked at us. "What can they do to me? Send me back to Poland?" He laughed harshly.

After lunch we sat in another big room full of people. The men and women talked while the children ran around yelling and chasing each other. Papa read his prayer book. From time to time he sighed heavily and wiped his eyes.

With my stomach full, I discovered I wasn't angry anymore. In fact a sprout of happiness began to grow inside me. Who cared if they wouldn't let us into America? That meant we were going home again! I pictured our return to Jibatov. Uncle Nahum would hire a carriage and drive to meet us at the train station in Lubov. In Jibatov, the whole town would be waiting. Maybe we would be home in time for Hanukah, and I would see the holiday candles gleaming in the windows as we rode through the cold. Mama would hug and kiss me and tell me how much she missed me and we would all eat potato latkes and sing happy songs. I was so excited I bobbed up and down on the bench. We were going home! What could be better?

Supper that night was almost as good as lunch. I ate a hard-boiled egg and cheese and fresh bread. Papa wouldn't let me eat the sausage. There was even a funny fruit. It was long and yellow. I took a bite out of it but it tasted like a piece of stringy cloth, so I spit it out.

"Greenhorn! Greenhorn!" The girl sitting next to me laughed so hard I thought the freckles would fly off her round face. "You have to peel it before you eat it. I did the same thing the first time I saw a banana."

Without the peel, the banana tasted sweet and creamy. I gave Papa a bite, but he didn't like it. He ate bread and one egg. The girl was eating something red and shimmery out of a bowl.

"What's that?" I asked. "My name is Raizel."

"I don't know, but it's good. Try some. I'm Haya. We're here because my mother bought a ticket for New York instead of Boston. So my father has to come all the way from Boston to get us."

I tasted the red stuff. It was sweet and cold, but had a slippery texture like jellied calf's foot. I took another banana. "Why can't you go by yourselves? You came all the way across Europe and across the Atlantic, didn't you?"

Haya's eyes grew wide. "They don't let women into America without their husbands. See that lady over there?" She pointed at a thin dark-haired woman with sallow skin.

"They say she's been here over two months. They sent telegrams to her husband to come and get her. They even sent policemen to look for him. But they can't find him."

"Poor woman. Maybe he died."

"Or maybe he found another wife and doesn't want her anymore. So they're sending her back on the next boat to Italy."

"They're sending us back, too."

"Why? Is your Papa ill?"

"No. But they think he can't work hard enough to support us."

Haya pulled down the corners of her wide mouth. "Too bad. I can't wait to get to Boston and go to school and eat bananas and oranges every day."

"I can't wait to get home to my mama's cooking. She makes the best challah and potato kugel and . . . everything! I'll take Russia over America any day!" I rubbed my stomach just thinking of all the good things Mama would make us to eat.

"Stop that, Raizel! You must not talk like that!" Papa's stern voice cut into my thoughts. His face was red with anger. "You should never say that again."

"What, Papa? What did I say wrong?" Why was Papa so angry with me?

"And don't answer back to your father!"

For a moment I thought Papa was going to slap me. "Yes, Papa," I said, and ducked my head so the people at the table wouldn't see my tears.

After dinner the matron with the tight bun gave me a hot bath and washed my hair with strong yellow soap. She scrubbed so hard I thought my skin would peel off like a banana. Then she combed my hair with a fine comb to take out head lice. Even though I combed my hair into braids every day, it was full of knots and tangles, but I bit my lip and didn't cry when she tugged too hard. There was no use wasting tears on little things.

When she was finished, she patted my shoulder and said "gut gur" or something like it in English. She took me to a long room with beds hung in three stories. The room was clean and bright and smelled like disinfectant. There were sinks along the walls, and they were clean, too. There must have been over a hundred people in the room, all with young children. Papa had a bed in a corner and I climbed up above him. There was no mattress over the canvass but the sheets were clean and I had a thin cotton blanket. How wonderful to feel clean and have a full stomach and no boat rocking under me. The only thing I didn't like were the bars on the high windows. We hadn't done anything wrong. Why were they treating us like prisoners? Suddenly I felt dirty, even after the bath and the clean sheets.

After they turned the lights out, I tried to sleep, but my mind kept running through all the things that had happened that day. I thought of home and how happy everyone would be to see us. Maybe we could even buy them gifts. Let's see, for Shloyme and Hannah I would get sweet red candy and bananas. What could I get for Lemmel? I know! A boy on the boat had a metal box he put in his mouth and made music with. Lemmel would love that! I decided to ask Papa in the morning if we had enough money. I was just drifting into a dream about dancing to the music of violins at a wedding party when Papa whispered in my ear.

"Raizel? You are still awake?" He was standing by my bed.

"Yes, Papa." I raised myself on my elbows.

"I am sorry I got angry with you. I know you are happy we are going back to Russia."

"You'll see, Papa. It will be all right. Uncle Nahum will lend you money to buy new goods, and I'll help Mama with the little ones and everything will be like it was before."

Papa sighed. "No, child, nothing will be like it was before."

"What do you mean, Papa? Why not?"

Papa stroked my hair. "You must be strong, Raizel. You have crossed the ocean to America, and I hope it has made you grow up. You will have to help your Mama."

"I always help Mama." Fear crept into my stomach. Was there something I didn't know? What was Papa trying to say?

"But now I will not be there."

"Why not?" Was Papa going to escape from Ellis Island? And leave me behind?

No, Papa would never do that!

"Do you remember how we had to sneak across the border? Why do you think we did such a dangerous thing?"

"Because we didn't have enough money for passports. That's what you told me, Papa."

"I told you only part of the truth. Now I will tell you the whole truth, because you are no longer a little girl. No matter what happens, you must be strong."

"Papa, what is it? You can tell me."

"I had to leave Russia, because they want to draft me into the Czar's army. They want to send me to fight in Siberia."

"You, Papa? But you're too old!" Despite the summer heat, I was shivering. All those hints I had overhead suddenly made sense to me. I clutched at Papa's hand. It felt like an icy fish.

"The Czar does not think so. As soon as we return to Russia, they will arrest me. And then they will send me to the army. To Siberia to fight their war."

Papa in the Czar's army? I threw my arms around him and buried my face in his shoulder. "No, Papa, you can't go! I won't let you."

If Papa went to the army, I would never ever see him again.

16

The Isle of Tears

I didn't sleep that night. After I had used up all my tears, I lay in bed listening to the clock ticking in the corridor. Snores echoed through the room and a woman cried out in a language I couldn't understand. Sometimes a guard padded up and down the corridor and looked into the rooms. Did he suppose we would try to swim back to New York City?

All I could think about was Papa. He would never survive the Czar's army. He was too weak and thin. He wouldn't eat the food and would get even thinner until he died—if the enemy soldiers didn't kill him first. Our only chance was to remain in America. There must be someone who could help us.

I could see from the dark circles under Papa's eyes the next morning that he hadn't slept either. At breakfast I took a few bites of hot porridge, but it made my stomach sick. Papa drank a cup of tea. After breakfast they let us go up on the roof. The grown-ups sat on benches while the children played in the open space.

A bunch of girls was skipping rope and singing:

"The dove flew all around the world
And saw a lovely land,
But the land was locked
And the key was broke.
One, two, three
Out you go!"

It was the same rhyme we had sung in Jibatov, but now it took on new meaning for me. Who would have suspected that we would find the golden door locked? If only we had known. I sniffed and wiped away a tear.

"Raizel, come play with us," Haya called.

I shook my head. I didn't feel like playing. I felt old and tired like my bones had grown into the bench.

Papa was reading his prayer book. "Isn't there anything we can do?" I asked. "Can't you tell the Americans about the army? Maybe they'll let you stay."

Papa patted my hand. He sat as limp as a rag doll.

A man stepped onto the roof. He had black curly hair and a smooth beardless face. He spun around on his heel looking for someone. He seemed to be in a hurry, not like the rest of us on the roof, who had nothing to do but wait. He stopped when he saw Papa and looked at the paper he held in his hand.

"You are Benjamin Balaban?" he asked in Yiddish.

"Yes."

"My name is Moyshe Stein—Murray they call me in America. I am from the Hebrew Immigrant Aid Society. I was told you need help."

I grabbed Papa's arm. Someone actually wanted to help us! Maybe everything was going to be all right, after all.

"If you don't mind, I want to ask you some questions. The examination board meets this afternoon. You have the right to appeal the decision to send you back."

For the first time, Papa raised his head and looked at the young man. "What good will it do?"

"Sometimes it helps," Murray explained. "They ask you questions. I will be with you and translate your answers. You will have a chance to tell them your story."

"And if they say no?" Papa leaned forward.

"Then they send you back. You are forbidden to attempt to enter again for twelve months after your deportation. Mr. Balaban, they're going to send you back anyway, so it can't hurt to try."

Papa nodded. Murray asked questions about Papa's age, his health, and what he could do. "Don't you have a trade, anything you can do with your hands?" he kept asking.

"I was a yeshiva student. Who needs a trade when you are a yeshiva student? A yeshiva student is not good enough for the Americans?"

"I'm afraid not. In America you have to work hard and earn your living."

"But Papa knows how to work hard." I burst into the conversation. "We always had enough to eat. Let me tell them!" I wanted to help so badly.

"Hush, Raizel. This is no matter for children."

"Your papa is right, meydele. They don't allow children in the hearing room. How did you support your family in Russia?"

"I had a horse and cart. I was a peddler," Papa said.

Murray sighed. "They already have too many peddlers in America. You should see the Lower East Side! Perhaps you have been a carpenter or a fur cutter?"

"Yes, Papa. You could tell them you know how to work with your hands!" Lemmel wanted to be a carpenter.

"With these?" Papa held out his smooth palms. "These do not belong to a man who works with his hands."

"Unfortunately, you are right," Murray said. "The committee is not stupid. They will know you are lying."

"So what do you think?" asked Papa. "Do I have a chance?"

Murray glanced down at his notes. "We will tell them what a hard worker you are, and that you are being drafted into the army. But I don't know . . . if only you had a trade. Well, we'll see. I'll come after lunch."

I watched him walk over to Haya's mother. He was nice, but somehow I didn't believe he could help us.

He gave Haya's mother a slip of paper. Her mouth opened in a smile. She was missing a front tooth.

"Children, children!" she called. "Your papa is coming. It says so right here in the telegram!" She grabbed Murray's hand and kissed it. His beard-less face went red. I was glad for Haya, but jealous, too.

After lunch, Murray came to take Papa to the board meeting.

"Please, can I come, too?" I asked.

"Children are not allowed in the hearing room." Murray patted my head.

"But I won't say a word. I just want to be with Papa. Please, Papa."

"You heard what the man said. It is forbidden."

I blinked away my tears as I watched the guard unlock the door of the detention area and let them out. I knew I should be there with Papa. I could tell them how hard Papa worked and how we never went hungry in Jibatov. I knew Papa would never become a public charge. He was too proud to accept charity.

I slowly climbed to the roof and sat down on a bench next to Haya.

"I'm so excited!" Haya bounced up and down. "Papa is coming to take us to Boston tomorrow."

"That's nice. What does your Papa do?"

"He makes chairs in a factory."

"My brother Lemmel wants to be a carpenter, too."

"Carpenter?" Haya snorted. "My papa isn't a carpenter. Back home he sold old clothes and rags to the peasants."

I couldn't understand. "But he must be big and strong."

"He's about the height of your papa, only fatter."

"Then how did they let him into America?" Haya's papa had no trade. He had a family to support in Russia. Why did the inspectors let him in and not Papa?

"I dunno." Haya shrugged her shoulders.

"Because he told them he could work with his hands, dummy," Haya's older sister said. "They told him on the boat to say he had a trade. So he said he was a carpenter."

"He lied?"

"Of course. The funny thing is it turned out to be true. Now he is a carpenter." The sisters laughed.

I felt like they had twisted a knife in my stomach. If only Papa had lied!

"Come on, Raizel, let's play. All you do is sit here and mope. Don't you like games?" Haya could never sit still for long.

"Of course. But I don't feel like playing. I'm waiting for the results of my Papa's hearing. I don't even feel like telling stories."

"You know stories? Tell me one, please." Haya's freckled face twisted into a pleading look.

"I don't feel like it."

"What a snob you are! I'm going to play with someone else." She tossed her braids and flounced over to a group of girls throwing a piece of wood and jumping on one leg. If only Susan and Reuben were here. They would understand why I couldn't tell a story today. They would sit with me and try to cheer me up.

Haya's sister was bouncing her little brother on her lap. She looked sixteen, old enough to marry. She acted like I was too little to talk with.

I got up and walked over to the wall. I could just see over the edge. Far below, the sea looked like a lace tablecloth with white waves criss-crossing into lines and patterns. Boats scuttled back and forth bringing new immigrants to Ellis Island and taking them back across to New York. The city shoreline was too far away to see clearly, but I could see the Lady. Only yesterday I had thought she was welcoming us to America. Today she seemed to be standing guard.

We don't want you here, I imagined she called to me. *Your papa isn't good enough for America.*

Please let us in, I pleaded silently. *You don't know how awful the Czar's army is. I love my papa so much. If you don't let us into America, he will die.*

Little girl, she answered coldly. *All the time people are coming and coming. Soon there won't be room for any more.*

But America is so big and there's still room for us. We won't take up much space and we'll work hard all the time. Please, Lady, please . . .

I felt a hand on my shoulder and swung around. Before Papa could open his mouth, I knew the answer. He looked like a handkerchief after too many washings.

"Papa . . . ?"

"We sail for Russia the day after tomorrow."

I nodded.

I had no tears left.

17
New Friends

We left Ellis Island two days later. Guards herded us onto a little boat and watched us while we boarded the Manitou. They made me feel ashamed, like a murderer or robber. In their eyes we weren't good enough for America, so they were sending Papa back to Russia to die. It was so unfair! I wanted to pound my fists against the guards' chest and scream at them to let us in, but I held my head up and followed Papa up the gangplank.

The matron had given me some bananas and oranges when we left, but Papa said I could eat the food on the boat this time. It was a long journey and he didn't want me to be sick.

I felt so miserable as I hung over the railing watching the little boats towing our ship out of the harbor. It was the saddest day of my life, even sadder than the day I left Mama and the little ones. The buildings of New York grew smaller and smaller until they seemed to sink into the ocean. It hurt too much to look at the Lady. I knew it wasn't her fault—she was only a statue after all—but I felt like she had lied and cheated us. Instead of welcoming us, she had closed the golden door in our face. Instead of raising her hand in greeting, she had raised it in farewell. I was terrified of what would happen to us in Russia. Would we ever be a happy family again?

The boat rose and fell under my feet in the familiar rhythm of the sea. This time I wasn't afraid of the ocean. My stomach felt steady as I walked around the deck observing the other passengers. Some I recognized from Ellis Island, including the man with the red eyes, while others were well-dressed in wool suits and hats. I couldn't find any children except for a big Polish family. The gate between the third-class passengers and the other classes was down so I had the whole deck to walk and play on. But who could I play with? The Polish children were too little, even if I could understand their language.

Finally I went below deck. We had been given a second-class cabin with two beds and a cabinet for our clothes. There was even a tiny bathroom. If I hadn't felt so miserable, I would have been happy with such luxury.

Papa was lying down with his prayer book propped on his stomach.

"Papa, will you teach me to read?" I held the book Leah had given me. Papa had been too sick on the first crossing, but maybe this time he would feel better.

"Not now, meydele. I'm too tired."

"I didn't mean right now. It's almost dinner time. I heard the steward ring the bell."

"Who has strength to eat?"

"Do you feel sick?" *Please don't let Papa be sick again.*

"Just tired."

"I'll try to bring you some bread."

Papa didn't answer. I bit my lip. Papa had barely eaten during our last days on Ellis Island. At mealtimes he drank a cup of tea and ate a banana or apple. But the worst part was that he barely spoke to me. He just wanted to sleep all the time.

A new worry chewed my thoughts. What if Papa got sick again? How would we get home? I felt so alone. If only Mama or Bobbe were here, they would know what to do.

Up on deck, I followed a group of passengers until we came to the first-class dining room. I remembered seeing it once before on the voyage out. One day Susan and I had found the gate leading to the first-class deck open. We had peeped in the dining room windows at the elegantly dressed ladies. A steward stormed out yelling and waving his fists at us. He was wearing the silliest black coat with two flapping tails like a giant bird. Susan and I laughed so hard we could barely run away.

I knew I wasn't allowed in the first-class dining room. But where was the second-class dining room? I was just going to look for it when someone asked in Yiddish, "You are coming to eat?"

I turned around. A tall man with a round red face and a shiny bald head was smiling down at me as if he had made a joke. Holding his arm was a white-haired lady wearing a black silk dress. Her long nose stuck out in my direction.

"I'm looking for the second-class dining room," I answered.

The man frowned and said something to the steward. "There are so few passengers that everyone is eating together."

"Of course, there are few passengers. Who is so crazy as to travel by sea during the stormy season?" The woman smoothed an invisible wrinkle out of the fabric of her dress. Her white hair was piled in waves on top of her head. She wore a large gold ring with sparkling red stones and a gold bracelet.

"Now, Mother, you know it couldn't be helped. Come, let's have dinner. You're welcome to join us, young lady, if you don't have anyone to sit with."

I followed them inside and stared at the splendid wood-paneled room. The tables were set with white tablecloths just like on the Sabbath. The silverware shone in the glow of candlelight. The room was hushed except for the clink of china and the low murmur of conversation. How could people eat so quietly? In the dining room at Ellis Island you couldn't hear your neighbor over the shouts and clatter. Then I saw the Polish family. The children were screaming and a baby was crying. The white-haired lady sniffed as we passed their table.

I felt funny sitting with grown-up strangers, but I didn't want to sit by myself either. If only Papa had come with me! The red-faced man seemed to read my thoughts as he pulled out my chair.

"I should introduce myself. I am Mr. Goldenberg and this is my mother. We are returning to Antwerp after a brief stay in the U.S."

"Not brief enough," said Mrs. Goldenberg. "Those Americans are so rude. I can't wait to get home where people are civilized."

I watched as the steward filled my water glass. "My name is Raizel Balaban."

"Speak up, child!" Mrs. Goldenberg tapped her fork on the table. She had a sharp voice, sharp like her long nose. She seemed to stare right through me.

"I said I'm Raizel Balaban. I'm traveling with my papa back home to Jibatov."

"Jibatov? Where's that?" The old lady turned to the red-faced man, who winked at me for some reason I couldn't understand.

"I confess I don't know either," he said. "Here, have a roll and butter." He put a roll on my little plate. I had so many plates and forks in front of me that I didn't know what to do with them. He put one on his mother's plate and spread it with butter. Then he guided her hand to the roll.

Suddenly I understood: Mrs. Goldenberg was blind!

"It's in Russia, in the Ukraine, near Lubov," I explained. The roll was soft as a cotton puff. "Do you think they would mind if I took a roll to my papa?"

"Is he ill, my dear?" Mrs. Goldenberg spoke more gently now.

"No, at least I don't think so. He's just too tired to come to dinner."

"I'll have the steward send food to his cabin." Mr. Goldenberg waved his hand in the air.

I couldn't believe it. In third class, if you missed dinner you went hungry. Here they brought the food right to your room. "Oh no, Papa doesn't want a whole dinner. Just some rolls would be fine. And fruit, if they have it."

"If they have it?" Mr. Goldenberg roared with laughter.

"Enough, Bernard." His mother put her hand on his arm. "Why won't he eat?"

"Because the food isn't kosher," I explained. "Papa didn't eat the whole way across the ocean. At Ellis Island he ate only fruit and hard-boiled eggs."

Mr. Goldenberg looked serious. "Now I understand. You are being sent back to Russia?"

"You don't have any contagious diseases, do you?" Mrs. Goldenberg shrunk away from me.

"Oh no! We are both healthy. They said Papa isn't strong enough to support a family, so they are sending us back. They said he's liable to become a public charge." The hateful words tasted bitter in my mouth. Just then a waiter put a huge tureen of soup down on our table. Clouds of fragrant steam tickled my nose as Mr. Goldenberg lifted the lid.

"Careful, Mother. It's very hot." He spooned some into a white china bowl. "Raizel?"

"I don't want any, thank you."

"You must eat, my dear," he said firmly. He put a little soup into my bowl. "You need your strength."

"Is the child very thin?"

"She looks about ten years old," Mr. Goldenberg said. "She has long brown hair which is doing its best to escape from her braids. She has a delicate face with pointed chin and large dark eyes. I think she's going to be quite lovely when she grows up." He smiled at me. "I am my mother's eyes these days. Was I right?"

"Almost. I'll be twelve soon." I took a sip of the soup. It was thin and clear, not like the thick soups Mama made at home.

"Then you must definitely eat more. You don't look a day over ten, and I should know. I have three daughters at home."

"Beautiful girls. I'm so sorry I won't ever be able to see them again." Mrs. Goldenberg dabbed her napkin to her eyes.

"We were in the U.S. to see about an operation," Mr. Goldenberg explained. "I heard that there was a specialist who operated on conditions like my mother's. But it didn't work out."

"Too old. He said I was too old for an operation." She sighed. "Well, I guess I have to be thankful that I saw so well for sixty years. It will be good to get home. I'm definitely too old for long journeys. Especially in the winter."

"Mother, we still have time before winter sets in. It's only October. How long have you been traveling, Raizel?"

"We left Jibatov in mid-summer. The cherries were coming ripe." The waiter cleared away our soup plates and another waiter appeared carrying a large silver tray. He presented it to Mr. Goldenberg who pointed and nodded. He put several slices of meat on Mr. Goldenberg's plate and a small piece of chicken on his mother's.

"Do you prefer meat or chicken, Raizel?"

I pointed at the meat. After that the waiter put mashed potatoes and peas on my plate. The food was delicious. The meat was so soft you could cut it like a ripe peach. I couldn't help watching Mrs. Goldenberg as I ate. She methodically collected her food into little piles and carefully raised her fork to her mouth. It took her a long time to finish, but she didn't spill a drop.

For desert we had a scrumptious vanilla pudding and bowl of fresh fruit. Mr. Goldenberg instructed the waiter to pack a bag of fruit and rolls for Papa.

"I hope we'll meet your papa in the morning," said Mr. Goldenberg as he helped his mother leave the dining room. "I want to tell him what a well-behaved little girl he has."

I felt my face burn.

"Good night, my dear. Sleep well." Mrs. Goldenberg said softly. Her face didn't look sharp to me anymore. She looked warm and kind, a little like Bobbe, but with fewer wrinkles and a lot more white hair.

I wanted to tell Papa about the Goldenbergs, but he was asleep when I returned to the cabin. He had been sleeping since we boarded the boat. How could anyone sleep so much? I took off my clothes and crawled under the chilly covers.

When I woke up in the morning, he was standing in a corner with his prayer shawl over his shoulders. I waited until he finished praying.

"Papa, I brought you some food. I met a really nice Jewish man and his mother. They're traveling to Antwerp and . . . "

Papa was rubbing his forehead.

"Do you have a headache, Papa?"

"A little. I did not sleep well."

"Shall I ask the doctor for some medicine?"

"No, I think I will lie down for a while."

"Why don't you come on deck? Remember how the doctor said you need fresh air?"

"Later, child." Papa lay down and closed his eyes.

I stared at him for a while trying to decide what to do. I couldn't force Papa to go on deck. But what was wrong with him? When I had a fever, I slept a lot. But Papa didn't look sick. Just sad.

I set the fruit on the table and left the rolls in the bag. After breakfast I would come back to check on him.

On deck it was a bright sunny day with a strong cool wind. The coast of America had disappeared behind the horizon and we were surrounded by water. I filled my lungs with the tangy sea air and wondered what I could find to do all day. If only Papa felt well enough to teach me to read. Perhaps there were other children on board and I hadn't looked hard enough.

The dining room was almost empty, but the steward showed me to a table and pulled out the chair for me. He served me a big bowl of oatmeal with sugar and cream. Then he asked me something I couldn't understand and pointed at another table where people were eating eggs.

"Eggs?" he repeated.

What a funny word! "Eggs," I said and nodded. Now I knew two words in English: eggs and banana. And greenhorn, of course.

A few minutes later he brought me a soft-boiled egg, toast and a big glass of milk. As I ate I looked around the dining room, wondering where the Goldenbergs were. I took a piece of toast and spread it with jam for Papa, but he was asleep when I returned to the cabin, so I went back up on deck.

I had wandered around the entire deck three times when I saw them. Mr. Goldenberg was helping his mother settle into a deck chair and covering her with a blanket. As I approached to say good morning, I could hear her scolding him.

"But Bernard, I don't understand how such a thing could happen. How many times have I told you to put your glasses back in the case?"

"Yes, Mother, I know. I was just about to put them back."

"Well, it was very careless of you. I don't know what I'm going to do on the crossing without someone to read to me. It's not as if I could knit or embroider, you know. It was simply thoughtless of you."

"Not having a second pair of reading glasses is the thoughtless part. I'm going to have two pairs made up as soon as we get home. Ah, good morning, Raizel! Perhaps you can help us."

How could I help the Goldenbergs?

Double Crossing

"Could you read to my mother for a while? My glasses unfortunately got broken."

"I sat on them." Mrs. Goldenberg made such a rueful face that I couldn't help laughing. "It's no laughing matter. Can you read Yiddish, child? Or French or English?"

Why did everyone expect me to know how to read? It wasn't fair. "No. I can't read except for a few prayers that Mama taught me. I was hoping Papa would teach me on the crossing, but he was too sick on the way over."

"Sorry to hear that," said Mr. Goldenberg. "I would teach you myself, but without my glasses, I can't read a thing. Why don't you keep my mother company, and I'll see if I can find someone to fix them?"

"Yes, dear. Sit down right beside me and tell me what you see." She patted the arm of the chair next to her.

"It's a bright sunny day. The sea looks like someone tossed a basket of laundry in the water and all the white handkerchiefs are bobbing in the foam. Two very elegant ladies are standing at the railing. One is wearing a green satin dress and a hat that looks like a molting bird. All the feathers are blowing in the wind and about to take flight. Oh, the hat blew in the water! Now she's got the steward by the arm and is pointing at the ocean. I think she wants him to jump in after it! He's shaking his head. Her face is as red as an over-cooked beet."

Mrs. Goldenberg was laughing so hard she had to wipe her eyes. "That's marvelous, Raizel. You have a gift for making words come alive."

"I like to tell stories," I said.

Mrs. Goldenberg clapped her hands. "So do I. Please tell me one."

"Oh no. I only tell stories to children. I tell them to Shloyme and Hannah, my little brother and sister."

Mrs. Goldenberg looked disappointed. "Can't you pretend that I'm a child? Close your eyes and pretend you're talking to Hannah. That's my name, too." She reached out her hand and pressed my arm gently. "Please. Humor an old lady. It will make the time pass so much faster."

What could I say? I leaned back and waited for a story to surface in my mind. I had never told a story to a grown-up before, except the Chelm stories to Papa on the train. I didn't think Mrs. Goldenberg would like Chelm stories. Bobbe hadn't liked them. Mrs. Goldenberg's lined face reminded me so much of Bobbe. Suddenly I knew which story to tell.

"Once there was a wise man with three sons. As the wise man lay dying, he called his sons to him.

"'Before I leave this world, I want to reveal a mystery to you, my dear sons. Somewhere there grows a magic tree with ten branches. Each branch bears a different fruit. The fruit on the tree has wonderful powers. It gives health to the sick, children to the childless, wisdom to fools, and much much more. I have learned that an army of demons has dug a deep ditch to prevent the waters of life from reaching the tree roots. If the tree dies, its blessings will be lost to the world forever. I charge you with the mission of finding this tree and ensuring that it is watered again. This is the last request I make of you.' With that the wise man closed his eyes and died.

"The two older sons set out in search of the tree. They searched for years and years, but in the end returned home tired, weary, and empty of hope. 'We could not find the tree,' they told the youngest son.

"'Then I will try,' he said.

"His two brothers laughed, because the youngest was lame and could not walk on his own. 'I will hire a wagon and driver to take me,' said the youngest son. 'I can travel as well as any man.'

"When the older brothers saw how determined he was, they paid for a wagon and driver to take him on his journey. One day as they were riding through a deep forest, a band of thieves attacked. The driver jumped down and ran away, but the younger brother could not move from the wagon. When the thieves saw that he was lame, they stole his supplies and the horse and left him to perish in the forest.

"Afraid that he would die of starvation if he stayed in the wagon, the younger brother crawled to the edge and rolled out. Then he pulled himself along the ground, eating herbs and berries to stay alive. Suddenly he saw an herb that was new to him. He pulled it out of the earth and found a large square rock entangled in the roots. Carefully he wiped it clean and was astounded to discover that the rock was a square diamond covered with writing. On one side was written that whoever grasped that side of the diamond would be transported to the spot where the sun and moon meet. This sounded more promising than the forest, so the younger brother grasped the diamond and was instantly transported to the end of the world where the sun and moon were talking to each other.

"'I am very worried about the tree,' the sun was saying. 'The demons are making the ditch even deeper and soon no water will reach its roots. All the blessings will be lost to the world.'

"'I know how to defeat the demons,' said the moon. 'There is a cross-road where ten paths meet. The dust on each path is magic. If you take the dust of righteousness and sprinkle it on the demons, they will be defeated.'

"The younger brother was overjoyed to hear this. *I must find the cross-road*, he said to himself. *Perhaps the diamond can help me.*

"Sure enough, on the next side of the diamond was written that whoever grasped it would be transported to the crossroads of the ten paths. Without wasting a moment, the younger brother gripped the diamond and found himself at the crossroads. Each of the ten paths was labeled with a sign: healing, love, youth, righteousness, and many more. The young man collected the dust from the path of the righteous and filled his pockets. Then he took out the diamond. On the third side was written that whoever grasped it would be taken to the life-giving tree. He was about to grasp that side when he had an idea. He pulled himself over to the path of healing and sprinkled a handful of dust on his lame legs. Instantly his legs became strong and healthy, and the young man could walk on them for the first time in his life."

"Praise the Lord," whispered Mrs. Goldenberg. Her eyes were closed but her face was turned to me. "Go on, child."

"Then the young man grasped the diamond and found himself confronting an army of terrible demons with hideous fearful faces. They spit fire from their mouth, and lightening from their eyes, and in their hands were enormous gleaming swords. The young man was filled with fear, but he knew what to do. He began throwing the dust of righteousness at them from his pockets. The demons laughed as they saw the dust flying though the air, but as soon as it touched them, they disappeared. When the demons were gone, the young man approached the pit surrounding the enchanted tree. It was so deep he could not see the bottom. Cold winds blew into his face and froze his blood. How could he cross the ditch? Just then the dust on his hands blew into the pit, and it disappeared."

"An illusion," murmured Mrs. Goldenberg.

"The young man approached the tree, which was withered and dry. It looked almost dead. He searched for water and found a trickle bubbling out of a rock. Using his bare hands, he gathered the water and carried it to the tree, going back and forth until his feet made a channel for the water to flow in. As he watched, the tree grew upright and its branches thickened. Buds formed and fresh green leaves unfurled. Blossoms perfumed the air and turned into firm ripe fruit, a different kind for each of the ten branches. The younger brother sat on the soft ground and feasted his eyes on the tree. A great happiness filled him, and he knew that the tree was blessing the world anew."

Double Crossing

Mrs. Goldenberg sighed. "What a beautiful story. It reminds me of a story I once read in a collection of Rabbi Nachman of Bratslav. There is much wisdom in it."

Mrs. Goldenberg was explaining the philosophical meaning of the ten branches when Mr. Goldenberg appeared smoking a pipe. "Bernard, is that you? I can smell you across deck."

"Yes, Mother. I'm afraid the glasses can't be fixed. I'm very sorry."

"It doesn't matter," said the old lady firmly. "Raizel and I can manage quite well by ourselves."

Mr. Goldenberg smiled. "And may I ask what you are doing?"

For a moment I was afraid she would tell him about the story. Telling stories to Mrs. Goldenberg was almost like telling them to Shloyme, but I didn't feel like having any more grownups around.

"You may not. It is our secret and we don't intend to share it with anyone. Do we agree, Raizel?"

I took her outstretched hand and squeezed it.

"And how is your Papa today, Raizel?" Mr. Goldenberg asked.

"He was still asleep when I came on deck."

"Are you sure he isn't ill? I could call the ship's doctor to look at him." I shook my head. "He isn't ill, just tired. He'll feel better later."

As I said the words, I realized I didn't believe them. Papa was more than tired. He was ill, but not with a sickness the doctor could cure. He was like a man who had lost something very very important, more important than reading glasses.

Papa had lost his hope.

18

A Sabbath Choice

Papa didn't leave the cabin that day, or the next. He ate only a few bites of the food I brought. I pleaded. I prodded. I spent hours with him in the cabin while he prayed and slept, prayed and slept. Nothing helped. I felt like Papa was slowly falling down a deep well. I could neither grab him nor catch him at the bottom.

"Papa, please come on deck with me," I pleaded on the fourth morning. "You need the fresh air."

"I was on deck at night when everyone slept." He rocked back and forth with his prayer shawl over his shoulders.

"At night? But you'll catch a chill." I shivered to think of Papa alone on the cold dark deck. The days were growing chilly and I could smell winter approaching in the wind.

"And you barely ate anything. Come to the dining room and have an egg at least. Please, Papa. I'm worried that you'll be sick."

"I am fine. Just tired."

I wanted to ask how he could be tired when all he did was sleep, but I bit my tongue. Children did not talk back to their elders.

Papa set his prayer book on the table and lay down on the bed. I sighed and closed the door.

Clouds scuttled around the blue sky, racing across the sun, and shifting the deck in and out of shadow. I hung over the railing listening to the sea slap the boat. Bursts of foam scattered like dandelion puffs in the wind. I felt so alone. Papa was drifting away from me like a moorless boat. He was getting thinner and weaker, and sleeping more and more. What if one morning he didn't wake up?

Who could I ask for advice? The ship's doctor? The Goldenbergs were the only people I knew on the boat. No, Papa would be furious at me for taking our troubles to outsiders. Mama always said, "Weep before God. Laugh before people." The Goldenbergs weren't family. You only share troubles with family.

"Good morning, Raizel."

Mrs. Goldenberg was sitting in her favorite deck chair as I approached. She liked to sleep late and have breakfast in her cabin. Then she took a stroll around the deck and we told each other stories until lunchtime.

"Good morning. How are you feeling today?" I asked.

"Just fine, thank you. You know the strangest thing keeps happening to me. Stories pop into my mind all the time. Stories I haven't heard for years."

"Where did you learn your stories?"

"From my aunt. She had a lame leg and couldn't do the hard work around the house. She would tell stories to keep the children amused or while she was knitting. She was a fabulous knitter. I wasn't always as well off as today, you know. My father was a fish seller. Our house stank of fish."

I stared at Mrs. Goldenberg. The white lace around her cuffs was as clean as fresh fallen snow. She wore a beautiful ruby brooch and her long fingers glittered with gold rings. Yet she was the daughter of a fish seller!

"Why are you so quiet, Raizel?"

"I'm trying to imagine you in a house full of smelly fish." Actually I was wondering if I should ask her about Papa.

"Then imagine me barefoot among my eight brothers and sisters. We were so poor we often had to make do with potatoes and onions for our Sabbath meal. How long ago that was!" She turned to me with a mischievous smile. "That counts as my first story. Now it's your turn!"

I closed my eyes and waited for a story to surface. But all I could think about was Papa. Why wouldn't he eat? Why did he sleep all the time? "I can't think of a story."

"Nonsense. Try harder."

"Well, once there was a house full of demons. No, I don't remember that one. Once . . . there was a young man whose father was dying." My throat closed up. Before I could help myself, the sobs bubbled over like a boiling pot of noodles.

"Raizel, child, why are you crying? Does something hurt you?" Mrs. Goldenberg put her hand on my shoulder. "Tell me, my dear."

I pulled back. "It's nothing. I just don't feel like telling stories today."

"Crying about stories? You can't fool an old lady. Something is troubling you. The greatest pain is the one you can't tell others about. If you tell me, perhaps I can help in some way."

The sobs boiled over again. I had to tell someone. If Bobbe were here I would talk to her, and Mrs. Goldenberg was so like Bobbe. "It's Papa. I don't know what's happening to him. It frightens me." If only Mama were here. I wanted Mama so badly.

"There, there." Mrs. Goldenberg handed me her white handkerchief. "Cry as much as you want. Then tell me what the matter is."

When the sobs had dried up, I told Mrs. Goldenberg how strangely Papa was acting. He never smiled or joked or asked about me. He was cold and distant, like someone I didn't know. I was afraid that he would be sick again. Or worse.

Mrs. Goldenberg listened closely. When I told her about the Czar's army and what would happen when we returned home, she pulled her gray shawl around her shoulders. "Oh my, oh my, the poor man. What a tragedy. If only there were something we could do."

"Do about what, Mother? What's the matter, Raizel? You look like a cat left out in the rain."

"This is no time for your jokes, Bernard. Sit down and put on your thinking cap."

Mr. Goldenberg sat down like a little boy whose hand had been slapped. "I'm sorry. I just assumed Raizel had been telling a very sad story."

So he knew! Just as long as he didn't ask me to tell him stories, too.

Mrs. Goldenberg repeated what I had told her. The cheery smile left his face. "I don't suppose it would help if I went to talk to him?"

"He won't talk."

"Or if I had food sent to his room?"

"He won't eat."

"Or asked the doctor to see him?"

"He's not sick."

"Bernard, you're not thinking."

"I'm thinking, Mother. I just think better on a full stomach. Why don't we have some lunch and put our heads to work while we eat?"

I barely tasted the food at lunch. Mrs. Goldenberg ate with her usual delicacy, taking small bites and chewing slowly. Only Mr. Goldenberg ate like a starving man, even asking for a second helping of the chicken potpie. When he had finished, he wiped his mouth with his napkin and patted his stomach.

"Nothing like sea air to make a man hungry. Perhaps your papa would join me in a brisk stroll? That would improve his appetite."

"What we need to do is improve his mood," said Mrs. Goldenberg firmly. "He is unhappy and needs to take his mind off his troubles. What makes your papa happy, Raizel?"

What made Papa happy in Jibatov? "Coming home to the family for the Sabbath. Conducting the Passover Seder. Playing with the little ones. Telling jokes with Uncle Nahum. Singing Sabbath songs after Mama's meal."

I remembered how Papa had sung our last Sabbath in Jibatov and wiped away a tear.

"Don't cry, meydele," said Mr. Goldenberg. "I can't make it Passover again, but do you know what day it is?"

I dabbed at my eyes with the handkerchief and shook my head. I had lost track of the days since we arrived in America.

"Oh, Bernard, that's a wonderful idea!"

I looked from one to the other without understanding.

"Today is Friday," Mr. Goldenberg said with a smile. "I'm sure your papa won't refuse to welcome in the Sabbath. We'll light the candles and have dinner brought to our cabin."

"With wine, of course." Mrs. Goldenberg clapped her hands. "Now where can we get a challah? If I had my sight, I would go into the kitchen and make one myself."

"I know how to make challah." I had been helping Mama for as long as I could remember.

"That's settled then! Bernard, talk to the steward. If we start now, there will be plenty of time for the dough to rise. And Raizel, it's your job to make sure your papa comes."

Mrs. Goldenberg gave orders like a general. Her face glowed as if she were sitting opposite a fire.

Mr. Goldenberg jumped up and went after the steward. A few minutes later I was in the kitchen giving orders to the cook, with Mrs. Goldenberg translating into English.

"Eggs," I said to the cook after I surveyed the flour, yeast, sugar, and oil he had set on the table.

"Why, Raizel, I didn't know you could speak English!" Mrs. Goldenberg was sitting on a tall stool.

"Just a few words that I learned on Ellis Island and here on the boat: bread, oatmeal, please, tankyou." I ran down the list. "Oh, and gut night and gut morning."

"I have a wonderful idea. I lived in England with my husband—may he rest in peace—for many years. I could give you English lessons every day after lunch. It would make the time pass even more quickly."

"All right," I said without enthusiasm. What did I need to learn English for? No one in Jibatov spoke English. But if it would make Mrs. Goldenberg happy, I could try.

I mixed and kneaded the dough just like Mama. The yeasty smell and soft sticky dough reminded me of home, but I wouldn't let myself cry. I had cried enough for one day. The cook watched with a big smile on his mustached face.

"He says you are as good as a professional baker. Let me feel the dough." Her fingers patted the round lump. "Yes, plump as a baby's bottom. Your mother is a good teacher. Now let the dough rise and go talk to your papa."

Papa was sitting at the table reading his prayer book. He didn't look up as I came in.

"Papa, guess what?" I paused and waited for him to make a joke about the Czar coming to visit or a dolphin jumping over the ship. But he kept on reading.

"Papa . . . ?" I called more loudly.

"What is it, Raizel?" Papa looked at me in surprise. His eyes were unfocussed as if he had been somewhere far away. I felt a chill blow through the cabin.

"It's the Sabbath, Papa. Tonight is the Sabbath and my friends, the ones I told you about, have invited us to their cabin to light the candles. And guess what, Papa? I even made challah. The cook let me work in the kitchen. There are so few passengers that he didn't mind."

"The kitchen is not kosher." Papa rubbed his forehead with a bony hand.

"I know, Papa. Please say you'll come. They'll be so disappointed if you don't."

Papa sighed. "How could I know it was the Sabbath? I have lost track of the days. I am so tired."

"No, Papa. Please don't go to sleep again." But Papa was already lying down on the bed.

I took a deep breath. "Honor the Sabbath Day and keep it holy is one of the Ten Commandments. We have to celebrate the Sabbath, Papa." Would Papa think I was being too forward?

Papa opened his eyes. "From a child's mouth. You are right, Raizel, one must welcome the Sabbath. I will come, but I will eat only your challah." He turned to the wall and pulled the blanket over his head.

He would come! I was so happy I felt like dancing around the room. Instead I returned to the kitchen to braid the challahs into the Sabbath loaves.

That evening I wore my embroidered blouse and almost-new skirt and brushed my hair into a single braid. I straightened Papa's coat and hat before we left the room. He followed me slowly, holding on to the wall as we walked up the stairs and down the corridor to the first-class cabins. Was it my imagination or was the ship rocking more than usual?

The Goldenberg's cabin was larger than our house in Jibatov. There were two separate bedrooms connected to a big sitting room filled with thick rugs and plump striped couches. Pictures hung on the wall like in a real house.

"How nice to meet you, Mr. Balaban." Mr. Goldenberg ushered us into the cabin. A table in the center of the room was set with a white cloth, polished silver candlesticks, and a bottle of red wine. A white napkin covered my challahs.

"I am pleased to meet you." Papa made a slight bow. "Raizel tells me how kind you have been to her."

"What a beautiful room you have!" I said to Mrs. Goldenberg who was wearing a gray wool dress and pearl earrings. I couldn't stop admiring the glittering chandelier and polished wood furniture. "It's too bad you can't see it. Oh, I'm sorry, I didn't mean . . . " What a horrible thing to say. I felt my face grow red with shame.

"Come sit beside me, child." Mrs. Goldenberg patted the empty seat on the couch. "Bernard has described the room to me so well, I feel as if I could see it. It's nothing compared to our living room at home."

"Come, Mother." Mr. Goldenberg took her arm. "It's time to light the Sabbath candles."

Mrs. Goldenberg slipped a veil over her head. She raised her hands to the flames and murmured the Sabbath blessing. Mr. Goldenberg blessed the wine and gave each of us a cup. Then we washed our hands in the enamel basin.

"Will you bless the bread, Mr. Balaban?"

Papa seemed to wake up. He lifted the napkin, stared at the challahs for a moment, and broke off a piece. Then he said the prayer and tore off chunks for each of us.

"Do you like it, Papa? Does it taste like Mama's?"

"It melts in my mouth just like your mama's," Papa said with a smile. He ate the bread and leaned back in his chair.

There was a knock at the door. "Ah, here's dinner." Mr. Goldenberg opened the door and a waiter pushed in a cart loaded with shiny covered platters. There was roast chicken and sweet potatoes and carrots and peas. Everything tasted so good that I ate almost as much as Mr. Goldenberg. For desert we had an apple pudding.

"Papa, just taste this. It's delicious."

Papa took another sip of wine. "I am not hungry, child." He nodded at Mr. Goldenberg. "Please do not be offended. I appreciate your inviting us to dinner."

"You've lost your appetite?" Mrs. Goldenberg asked. "I have some excellent tonic that my doctor gives me when I'm feeling under the weather. It will perk you up in no time."

"No, thank you. I am not ill."

"But all you've eaten are two pieces of bread." Mr. Goldenberg sounded annoyed. "How will you keep your strength up on so little food? It's a long trip back to Russia."

Papa's face turned red. I could see he was struggling between his duty not to offend his host and his desire to defend himself.

"Bernard . . . " Mrs. Goldenberg's voice held a warning. "Be my eyes, please."

"Yes, Mother. Mr. Balaban is a small man and very thin. He has a black beard with no gray in it and side curls. He is wearing a long black coat and a large black hat."

"Just like my papa," whispered Mrs. Goldenberg. "Tell me about his face."

"His eyes are sunk into his face. His cheeks look like they've been gouged out with a spoon. His skin is almost transparent. His bones stick out like a skeleton."

"No!" Papa cried out suddenly. Everyone stared at him. "What are you saying? I don't look like that."

"Papa, you do," I whispered.

"When was the last time you looked in a mirror?" Mr. Goldenberg asked.

I took Papa's hand and led him to the full-length mirror hanging on the wall. Papa stared at himself for a moment. He took off his hat.

"I look like a man with the consumption. Is this the way I looked at Ellis Island?" he asked.

"Yes." I wanted to put my arms around him.

Papa rested his hand on my shoulder to steady himself and sat down again.

"I did not know. I had no idea." He covered his face with his hands. Mrs. Goldenberg put her finger to her lips. Papa sat in silence for a few minutes. When he raised his face, it was full of pain. "Now I see why they would not let me in. I look like a walking dead man."

"Oh Papa, it's not that bad. If you would only eat more . . . "

"No, Raizel, it's not just food." Mr. Goldenberg's voice was harsh. "It's the hat and the coat and the beard. This is 1905. No one dresses like that anymore."

"In Jibatov they do," Papa said.

"Yes, but not in America."

I nodded. In Berlin, Antwerp, and New York, the men wore short jackets. Their faces were clean shaven or had a neatly trimmed beard. Even among the immigrants on Ellis Island, Papa looked out of time. "You mean that if Papa shaved his beard and wore modern clothes they would have let him into America?"

"Bernard, you're a genius!" Mrs. Goldenberg clapped her hands. "Why, I bet one of your suits could be altered to fit him. There must be a tailor on board. And of course there's a barber. Why we could fatten him up and—"

I looked from one to the other, not sure if I understood what they meant.

"Stop!" Papa put his hands over his ears. "I will not listen to this blasphemy anymore. Eat tref? Shave my beard? Cut my hair? What kind of Jew do you think I am?" He glared at Mr. Goldenberg. "Why, you do not even wear a skullcap. And you eat tref, the both of you." He stood up and grabbed my hand. "Come, Raizel. Thank these people for their food. We are going back to our own cabin."

"But Papa . . . " I turned to Mr. Goldenberg for help.

"Do as I say!" Papa shouted. "I am still your father!" He opened the door and stormed out.

I remained standing in the middle of the room. My thoughts were galloping in too many directions at once. "I'm sorry for Papa's rudeness. Please don't be angry with him. Thank you so much for dinner."

"We understand, Raizel." Mrs. Goldenberg smiled sweetly. "We'll talk in the morning. Everything will be all right."

"All right? That stiff-necked fanatic!" Beads of sweat glistened on Mr. Goldenberg's flushed face. "A family man has responsibilities. He must put his family's welfare first."

"That's enough, Bernard. You've done enough for one night. You've given Mr. Balaban a choice. He has a lot to think about. Good night, child."

"Wait, I have to know." I turned to Mr. Goldenberg. "Do you really think that if Papa looks more like an American, they will let him in?"

Mr. Goldenberg pulled out a handkerchief and mopped his face. He was silent a moment. "I think that if he goes back to Russia, they will put him in prison or worse. And I know there is no country in Europe—not Belgium, not Germany—that will let you stay. As a businessman—and a successful one—I would say that your Papa's options are limited. That may be the only option he has."

"And as a Jew? What is his option as a Jew?"

"That's a question only he can answer, Raizel."

I walked slowly back to our cabin. The boat was definitely rocking more than usual. I had to clutch the railing with both hands as I walked down the stairs. I found Papa pacing the floor.

"What foolishness that man talks. What kind of Jew is he, anyway? How dare he tell me what to do?"

"He's only trying to help us, Papa." I wrapped myself in my winter shawl and sat down on the bed, my teeth chattering.

Double Crossing

"Help like that I do not need. Just because he is rich does not mean he can tell me what to do."

"But Papa, what are we going to do? We can't go back to Russia, and no other country will have us."

Papa stopped pacing. His shoulders slumped as if they were carrying a heavy load of wood. "We have no choice. We have to go back to Russia. Perhaps Nahum can help us. Perhaps . . . " He sat down on the bed and covered his face with his hands. His shoulders shook.

"Papa . . . ?"

"All I wanted was to make a good life for your mama and the children. Now you will be orphans. What have I done?"

I had never seen Papa cry before, not even at Bobbe's funeral. I felt my world splinter apart like rotten wood. "Papa, please. The family will help us. Everything will be all right." I put my arm around his shoulders. I didn't believe my own words and neither did Papa. We sat in silence for a long time until my eyes closed with tiredness and wine.

When I woke up, I was under the covers, fully dressed. The cabin light was on.

"Papa?" He was swaying back and forth in the corner of the cabin with his prayer shawl over his head. "Papa, it's late. Come to bed."

Papa turned around. His eyes were red. "Shhh. Go back to sleep, child. I need to think. And pray."

"Are you praying for a miracle?" I sat up in bed and began undressing. I didn't want my good clothes to get wrinkled.

"Miracles are scarce these days."

"Papa, if you shave your beard, change your clothes and eat unkosher food, will you still be Jewish?"

"My father, may his memory be blessed, would rise up from his grave and beat me over the head with his gravestone if he heard. Does that answer your question?"

I thought a moment. "No. I've been eating the food on Ellis Island and the boat and I still feel Jewish."

"For men it is different."

That made me mad. "Why?"

"Because men are charged with following all the commandments and laws. It is men who preserve the knowledge of the Jewish tradition."

"But women determine who is Jewish and who isn't. A child with just a Jewish mother is Jewish. A child with a Jewish father isn't." Bobbe had told me that.

"Raizel, you are a child. The law is not as strict with children. Children are allowed to eat on the Day of Atonement instead of fasting like the adults. Now go to sleep."

That was true. I leaned back and closed my eyes, but my mind wasn't sleepy. What made me Jewish? Was it the food I ate and the clothes I wore? Or being born to a Jewish mother? Or observing the Jewish laws and customs? What about the Christians in our village? What if one of them— say, the blond-haired boy—decided he wanted to be Jewish? What if he came to live in our house, studied with Lemmel at the cheder, and kept all the laws? Would that make him Jewish?

What if a Jew wanted to become a Christian? Mama said Christian babies had to be sprinkled with holy water in order to become Christian. I had heard stories about little Jewish boys who were kidnapped by the Russian army and sprinkled with the water while they slept. So while they still wanted to be Jewish, they couldn't be anymore. Or maybe they stayed Jewish inside but were Christian on the outside.

Inside. Outside. My head began to spin. Did your outside matter if your inside was still the same? If I put on Lemmel's clothes and cut my hair, I would still be a girl. Nothing could change that. If Papa put on Mr. Goldenberg's clothes, he would still be Papa. So why were clothes and food so important, anyway?

Papa got into bed, but I still couldn't fall asleep. Everything had been so simple in Jibatov. I just did what Mama and Papa said and it all felt safe and right. I knew they would take care of me.

But in the world outside of Jibatov, things were different. You couldn't be sure of anything. People weren't what they seemed. Bad people like Ivan were really good. America had closed the golden door and sent us back to Russia. Now I couldn't even be certain what a Jew was.

It scared me.

How nice to be that little girl again, back home where everything was safe and simple. But would home still be the same? Jibatov hadn't changed, but I had. I was outgrowing the scared timid Raizel who always did what she was told like I outgrew Leah's hand-me-downs. I hadn't lost Papa on the crossing as I had feared.

I had lost myself.

19
The Storm Erupts

"Papa's fasting," I said to Mrs. Goldenberg on Sunday morning. We were sitting on the couch in her cabin. It was too cold and windy for her on deck.

"Oh!" She touched her fingertips to her cheeks. "It isn't a fast day, is it?"

"No. Papa says when the body is pure, the mind is free of earthly thoughts. He always fasts on Yom Kippur to atone for his sins and on Tisha B'Av in commemoration of the destruction of the Temple in Jerusalem, but this is different."

"You are worried about him." It wasn't a question.

"I think he is too weak to fast. I told him he would be sick. But he wouldn't listen."

"Your papa is a stubborn man."

"Mama always told him, 'Better to ask the way ten times, than go astray once.'"

"Men never ask the way," Mrs. Goldenberg said with a little smile. "My mama always said, 'Better a Jew without a beard, than a beard without a Jew.'"

"Yes." I smiled. "Mama says that, too."

"Anyway, perhaps fasting is a good sign. It means he is weighing the idea with utmost seriousness."

"I hope so. If only there were something I could do to help!" I felt like Hannah who could only suck her thumb and stare at the grown-ups.

"It is adult of you to want to help your parents," said Mrs. Goldenberg. "But only your papa can make the decision." She pressed my hand. "Now tell me a story."

I closed my eyes to think. I knew Papa wouldn't listen to me because I was only a child and a girl at that. He wouldn't listen to the Goldenbergs because they were strangers and not observant Jews. He might listen to Mama or Uncle Nahum or the rabbi of Jibatov, but they were too far away. Suddenly I sat up straight. Our storytelling had given me an idea! Perhaps there was one thing I could do. I promised Mrs. Goldenberg I would return and ran to our cabin.

Papa was lying in bed with his eyes wide open when I entered.

"The steward said there will be a storm." I noted that the bag of rolls I had brought earlier was unopened.

"The wrath of God is upon me," Papa murmured.

I shuddered. Reuben had said the Manitou was a strong boat. But Reuben was safe in America, and we were in the middle of the Atlantic Ocean. I hoped the steward was wrong.

"Papa, may I tell you a story?"

Papa turned his head and looked at me. His eyes stared through his thick lenses like giant eggs. "A story? Now?"

"Why not? We used to tell stories on the train to pass the time, remember?"

"It seems so long ago. Why not? But not Chelm stories."

"I don't feel like a Chelm story either," I said, sitting down on my bed. I knew exactly which story I wanted to tell him. "Once there was a famous sage named Rabbi Adam who possessed mighty powers. Unlike magicians and sorcerers who use the forces of evil, Rabbi Adam used the force of good, the secret Name of God. The Rabbi's fame reached the ears of the king's minister. He was jealous and determined to bring about the rabbi's ruin and cast shame on the Jews of the kingdom."

Papa was lying in bed with his eyes closed. Had I put him to sleep?

"The evil minister told the king about the Rabbi and suggested he invite him to dinner. He knew the Rabbi lived in a poor hut and had nothing but old worn clothes to wear. To appear in court like that would bring shame on the Rabbi and the Jews.

"The Rabbi was invited to the palace. When he appeared, he was dressed in the finest clothing, as rich as that of any noble in the court. The minister couldn't understand what had happened and suspected that the Jews of the kingdom had contributed money for the Rabbi's clothes. But the truth was different. The clothes were an illusion, for Rabbi Adam knew how to use the power of illusion to create whatever he desired."

Papa had rolled over on his side and was watching me. Was that a half-smile on his face?

"The minister was cunning. After dinner he suggested that the Rabbi demonstrate his powers for the king, hoping to disgrace him. Rabbi Adam asked the king to imagine something he wanted and whisper it to the minister. Then he told the king to put his hand in his pocket. Lo and behold, the king took out an enormous diamond, the purest he had ever seen.

"'That is exactly what I wished for,' he said.

"The evil minister didn't lose his composure. He suggested that Rabbi Adam invite the king to his home, just as he had been invited to the palace. This would surely disgrace him for he would be unable to entertain the king as he deserved."

Papa sat up. He crossed his arms and rested his chin on his hand.

"Of course Rabbi Adam had to agree, even though he lived in a one-room hut in the forest. As the day of the visit approached, the minister sent spies to see if the Rabbi was building a larger house and preparing for the banquet he was about to serve the king. The spies reported nothing had changed in the little hut.

"Imagine the minister's surprise when they approached the Rabbi's house on the evening of the dinner and found a magnificent marble palace in its place! Rabbi Adam's servants served a banquet more lavish than that of any king, at a table set with golden plates, cups, and silverware.

"Furious that he had failed to humiliate the Rabbi and bring disgrace on the Jews, the evil minister determined to profit from the evening—he hid a beautiful gold wine goblet in his robe.

"When the time came to leave, everyone rose except the minister.

"'Come along,' said the king. 'Why don't you rise?'

"'I can't move,' said the minister, his face red with exertion.

"The king turned to Rabbi Adam for an explanation. 'It is his own fault,' explained the rabbi. 'He is unable to rise because he has stolen something that does not belong to him.'

"The king ordered the minister searched and the gold goblet was found. Of course, the minister was disgraced and thrown in prison. Rabbi Adam was honored by the king and the Jews of his kingdom enjoyed good treatment for the rest of his long reign."

I looked at Papa expectantly. Had he understood why I told him the story?

"That's a lovely story, meydele."

"Thank you, Papa. Did you notice the part about Rabbi Adam using the forces of good to change his appearance and then his house?"

"Yes. It would be nice to have magic powers."

"No, Papa, that's not what I meant."

"Raizel, do you think I have such a thick head that I don't understand why you suddenly chose to tell me that story about Rabbi Adam changing his clothes and his house?"

I sighed. Had I really believed a story could make up Papa's mind? "Papa, I was just trying to help."

"Meydele, stories are nice, but I could tell you a story for everything. For example, I could tell you a story about the Baal Shem Tov who wanted to enter the Holy Land, but was forbidden by God himself."

"Why, Papa?"

"Because if he entered, it would bring the Messiah and the end of the world before the time was ripe. But a demon tempted him and he almost lost himself to temptation. At the last moment he saw the demon had no shadow and was able to avoid falling into the pit the demon had prepared for him."

"And did he finally enter the Holy Land?"

"No. He bowed to God's will and never tried again. So you see, for every story you tell me, I could tell you an opposite one. Now let me go back to my prayers, and don't disturb me with any more stories."

"I'm sorry, Papa," I said, but Papa had turned his back and wasn't listening. I wrapped my shawl around me but I still felt the chill inside me.

That night at dinner, the waiter spilled the tureen of soup before he could set it down on the rocking table. Potatoes rolled around on my plate like marbles. The dining room was half-empty. My stomach felt so queasy I could only force myself to eat a few spoonfuls.

"If this weather continues, I shall keep to my cabin tomorrow," said Mrs. Goldenberg.

"It's fortunate we don't suffer from sea sickness." Mr. Goldenberg cut into his roast beef. "How is your father feeling?"

"He didn't sleep last night and he hasn't eaten anything today."

"Perhaps I should speak with him."

"Bernard, you know that would only make things worse. We have planted a seed and it will take time to sprout. I'm sure Mr. Balaban will work things out in a few days."

A few days! How would Papa survive so long without eating? I put down my fork. The boat was bouncing and jouncing like a runaway carriage and my stomach bobbed with it. "I think I'll go back to the cabin," I said.

"Be careful. Don't wander around the deck in this weather," said Mr. Goldenberg. "Don't you want to take anything for your papa?"

"It's no use. He won't eat until he comes to a decision."

As I stepped on deck, the wind grabbed my shawl. I snatched at the fringe before it disappeared in the ocean. I leaned against the wind and struggled forward. It was like pushing through thick cold mud. It was too dark to see the ocean, but I could hear it howling like wolves outside a cottage door. The air smelled of the churned muck and vegetation of the ocean floor.

I remembered how frightened Mrs. Feinstein was of storms at sea and how Reuben had reassured her. If only Reuben were here right now to hold my hand and tell me everything would be all right. What were Reuben and Susan doing right now? Had they started school already? I would ask Mama to help me write them a letter when we got back to Jibatov.

"The storm is getting worse." I burst into the cabin stamping my feet and rubbing my hands to warm them.

Papa took no notice of me. With one hand he held onto the table to steady himself, with the other he held his prayer book.

I took off my clothes and crawled shivering under the covers. Perhaps when I woke up in the morning the storm would be over. Perhaps Papa would have made up his mind.

"Papa, aren't you coming to bed?"

Papa's face was as pale as moonlight, his skin transparent as glass. Under his eyes were dark black smudges. "Soon, child. Go to sleep."

I watched as Papa swayed back and forth with his prayer shawl around his shoulders. Since he began his fast he had barely slept. What would he decide? Both choices were terrible. To go back to Russia meant imprisonment and certain death. It meant our family would have to depend on Uncle Nahum's charity. Lemmel would stop his studies and go to work. I would have no money for a dowry and would spend my life taking care of other people's children. But worse than anything, it meant we would never see Papa again!

And what if Papa did as Mr. Goldenberg suggested? The barber would cut his hair and shave his beard. He could wear an old suit of Mr. Goldenberg's. And there was plenty of nutritious food to eat on the ship.

"Forbidden!" I heard the voice of my grandfather and felt the sharp slap on my hand. How old had I been when it happened? We were in the market. It was summertime and a dusty wind was blowing my curly hair. I was thirsty and wanted to go home. I clung to grandfather's long coat as he bargained with the peasant woman over a dozen eggs.

Then the piece of smoked meat was in my mouth, hard and chewy. Had the woman given it to me or did I snatch it from the stand?

Suddenly Grandfather saw me. The sky was full of his white beard and angry black eyes. The meat was in the dust and I was crying because my hand hurt and Grandfather had turned into an angry stranger.

Did Mama comfort me later or was she resting after having a baby? I just remembered Grandfather shaking my shoulders and telling me I must never eat tref again, even if I were starving to death.

But I had eaten tref on Ellis Island and now on the boat and nothing happened. Grandfather didn't rise out of his grave and lightning didn't strike me down. But with Papa it was different. He was the grandson of a famous rabbi, and a scholar. He wanted nothing more than for Lemmel to study in the yeshiva in Lublin. There were too many generations of tradition marching behind him. For Papa there was no choice. He would go back to Russia and face death rather than break Jewish law. I turned my face to the wall as the tears sank into the pillow.

I dreamed I was riding a great horse along the seashore. I clung to the horse's mane as we rose and fell, digging my fingers into the coarse hair. Below me the sea raged and roared and the horse galloped faster and faster to escape the hungry waves.

A sudden crash awoke me! I sat up and looked around. The cabin was surging up and down. In the dim gaslight I saw the metal washbasin had fallen to the floor. Papa's bed was empty. The beds and table were nailed down, but Papa's prayer book and an apple were sliding back and forth along the floor. I gripped the edge of the bed to keep from rolling off and looked around.

"Papa?"

No one answered.

I got out of bed, shivering in the cold. The bathroom door swung back and forth.

"Papa?

The cabin was empty!

Quickly I pulled on my clothes and shoes. The cabin was rocking so hard I could barely stand. Where was Papa? Why would he go up on deck in the midst of this terrible storm? I had to find him. I took my thickest shawl and tied a kerchief around my head.

Then I pushed open the cabin door.

I had to hold the railing with both hands. Inch by inch I crept up the stairs. My teeth were chattering with cold and fear by the time I reached the deck door. I pushed against it with all my might, but it remained shut. I threw myself against the door until it fell open. A fist of water smashed my face as I stumbled on deck. The door slammed shut behind me.

I held to the handle and tried to think. It was raining hard and the deck was so slippery I could barely stand. I knew it was too dangerous to be on deck. I should return to our cabin.

But where was Papa?

I had to find him and bring him back to the cabin. The curtain of wind and rain drenched my clothes. I peered through the darkness. The night was as black and cold as a bread baker's oven on Yom Kippur. Wind howled around the deck like a sea monster. The ship leaped and groaned as gigantic waves roared against the hull, crashing over the railing and sending sheets of water hurtling across the deck.

"Papa! Papa!" I screamed, but the wind swallowed my cries. I pulled myself from one nailed-down deck chair to another, grasping the cold wet metal with frozen hands. A wave caught me between chairs and slammed me against the wall. A stab of pain sliced my shoulder, but I grabbed a chair as the wave swept my feet out from under me. I gasped for breath as the wind struck my face again and again.

"Pa-a-a-pa-a-a!"

If Papa were outside in this storm he would be swept away. Perhaps even now he was struggling in the water or sinking down down down to the bottom of the sea!

"Pa-a-a-pa-a-a!"

Suddenly a strong arm lifted me off my feet. A sailor in a black rain slicker shouted words I couldn't understand. Holding me under his arm like a sack of potatoes, he started back in the direction of our cabin.

"Papa! Papa!" I beat my fists against his chest. He stopped and looked at me.

"Papa?" He shouted above the din. "Yah. Yah." He changed direction and fought his way against the wind until we came to the dining room. He fell against the door and we both collapsed on the wooden floor.

I lay in the puddle like a drowned spider. I was shaking so hard I could barely breathe. The sailor pulled me up and led me through the entrance into the darkened dining room. In a sudden flash of lightening I saw a figure standing by the window.

"Papa!"

The man turned around.

"Raizel?"

Papa rushed toward me and hugged me in his arms. "How did you get here? The storm is so terrible. Oh, my poor child, you're soaking wet. You'll catch your death of cold."

"P-please, Papa, I don't want to go outside again." I was sobbing so hard I could barely speak, whether from fear or relief or both.

"Of course." Papa thanked the sailor who shook his finger at me in warning and strode back into the storm. "Take off your wet clothes. Put on my coat." Papa helped me change my clothes. He wrapped me in a tablecloth and carried me over to a couch.

"Papa, why did you go outside? I woke up and you weren't there. I thought . . . " I began crying again.

"Shhh, meydele. Everything will be all right. I couldn't sleep so I took a walk on deck as I often do at night. Suddenly it began to rain and I dashed in here to keep dry."

"Papa, I was so frightened. I thought something had happened to you. I thought you had been swept overboard . . . "

Papa hugged me. "Shhh, Raizel, listen to me. I am so sorry. Who thought you would go out in such a storm? Such a brave girl you are. Braver than your papa."

I curled into a ball and put my head on Papa's lap. "I'm not brave, Papa. I was frightened of the storm, but I had to find you."

"You think brave means not begin frightened? It means having the courage to act no matter how afraid you are." Papa stroked my cheek.

"I'm so tired. You won't let me fall?" I felt like my body was sinking into a deep cloud.

"Go to sleep. I won't let you fall. Ever."

The steward shook us awake. Pale gray light shone through the dining room windows. The ship was still bobbing up and down, but the wild horses had slowed to a trot.

"Is the storm over?" I rubbed my eyes and sat up. Waiters were rushing around setting the tables. They didn't even glance at us.

"The rain has stopped," Papa said. He was still holding me tightly. "We should be free of the storm by the afternoon."

Papa gathered up my wet clothes. I felt silly wearing his coat. "Come, let's go to the cabin and change." Papa took my hand as we stepped on deck. The cold wind slashed right through me. The deck was slick with salt and seaweed. I was glad to go below again.

"Shall I bring you some rolls from breakfast?" I asked when I was dressed in dry clothes.

"No need."

"Papa, you can't go on fasting forever. You'll make yourself sick."

"Who said anything about fasting?" Papa smiled at me. How long had it been since Papa smiled? "Today I am going with you to the dining room and I am going to eat a big bowl of oatmeal and a soft boiled egg and a mug of coffee. With cream!" Papa smacked his lips.

"Papa!" I grabbed his hands. I felt like a huge stone had rolled off my back.

"I am going to the dining room today and tomorrow and the next day and the next."

"Does that mean you've made up your mind? Tell me, Papa, please."

Papa sat down on the bed. "I have decided to accept Mr. Goldenberg's suggestion. It will be hard, but it will be worth it if I can save the family and bring everyone to America."

"I would very much like to know what made up your mind, Papa. If you will tell me, that is."

Papa's eyes smiled at me. "Yes, you deserve to know. Last night I realized that it was more than belief that was keeping me from making a choice. It was fear."

"Fear of what? Of God's wrath?"

"God is too busy to concern himself with the kind of clothes Benjamin Balaban wears. No—fear of the unknown. Fear of change. Fear of leaving my tradition behind and stepping naked into a new world."

"And you're not afraid anymore?" I didn't understand.

"Now I'm more afraid than ever. But when I saw you brave that dreadful storm last night, when I saw you half-drowned and risking your own life to look for me, I felt so ashamed. Because you have more courage than I have, Raizel. You are the brave one in this family."

I buried my face in Papa's coat. "You're brave, too, Papa. You're the one who decided to go to America. I was afraid to leave Jibatov and Mama."

"So maybe two cowards together make a brave man." Papa winked at me. It felt warm and wonderful to have Papa's respect. I felt like I had grown half a meter overnight.

"I'll help you, Papa. I'll remind you to eat and act like an American and . . . I have an idea. Maybe we can even learn English!"

"What is this hurry? Right now, all I can think about is how good a nice piece of bread and butter will taste. Come, my brave one. Let us get something to eat."

20

The Gift of Friendship

A stranger stepped out of Mr. Goldenberg's bedroom. His clean-shaven face was ruddy from the cold sea wind. He wore a short black coat and gray hat in a modern style. If I passed him on the streets of Antwerp, I would never guess he was a Jew, let alone my papa.

"Papa, you look so different! No one in Jibatov would recognize you."

Papa squirmed. His arms disappeared inside the over-long sleeves. He looked as if he had shrunk in the wash.

Mr. Goldenberg stepped out of the bedroom with a huge smile on his face. "Very nice. It needs alterations, but I'll take you to my tailor when we get to Antwerp."

"Does he look like an American?" Mrs. Goldenberg coughed into a handkerchief.

I tried to remember the inspectors on Ellis Island. I had seen so little of America. "I think so. But he's too thin. Without his beard, Papa looks like a sheep after shearing."

"I feel like one, too. I never knew how useful a beard was in keeping my face warm."

"You'll get used to it. Now let's go to dinner. Mother, you need your warm coat." Mr. Goldenberg draped a thick fur coat around her shoulders.

I took Mrs. Goldenberg's arm and buried my chilly hands in the silky brown fur.

At dinner Papa sipped the soup, straining it between his teeth and plucking out tiny slivers of meat. This was an improvement over last night when he ate only bread and potatoes.

The waiter brought the main course and set a thick slice of rare roast beef on Papa's plate. He ignored it and ate his potatoes and carrots. I sneaked a glance. Now he had finished and was searching carefully around his plate. There was nothing left but the meat. He couldn't avoid it anymore! Yes, he could. Methodically he cut his meat into pieces and then even smaller pieces. He had done the same thing yesterday, pushing the meat around and around his plate and finally leaving it buried under a slice of bread.

"Today, I really am going to try it," he announced as he caught my eye.

"You must." Mr. Goldenberg looked serious. "It's the only way you'll fatten up and gain strength."

"I know. I know." Papa stared at his plate like an unhappy little boy whose mama had ordered him to finish every scrap. I felt sorry for him.

"It's pikuekh-nefesh, Papa," I whispered.

"It is not. I am not starving to death. And anyway, the laws do not apply anymore."

"Why not?" I was shocked. "You are still a Jew, Papa. You can still pray and go to synagogue and . . . "

"Enough!" Papa slammed his hand on the table. The wine glasses shuddered and the people at the next table glared at us. "I'm sorry," he said in a lower voice. "But I cannot pick and choose which laws to follow and which to break. It is not my right."

I stared at Papa. By taking off his coat, hat, and beard, did Papa mean he had taken off his religion?

Looking straight into my eyes, Papa thrust a piece of meat into his mouth, and began chewing violently. Then he ate another and another. I dug my fingernails into my palms and held my breath.

Suddenly Papa gagged on the meat. His face went chalk white. He pushed back his chair and ran out of the room. I got up to follow, but Mr. Goldenberg put his hand on my shoulder.

"No, Raizel, leave him alone. It's hard for him now."

"The meat made him sick?" Mrs. Goldenberg asked.

"Not the meat itself, I expect, but what it symbolized," Mr. Goldenberg explained. "I remember feeling nauseous the first time I ate unkosher meat."

"He doesn't have to eat meat," said Mrs. Goldenberg. "Some people don't."

"Papa never does anything half-way," I said. "When he had to leave the yeshiva to support his family, he gave away the few books he owned. When the time comes to break the fast on the Day of Atonement, he waits an extra hour after everyone else has begun eating."

"That doesn't make for an easy life." Mr. Goldenberg helped himself to a large portion of rice pudding.

"Not only that, but he doesn't pray anymore. I looked all over the cabin, but I can't find his prayer shawl or phylacteries or prayer book anyplace." I looked at Mr. Goldenberg and brushed away a tear. "I think he threw them overboard!"

"There, there, child." Mrs. Goldenberg patted my hand. "The change isn't easy for him."

"Think of your father as a man recovering from surgery," said Mr. Goldenberg. "Part of his body has been cut away, the part that connects him to his past and everything he believes in. The wound will be painful for a long time."

That made sense. "But the wound will heal, won't it?"

"Some wounds fester, but yes, most heal."

I liked Mr. Goldenberg for being honest with me. He didn't promise everything would be all right. He talked to me like a grown-up.

Since Papa had made his decision, I had felt as weightless as a seagull hovering above the waves. True we weren't returning to Mama and the family, but now we would all have a chance at a new life. I was even happy we were going back to America. Although I had seen for myself that the streets weren't paved with gold, the devil wasn't so bad after all. The only thing that worried me was where we would find the money to pay for the return passage. Papa was certain Uncle Nahum would send it to us.

Mr. Goldenberg was right. I needed to be patient with Papa. You couldn't just put on a new life like a new coat—not when the one you cast off had been the life of your father and your grandfather and all your ancestors before you.

I giggled.

"Raizel, what is the joke?" Mrs. Goldenberg asked in surprise.

"I was just picturing all of Papa's ancestors turning over in their graves at one time. What an earthquake that would make!"

"I wouldn't mention that to your papa, if I were you," she said.

"Of course not."

With the passing days, Papa succeeded in eating almost everything on his plate. He took long walks around the deck with Mr. Goldenberg. They talked about business and how to invest your money and other things I didn't understand. They also decided that Papa shouldn't return to New York City, since it was forbidden to attempt to enter America less than a year after rejection. They mentioned Boston and Baltimore, places I had never heard of.

Mrs. Goldenberg kept to her cabin with a cold, but she liked to have me for company. Of course we told stories, but we spent even more time studying English.

"Bed. Book. Table." I pointed to all the objects in the room.

"Good." Mrs. Goldenberg sat in bed wrapped in a pale blue shawl. "Now we will have a conversation. Where is the book?"

"Da boook is on da taable."

"Good, but touch your upper teeth with your tongue when you say 'the.' Try it again."

"Da. Dha. Ta." I felt ridiculous. "My teeth get in the way. I sound like a greenhorn."

"All you need is practice. With your good ear for stories, you should learn a new language in no time. Try practicing with people on the boat. Talk to the cook and the waiters. The more you practice, the better your English will be. How are you today?"

"I am fine, dank you." I didn't tell Mrs. Goldenberg I was too embarrassed to speak English with anyone else. I knew they would laugh at my mistakes and funny accent. Why was English such a hard language anyway?

Papa thought it was hard, too. He came with me a few times, but he couldn't keep his mind on the lessons. "I'll just have to learn English when we get to America." He apologized as we left Mrs. Goldenberg's cabin. "I can't keep the words straight in my mind right now."

"Are you worried about money, Papa?"

"The money, too. We do not have enough for a return ticket. I will ask Nahum to sell Bunchik."

"Make sure he sells him to someone nice," I said. Bunchik was old and sway-backed, but he had pulled Papa's wagon for so long that he was like part of the family.

On our last evening aboard, Mr. Goldenberg invited us to stay in his home in Antwerp. I was afraid Papa would be too proud to accept, but he thanked Mr. Goldenberg politely. He looked relieved.

We docked in Antwerp on a cold rainy day. A large black carriage was waiting for us as we walked down the gangplank. A man rushed out with an umbrella and held it over Mrs. Goldenberg's head as he helped her into the carriage.

Mr. Goldenberg's house was in a neighborhood I hadn't seen before, far from the port. The horses trotted along a tree-lined street with large stone houses set off from the road and protected by wrought-iron fences. We turned into one of them and I caught a glimpse of a huge garden with trimmed shrubs and tall leafless trees. The coachman carried our things into a two-story house with dark green shutters. Inside, the polished wood floors were covered with thick rugs, and the tables in the entrance hall gleamed with silver and crystal bowls. I had never been in such a fine house before.

"Bernard!" called a woman's voice.

A blond-haired lady dressed in an emerald-green dress seemed to float down the stairs. She kissed Mr. Goldenberg on both cheeks and spoke quickly in a language that sounded like a flock of blackbirds beating their wings. Then she repeated her kisses with Mrs. Goldenberg and clapped her hands. A woman dressed in white appeared and helped Mrs. Goldenberg up the stairs.

"Colette! Madeleine! Juliette!"

Mr. Goldenberg looked around expectantly. Three little girls bounced down the stairs. They were all dressed in identical yellow dresses with large pink bows in their long blond hair. The oldest looked about Lemmel's age. They approached Mr. Goldenberg and curtsied. He stretched out his arms, and the little girls jumped all over him, hugging and kissing, patting his pockets, and pointing their fingers at his suitcases. I watched as memories of Mama, Shloyme and Hannah pinched my heart.

At a word from their mother, they left Mr. Goldenberg and followed her into the next room like a flock of ducklings trailing a mother duck. The blond-haired woman sat down on a plump green sofa, smoothed out her dress, and looked at us expectantly. The expression on her face froze as Mr. Goldenberg spoke in the bird language, gesturing with his hands.

"This is my wife, Louisa," said Mr. Goldenberg.

"Parlez-vous Francais? Do you speak French?" Papa shook his head. "You may call me Madame Louisa. Welcome to our home." She spoke Yiddish haltingly. Her cold blue eyes belied her warm words. "These are my daughters."

The little girls sat in a row on another sofa. They stared at me, whispering behind their hands. The oldest giggled at something, and the younger two laughed out loud.

"Shhh!" Madame Louisa tapped her finger to her lips. The girls lowered their eyes, but made faces at each other when they thought their mother wasn't looking. I sipped the cup of hot tea a maid had brought and pretended I didn't see them. I refused the tiny cookies the maid offered. I didn't feel hungry.

"I don't like it here," I said to Papa as we arranged our clothes in the enormous wooden chest in our bedroom a few minutes later. Our room had lacy white curtains and dark wood furniture carved with flowers. I sank into a bed soft as a mound of fresh cut hay. The violet-colored comforter smelled like lilacs.

"The room is not elegant enough for you?" Papa asked with a smile.

"It's beautiful, Papa, but I don't think Mr. Goldenberg's wife likes us. She probably wasn't expecting houseguests. And the girls were laughing at me."

Papa sighed. "Not everyone welcomes poor rejected immigrants into their home, even into a wealthy home like this. I hope we won't have to stay here long."

"Houseguests and fish spoil on the third day."

"That is your mama talking." Papa wagged his finger at me.

I missed the elder Mrs. Goldenberg at dinner that night. The family ate in a huge dining room. Fine china lined the glass cabinets. The table was set with a white linen cloth and silver candlesticks. I couldn't take my eyes off the red and yellow roses in the center of the table. It was cold and rainy outside. How could flowers bloom in the garden in this weather?

When I asked Mr. Goldenberg, he burst out laughing and translated for the girls into French. Madame Louisa and the three girls laughed, too.

I stared at my soup. For a moment I thought the tears would start, but a wave of anger blocked them. At home we never laughed at our guests, no matter how ragged their clothes were. The Goldenbergs might be rich, but they had bad manners.

"I'm sorry, my dear," said Mr. Goldenberg. "You're right. Of course there are no flowers in our garden at this time of year. These are grown in special glass houses which stay warm all year round." Mr. Goldenberg frowned at the little girls and they stopped laughing, but they giggled and whispered behind their hands all through dinner.

"I think you will find the meat to your liking." Mr. Goldenberg carved the tremendous chunk of roast beef. "We keep a kosher home for my mother's sake."

Papa looked pleased and accepted a large portion. Madame Louisa pursed her lips. She barely touched her food, chewing very slowly and keeping her eyes on the three girls.

"Where's your appetite, Raizel? Did you leave it on board the boat?" Mr. Goldenberg looked concerned.

"I don't feel hungry. The food is delicious, though," I added quickly. Madame Louisa gave me a frigid smile. Then she began asking Mr. Goldenberg questions in French. With her attention off me, my appetite returned and I ate a few pieces of roast potato.

Sleeping in the feather bed with the down comforter that night was like sleeping in a toasty warm snowdrift. The maid woke us in the morning and set a pot of coffee and milk on the dresser.

"Papa, it's still dark out. Why do we have to get up?"

"We're going into the city with Mr. Goldenberg. He's taking me to his tailor and to the shipping office to buy our tickets."

Outside it was still raining. Drops of ice stung my face as we stepped into Mr. Goldenberg's carriage.

"Did you sleep well?" he asked.

"It was like sleeping in a bed of flowers," I said. "How is your mother?"

"She's weak, but well. The trip was hard, although you made it easier by spending so much time with her. Come, the first stop is to have my glasses repaired."

We made several stops to fix Mr. Goldenberg's glasses and have his suits altered for Papa. We even stopped for hot chocolate and pastry.

"This is to keep up our strength," Mr. Goldenberg said as he bit into a huge almond tart. Afterwards he dropped us off at the steamship office and continued on to his office in the diamond district. He arranged for his carriage to pick us up and return us to his house.

I remembered the steamship office from our previous visit. There was the same smell of stale smoke and the same bored-looking clerk sitting behind the counter reading a newspaper.

"We would like to book passage to America," Papa said.

The clerk ran an ink-stained finger down the list. "S.S. France sails in three days. Or you have the Bremen in two weeks. It is winter now and the slow season." He looked at us through tiny gold-rimmed glasses.

"We do not want to land in New York," Papa said. "We want Baltimore or Boston."

"Hmmm. There is a ship to Boston in five weeks. Nothing to Baltimore until the spring."

"Five weeks! Papa, that's so long."

"Hush, child. How much for two third-class tickets?"

"Sixty dollars."

Papa took out his leather moneybag and did some calculations. "Why, that is twice what we paid, uh, what we heard you pay on the Manitou!"

"It's off-season. There are no third-class accommodations to Boston this time of year."

"But there must be something cheaper. I was told my daughter's ticket would be half-price."

The clerk lit a cigarette and picked up his newspaper. "Not in second-class. Now, good day to you."

"We don't have enough money, do we, Papa?" I asked as we stepped outside.

"I never thought it would cost so much." Papa's voice shook like a dry leaf in the wind.

"Are there any other ship lines?"

The story was the same at two other offices. There were few boats to Boston at this time of year and prices were high. When we returned to the first office, Mr. Goldenberg's carriage was waiting. Papa asked to stop at the telegraph office where he sent a message to Uncle Nahum: "Rejected America. Need sixty dollars ship Antwerp Boston. Sell horse. Wire immediately. Both well. Binyumin."

"How long will it take for the money to come?" I asked as we rode home.

"I don't know." Papa sounded tired.

"It should take two weeks," Mr. Goldenberg said that night at dinner. "Are you sure your brother-in-law will have the money?"

"He has a big lumber mill. And I left my horse with him, which he will sell. It should be alright." Papa sounded more confident than he had this morning. "But I am sorry to impose on you for so long. Perhaps we should go to the inn?"

"Nonsense! I won't hear of it. Why, my mother would never forgive me. Louisa says she has been asking for Raizel all day."

"I want to see her, too," I said. Even though I didn't feel welcome in the house, I knew we needed to save the little money we had.

"You shall take breakfast with her tomorrow morning," Mr. Goldenberg promised.

The next day I had delicious crispy rolls, jam, and coffee with Mrs. Goldenberg. We continued our English lessons until Madame Louisa came in and began scolding the elderly lady.

"She says you must go now because I have to rest. She doesn't understand that when I'm with you, I don't feel tired at all."

Madame Louisa pulled the curtains and shooed me out of the room. I stood in the long hallway and looked around. What was I to do in this big house all day? Except for the baby, the little girls were in school. And they wouldn't play with me anyway. For once Madame Louisa seemed to understand. She motioned for me to follow her to a room filled with books. Papa was sitting in the corner reading a newspaper in Yiddish that Mr. Goldenberg had brought him. Madame Louisa pointed at a low shelf.

"Pour les enfants. For children."

I looked away. "I can't read," I whispered.

Madame Louisa cocked her head. "What?"

"I can't read." I wanted to hide behind the thick green curtains.

"Tsk. Tsk." She shook her head and mumbled something. Then she pulled out some books.

"These have pictures," she said, as if she were talking to a five-year-old.

"Thank you." I sat down at a table and examined the beautiful black engravings. The figures looked strangely old-fashioned, as if they belonged to another time. They were full of tiny little details. One picture in particular fascinated me: four horsemen were riding fiercely through a crowd of people with an angel flying overhead. One of the horsemen was almost a skeleton. Soon my mind filled with stories, and the time passed like waves rolling against the deck.

"What did you do today?" asked Mrs. Goldenberg late that afternoon. We were taking tea together. It was already dark outside. The girls had come home from school and I could hear them playing in their room down the hall.

"I looked at pictures in the library. And made up stories." I told Mrs. Goldenberg about the book.

"Durer, from your description. I loved art very much. Now I must make do with music. I should so like to hear a concert! I don't suppose you have ever been to one?"

"No. Just to weddings where they played the fiddle. Is it like that?"

Mrs. Goldenberg laughed. "Something like that. Only there are many more musicians and not just violins. If I feel better, perhaps I can take you."

"I would like that," I said. Maybe five weeks in Antwerp wouldn't be so hard after all.

The next day Papa sat down in the chair opposite me in the library. "Here's a book by Mendele Mocher Sfarim. Shall we read together?" he asked.

Papa was finally keeping his promise, but suddenly I had no desire to read Yiddish.

"What's the matter, Raizel? I thought you wanted to learn to read."

"In America they read English, Papa," I said.

"And if we never get to America?"

"But we have to. We can't go back to Russia!" How could Papa talk that way? Was he giving up already?

He sighed and rubbed his bare chin. "I miss my beard. The tickets are a lot of money. Perhaps too much."

"But Uncle Nahum will help us! We can't go back." As much as I wanted to see Mama and the little ones again, I knew we couldn't go back to Russia.

I pushed the Yiddish book away. "I am not going to learn Yiddish, only English."

No matter what Papa said, I was not going to give up.

21

The Freedom to Choose

Perhaps Papa already suspected. Perhaps he had a premonition. In any case the telegram came the next day. Madame Louisa called us from the library. As soon as Papa read it, I sensed the answer.

"What does it say?"

"Not here, child." I followed Papa up the stairs to our room.

"Nu, Papa, is everyone all right? Is Uncle Nahum sending the money?"

Papa sat down on the bed. He took a long shaky breath. "Everyone is well. But the lumber mill did poorly this year. Someone set fire to the lumber piles."

"That's terrible!"

"And that is not all. Nahum already sold Bunchik and gave the money to your mama. He has nothing to send us."

Papa and I sat like statues in the darkening room. After a while I realized my face was wet. I dried the tears on my sleeve. What could we do now? Who would help us?

"You must go to the Jewish charity organizations," Mrs. Goldenberg said firmly when I told her what had happened. "They will help you. We have been donating money to them for years."

"They'll give us enough money to go to America?" It was too wonderful to be true.

When I told Papa, he shook his head.

"But Papa, we have no choice."

"I do not take charity. Does Benjamin Balaban look like a pauper?"

"Then I will go alone, Papa." I tried to keep my voice steady.

"You will not." Papa sighed and rubbed his chin. "I will think on my—what does Mr. Goldenberg call them—options, and decide in the morning."

The next morning Mr. Goldenberg dropped us off in front of a shabby building down the block from the inn where we had stayed. I didn't ask Papa why he had changed his mind. I knew when to let well enough alone.

The over-heated waiting room smelled of garlic and was full of people speaking Yiddish. For a moment they looked strange to me: the men in their long black coats and fur hats, the women in their black skirts and thick shawls. I hadn't seen Jews from Eastern Europe since Ellis Island. Here it was Papa, beardless and wearing a short gray coat and hat, who looked out of place. We didn't talk to any of them, but I listened.

"My little one is ill. She has the scabies. We sail tomorrow and they won't let her go."

"They won't let me go because of this cough. I tried to tell them I've had it for years, but they won't listen."

"With me, it's different. The tickets were supposed to be waiting for us at the steamship office. I gave my money to the company representative. Now they say they have never heard of him!"

We sat for hours. Everyone had a story. The women were red-eyed. The children had runny noses and couldn't sit still. A tired woman with graying hair came out to shush them. At lunchtime she brought everyone a cup of tea and a hard roll. The afternoon light was fading when we finally entered the office.

Two men sat behind a desk piled with stacks of paper. The younger one motioned to us to sit down. They listened while Papa told his story.

"Exactly how much do you need?" asked the older man. He had a long white beard and bushy gray eyebrows.

Papa told him.

The two men looked at each other.

"I'm sorry, Mr. Balaban," said the man with the bushy eyebrows. "That is too much money."

Papa sat up straighter. "I have never asked for charity before. I am not asking now. I will pay you back the money, I swear it."

The younger man shook his head. I didn't like the half-smile on his face. "You have to understand, Mr. Balaban. Everyone tells us that, but when they get to America, they somehow forget."

"We do not have that much money to give," said the older man more gently. "You have seen how many people are in need. Sick children. Women about to give birth. We try to help everyone as best we can. If you need money for tickets back to Russia, we can help you."

"My papa can't go back to Russia! They'll put him in prison or send him to Siberia!" I said.

"Hush, Raizel. It is not for children to talk."

I bit my lip.

"We understand the situation, but aside from the money, we are not permitted to pay passage to America. We would have all the Jews in Russia knocking on our door if they knew we would pay their steamship ticket. We are committed to helping in cases of life and death," the older man said. I could see he felt bad that he couldn't give us the money.

"Now, do you need the money for train tickets?" The younger man looked at his gold watch. "We have more people to see today."

Papa stood up. "No, thank you. We can manage." He bowed stiffly. I followed him out of the room.

"Papa, isn't there someplace else we can go?" I asked as we stepped out into the cold. Snowflakes kissed my cheeks. I remembered how Shloyme loved the snow.

Papa shook his head. "It is wrong to ask for money from strangers. Others need it more than we do."

"But Papa . . . !"

"Enough! If I must go back to Russia, I will go with my head held high, not crawling like a dog begging for a bone." He strode purposefully down the street to the carriage stand.

I told Mrs. Goldenberg what had happened when we got back.

"Your papa is a proud man," she said, sipping her tea from a china cup painted with delicate pink roses.

"Papa doesn't know how to fight." My tea tasted bitter, despite the lump of sugar I gripped between my teeth.

"He is a man of the book, not a soldier."

"That's the trouble. How will he manage in the army?" I could feel the tears gathering behind my eyes.

Mrs. Goldenberg didn't answer. She sipped her tea in silence for a while. "Raizel, I want to ask you something. Don't answer right now. Take your time to think about it."

I put down my cup and looked at her round face with the gentle smile I had grown to love. She lived in a world of darkness, but her kindness shone like the Sabbath candles.

"You don't have to go back to Russia with your papa," she said. "I would love for you to stay here with me, as my companion. You would go to school with the girls and visit me in the afternoons. We could attend concerts together and tell stories. And soon you would be able to read to me. I can promise that you will want for nothing."

Not go back with Papa?

"Oh no, I couldn't!" The words rushed out before I had a chance to think.

Mrs. Goldenberg put her finger to her lips. "No, don't say anything. I asked you to take time with your answer. Talk with your papa. Think deeply about it. It is a chance for a wonderful life, my dear."

I promised to take time before I made my decision. After I left Mrs. Goldenberg to her nap, I went into the library where Papa was absorbed in a book.

"Papa . . . ?"

He shut the book and looked at me like a child caught with his fingers in the jam pot. Then he smiled and opened it again.

"What are you reading, Papa?"

"A book by a man named Spinoza. We used to whisper about him when I was in yeshiva, but no one had actually read him. He was cast out of the Jewish religion for his beliefs."

"How can you be cast out, Papa? If you were born a Jew, you always remain a Jew."

"Not if you become a heretic. The rabbis of his day believed Spinoza was dangerous to the rest of the Jews because he questioned Judaism and expressed his own ideas about free will. But many considered him one of the most brilliant men of his time. I see that they were right."

Suddenly Papa stood up and walked restlessly around the library. Shelves of books reached to the ceiling, their dull leather bindings glowing like jewels in the gaslight.

"Just look at all these books, Raizel. I feel like a man who has been starving all his life and is suddenly confronted with a banquet. What should I read first? How much nourishment can my mind absorb at one time? I have so much catching up to do." He sat back down and grasped the book by Spinoza in both hands. "What did you want to talk to me about, meydele?"

"Nothing special, Papa."

I pulled aside the heavy green curtain and crawled into the chilly window seat. I could see the garden below, dull and gray in the winter light. What did it look like in the spring when the leaves pushed into the sun? What would it be like to live permanently in this fine house? I would learn French and Flemish, the languages of Belgium, and go to school with Madeleine. In the afternoons I would visit Mrs. Goldenberg and keep her company. I would dine on rich food every evening with the Goldenberg family and celebrate the holidays with them. No longer would I have to watch my little brother and sister, or clean house and cook with Mama. Servants would take care of everything. I felt like one of my stories had come true.

I clasped my knees to my chest. Daydreams of concerts and theatre and trips to the seaside filled my head. I imagined myself wearing yellow and pink dresses like Colette, Madeleine, and Juliette. Of course, I would never have long blond curls like theirs, but I would get an education and . . .

I pressed my forehead against the icy windowpane. My daydream dissolved like the thin frosting of ice on the glass. What was I thinking? What did fancy clothes, food, and servants matter when weighed against my love for my family? Who would help Mama if I stayed in Antwerp? Who would take care of Shloyme and Hannah? If something happened to Papa, Mama would need my help more than ever.

Why, remaining in Antwerp meant I might never see my family again!

"I've decided," I said to Mrs. Goldenberg the next day as we sipped our café au lait.

"I hope you didn't spend a sleepless night."

"No, I slept well, thank you. I have decided to return with Papa."

Mrs. Goldenberg sighed. "I expected as much. Your papa must have been opposed to the idea."

"I didn't tell him."

Mrs. Goldenberg cocked her head. "Such an important decision and you didn't consult your papa?"

"It was my decision to make, not Papa's. I thank you for offering me the chance." I kissed her on the cheek.

Mrs. Goldenberg took my hands in hers. "You know, Raizel, I wanted to give you the choice, but I believe you will have a wonderful life wherever you are. Your imagination is a gift. Together with your loving heart, it will stand you in good stead." She kissed my hands. "I am an old lady and have known many many people in my life. You are special."

I hugged Mrs. Goldenberg, breathing in the smell of lavender and roses from her gray silk dress. "I love you almost as much as Bobbe," I said.

"That is the most wonderful thing you could say to me," she whispered.

I didn't tell Papa about Mrs. Goldenberg's offer. Things were hard enough for him. Mr. Goldenberg gave Papa the addresses of more Jewish charities. He went because he knew he should, but I could tell his heart wasn't in it. Wherever we went, the line of people waiting was the same. The answer was the same.

I spent my remaining days with Mrs. Goldenberg. She insisted that we keep up our English lessons for "someday." In the morning Juliette would play on the floor with her dolls. When her sisters came home from school, she ran to join them without so much as an "au revoir."

A letter came from Uncle Nahum, telling how a man had tried to force Nahum to sell the mill at a low price, and, when he refused, had paid one of the mill workers to set a fire. The police would do nothing to catch the criminal. The man had paid them off in advance, and Nahum, after all, was only a Jew. Luckily the mill had been spared.

"And that is the Russia you must go back to," said Mr. Goldenberg when he heard the story. We were finishing a late dinner. The little girls were already in bed. "Here in Belgium it is better, but anti-Semitism knows no geographical boundaries. Just look what happened to Alfred Dreyfus in France a few years ago.

"Who is he?" I asked.

"A French army officer who was falsely accused of treason. He was Jewish," explained Mrs. Goldenberg.

"Do you think there is anti-Semitism even in America?" I asked.

"I have never heard of a Jew being killed in a pogrom in America, but in the South they hang black men from trees," said Mr. Goldenberg.

"In America?" I couldn't believe it.

"There is hatred every place," said Mr. Goldenberg. "Sometimes I wonder if people don't enjoy hating each other."

"It is easier than loving," said Papa. "'Love thy neighbor as thyself' is more difficult to observe than the Ten Commandments."

We finished our pudding in silence.

"We plan to leave next week for Russia, if it's all right with you," Papa said. "After the Sabbath."

"Of course," said Mr. Goldenberg. "You may stay as long as you like. My mother will miss Raizel very much. I'm afraid my girls don't have her patience for their grandmother."

The next day was Friday. The little girls dressed up in pretty green frocks. I had just put on my best blouse and skirt when Madame Louisa knocked on our door. She was holding a bundle wrapped in tissue paper.

"Pour vous," she said with a smile.

"Papa?" Would he permit me the gift? He nodded and smiled. I set the package on the bed and carefully unwrapped the crinkly paper. Inside was a beautiful brown velvet dress! The collar and cuffs were trimmed with white lace. A row of tiny silver buttons marched down the front. Even Leah never had such a beautiful dress!

"Well, does it fit?" Mrs. Goldenberg walked into the room. "It's a going-away present from Madame Louisa and the girls."

I ran my fingers over the velvet, soft as rabbit fur. "It's beautiful!" I stepped behind the changing screen and took off my clothes. My fingers shook with excitement as I worked the tiny buttons. "How do I look?"

Madame Louisa clapped her hands. "Voila! Fantastique!" She spoke to Mrs. Goldenberg in her lilting French.

"She says you look like a princess. She wants to fix your hair so it will be more elegant."

"This is the first dress I ever had that wasn't a hand-me-down! Thank you so much!" I kissed Madame Louisa on the cheek and she kissed me back.

I stood before the mirror as Madame Louisa unbraided my hair and combed it into a swirl upon my head. I looked so tall and grownup. The new dress was the same color as my eyes and made them look bigger. "Why, I look like Mama," I said. If only Reuben could see me.

The dinner bell rang. I took Mrs. Goldenberg's arm as we descended the stairs. The little girls were waiting for us in the salon. They smiled and clapped their hands when they saw my new dress. "Tres joli," said Madeleine. I could guess what she meant without translation.

But where was Mr. Goldenberg? Last Friday he had come home early to eat dinner with the family. Madame Louisa glanced out the window at the dark sky and shook her head. She covered her hair with a lace cloth and lit the Sabbath candles, reciting the familiar prayer in her French accent.

"Where is Mr. Goldenberg?" I asked when she had finished.

"Oh, he'll be here soon." Mrs. Goldenberg didn't seem worried. "He is a busy man, you know."

The girls fidgeted and pulled at their mother's dress. Juliette rubbed her eyes and stuck her thumb in her mouth. Finally Madame Louisa shrugged and called to the maid. We all followed her into the dining room where the table looked even more elegant than during the week. Papa recited the blessings over the wine and the challahs. We were just finishing the soup when Mr. Goldenberg walked in, his nose glowing red from the cold.

"I am so sorry I'm late. Business, you know." He washed his hands and took his place at the head of the table. Madame Louisa glared at him. She disapproved of lateness at meals. We ate in silence for a while.

The roast chicken and potatoes were delicious. There were glazed carrots with raisins and a funny round vegetable that looked like tiny cabbages. I felt so grownup in my new dress. If only it weren't a going-away present and we could stay here longer. I had grown to like the family so much. Even Madame Louisa had warmed up to me when she saw how much Mrs. Goldenberg enjoyed our time together.

"Papa, are you going to grow your beard again?" What would people in Jibatov say when they saw him? Would they think he was no longer a Jew?

"Perhaps. I have gotten rather used to my bare face. Although I can't say I enjoy shaving every day."

"Neither do I!" Mr. Goldenberg laughed. "Perhaps I will grow a beard? Just a little one that ends in a point?" He turned to Madame Louisa who smiled and shook her head.

As the plates were cleared away, Mr. Goldenberg took a small package out of his coat pocket. "I got the tickets like you asked." He handed the package to Papa.

Papa unwrapped the paper with a puzzled expression on his face.

"Those don't look like train tickets," I said.

"These are steamship tickets!" Papa's head shot up. "How . . . ? I can't pay for these."

"Who said anything about paying? Wait, I know what you are going to say." Mr. Goldenberg spoke quickly before Papa could open his mouth again. "Something came up at work today. I need an important package delivered to a client in Boston. It's too valuable to send through the mails. In cases like this, we usually hire a messenger and pay his boat passage." He paused for breath. Papa was staring at him, his lips pursed.

"So I said to myself, why pay a messenger to sail back and forth? Mr. Balaban is as trustworthy as any messenger I could send. I can pay his passage and he will deliver the package for me. What could be simpler? I'm sorry I couldn't consult with you, but the matter was urgent." Mr. Goldenberg leaned back in his chair. His eyes darted around the empty plates, avoiding Papa's eyes.

Papa looked at the tickets, at Mr. Goldenberg, and back at the tickets. Mrs. Goldenberg and Madame Louisa stared at their plates. Had they known? Papa wouldn't take the tickets if he thought he was accepting charity. I bit my lip. What would Papa say?

"I must refuse," he said finally. "I understand what you are trying to do. You have done so much for us already. This is too much."

"You mean you won't help out a friend?" Mr. Goldenberg raised his voice. "Why, I only had to buy a one-way ticket. And I won't have to pay the messenger a salary. Think of all the money I save. This is purely a business deal!" He sounded outraged.

"Please, Mr. Balaban, think of your family," said Mrs. Goldenberg. "This is your last chance to save yourself. Don't let your pride be your gravestone."

Papa turned red. He got up from the table without a word. We could hear him stomping up the stairs.

"Now you've done it," said Mr. Goldenberg to his mother. "Why couldn't you leave well enough alone?"

"He isn't a child, Bernard. He knows what you are trying to do."

"I'm trying to help a fellow Jew and a friend. Is that so terrible?" Madame Louisa rested her hand on his arm.

I wanted to rush after Papa and try to convince him to take the tickets, but I didn't. I knew he needed time to think things through and make up his own mind. Instead I sat with my friends and felt love expand inside me like an ocean swell.

After dinner I rewrapped the tickets carefully and carried them to our room.

"It was rude of me to leave the table like that." Papa was standing at the darkened window with his hands clasped behind his back.

"No one was angry." I began unbuttoning the tiny buttons of my new dress. I had made up my mind not to ask Papa questions.

"That is a very pretty dress they gave you," Papa said suddenly. "You have made good friends here."

"Yes, I'll miss them." I carefully hung the dress in the wardrobe.

"Mr. Goldenberg is a true friend," Papa continued. "I never had a rich friend before. Nahum is family. He doesn't count. But even friendship has limits."

"But you'd be helping him out if you take the tickets, Papa!" The words shot from my mouth like a runaway horse.

"Do you suppose I believe that story? I am not a child who can be tricked with a piece of candy."

"Of course not, Papa," I said.

Papa paced back and forth in front of the window. Then he spun around and looked at me. "And that is why I am going to accept the tickets."

I stared.

"After all, what is the use of a good head if the feet can't carry it? My friend wants to give me tickets. Am I such a fool as not to accept?

Benjamin Balaban has been called many things, but never a fool." He scooped up the tickets from the table.

Papa was going to accept the tickets! Even though he knew Mr. Goldenberg had invented a story. Even though it meant taking money like charity. Suddenly I realized that Papa, too, had changed on this journey.

"Where are you going, Papa?"

"To thank our friend for his generosity. And to let him know that I intend to pay him back, as soon as our family is safely reunited in America!"

22

The Double Crossing

The ocean tossed the ship like a bottle, but I barely noticed. The last three weeks at sea had been a rough crossing. Mrs. Goldenberg had begged us to wait until spring when the sea would be calmer, but Papa wouldn't hear of wasting time. With Nahum in financial trouble, Papa wanted to reach America and find a job to support Mama and the children.

"Guess what, Papa?" The soup slid off the spoon as I raised it to my mouth. "The steward says we land tomorrow!"

"Good news." I could sense the worry behind Papa's smile.

Instead of two weeks, the crossing had taken three. A ferocious storm had blown us off course. It was so violent that the previous storm seemed like a tiny squall. We had stayed in our second-class cabin for three days, while the steward brought us food and fresh water. Not that we could eat anything. I thought I was an experienced sailor, but I spent the three days on my bed praying the ship would stay afloat long enough to reach the Boston harbor.

"Do you want more bread?" I offered Papa. He barely ate meat, but he made sure to eat plenty of bread, potatoes, and vegetables.

The waiter came over to the table.

"Please, more bread," I said in English.

"Your little girl has a smart head on her," said Misha who often joined us at mealtimes. He was a horse dealer who had lived in a town not far from Jibatov. He had approached us the first day on board, claiming he remembered Papa from somewhere. Misha wore high leather boots and had a curly black beard like Ivan's. He had the same loud voice, too.

"I studied English hard," I said. Mrs. Goldenberg had given me an English-Yiddish dictionary as a going-away present. Papa and I studied together, but while the words stuck in my mind like flies in a pool of honey, Papa had to struggle to remember every syllable. Because of the dictionary, I could now read Yiddish and English!

"I will learn English in no time," Misha boasted. He was always bragging how he would be rich in a year. I think he believed Papa was rich, because of Mr. Goldenberg's fine clothes. "I don't know why you want to go to New York after Boston," he continued. "I hear Boston is the wealthiest city in America."

"We have a relative in New York," Papa said, finishing the last of his pudding. He had warned me not to tell Misha that this was our second crossing. No one must know we had been rejected once before.

"Relatives! Phew!" Misha spat on the floor. "I'm going to America to get away from relatives. They're parasites. When you have money, they suck your blood. When you need money, they forget who you are."

"That's not true!" I said. "Our relatives help us. Why, my uncle gave us the money for our tickets!" Misha made me so mad I felt like hitting him with a plate.

Misha sneered. "I spit on my relatives, may they rot in their graves!"

Papa put his hand on my arm. "We must be going to bed now. We want to be up early for our first glimpse of America."

"Sure you won't join me for a schnapps?" Misha pulled a bottle of vodka from his coat pocket. When Papa shook his head, he took a swig. "I'm going to look for a card game." He walked over to a group of Polish men who had already taken out a pack of cards.

As we stepped outside, I took a deep breath of sea air to clear my lungs of the smell of smoke and grease that permeated the second-class dining room. The wind froze my face and pierced the thick fabric of the coat the Goldenbergs had given me.

Our parting had been hard. The little girls had cried and even Madame Louisa dabbed her eyes with a lace handkerchief. Mrs. Goldenberg stayed in her room. I knew she was too upset to come down to say good-bye. Finally Mr. Goldenberg lost patience with her and yelled that we would miss the boat if she didn't come down to say good-bye. She made me promise to write her a letter as soon as we got to America. We both cried and hugged each other. It was almost like leaving Mama all over again. And Mrs. Goldenberg was not well. I would never see her again unless— I pushed the thought to the back shelf of my mind. We had to get into America this time.

"I'm sorry, Papa," I said when we were safe in our little cabin. "That man made me so angry with his talk about relatives."

"He annoyed me too, but we have to be very careful around him."

"What do you mean?" I took off my coat and hung it in the closet.

"He is dangerous. I've met men like him on my travels. He acts like a friend, but he drinks too much and talks too much. Who knows why he left Russia?"

"Do you think he's a criminal, Papa?" I hated when Misha looked at me. His stare felt like frozen knives.

"I don't know, but we must be careful."

Papa had been saying that the whole voyage. He stayed away from the other passengers, speaking only when spoken to. It wasn't hard to avoid people in the rain and cold. No one sat on deck. They played cards in the dining room or stayed in their cabins. There were a few Jewish families with small children, but no one my age. Sometimes I told stories to the little ones, but more often I would go into the kitchen and talk with Jacques, the cook. He had a hot temper, but he liked to have someone to talk to. He had worked in a restaurant in a city called Philadelphia for many years and knew English well. I would knead bread or shell beans and he would tell me about his sailing adventures. Mostly I just listened. I was embarrassed when I spoke English and people corrected my mistakes. I knew I should practice speaking more, but I didn't.

We went to bed early, but I couldn't fall asleep. The sea pitched and churned underneath us and my thoughts churned with it. I remembered Susan's excitement about seeing the Statue of Liberty and how certain I had been that soon we would be living in America. It had never crossed my mind that Papa would be rejected. The Raizel who left Jibatov a few short months before had been so ignorant and trusting. She always did what she was told. She never spoke back to grown-ups. Looking back at her, I felt like my own older sister. In a way, I felt sorry for her. But I missed her, too.

I lay there going over all the details of the landing in my mind for the hundredth time, as if by imagining the events, I could somehow control them. We were second-class passengers now so no one would herd us to another Ellis Island. Papa looked healthy. His hair was neatly trimmed and his expensive clothes fit well. I would wear the lovely dress the Goldenbergs had given me, even if no one would see it under my coat. Wearing it would make me feel braver. Papa would tell the immigration people that he was a bookkeeper and hoped to get a job in his cousin's factory. Never mind that the cousin, or rather second cousin, was only a cutter, and Papa had never done bookkeeping. At least they would think he had a trade that didn't require physical strength. The only thing that remained was the problem of the name.

What would happen if the immigration people in Boston had a list of people deported from Ellis Island? Mr. Goldenberg had advised Papa to give a different name. But the tickets were in the name of Balaban. The name Balaban appeared on the ship register. Papa was afraid that lying would be dangerous. If they discovered he was trying to change his name, they might put him in prison. I shuddered and pulled the blanket around my neck.

We had talked about it that last night in Mr. Goldenberg's house. "They won't put you in jail," Mr. Goldenberg had said in a confident voice. "Deportation is punishment enough."

But Papa wasn't so sure. "Balaban was my father's name and my grandfather's name," Papa kept repeating. "I have given up so much to get into America. Must I give up even my name?"

"But Papa, you can always change it back."

"Like I can always go back to keeping the Jewish laws?" Papa shook his head. "I have never been a good liar, which is why I was not a successful salesman. Silk-coated words are not in my nature."

"But, Papa . . ."

"Enough!" Papa pushed his chair away from the table. "This is not a discussion for children." Then he sat back down and said in a softer voice, "I want you to understand, Raizel. In this world there are two types of people—those who value self-respect and honor above all and those who don't. You cannot walk both paths at the same time without muddying your feet. Now that is the end of the discussion."

I didn't give up. Over and over again I talked to Papa, trying to prepare him for the moment we would stand in front of that immigration official, a man with the power to admit us to America or send us back to Russia forever. But Papa had made up his mind, and there was nothing I could do to change it.

I tossed and turned while Papa snored quietly in the chilly darkness. How could he sleep on a night like this? Finally I did what I had done on other sleepless nights. I imagined myself back in our house in Jibatov with Hannah on my lap and Shloyme's head pressed against my shoulder—

Raizel, tell me about America.

In America the streets are paved with gold, I began. People ride in silver carriages dragging peacock feathers behind them to dust the streets. In winter it snows goose down. They gather it to make feather comforters. And when it rains, it rains . . . can you guess?

Honey!

Wrong! I cried. In America the streets are paved with dusty gray stones. People walk or take crowded streetcars. The snow lies in hard dirty piles just like in Jibatov. And when it rains, you get wet and have to change your clothes, or you'll catch cold.

I don't like that story, Raizel. Tell me another. Shloyme had tears in his eyes.

I don't know any others, I said. My stories sank down to the bottom of the sea and the fishes ate them. To this day the mama fish tells my stories to the baby fish and they all dream of going to Amer . . .

"Wake up, Raizel. It's time for breakfast."

I pried open my eyes. Papa was already dressed. He put the last of our clothes and the small package he was delivering for Mr. Goldenberg into the worn suitcases. My hands shook as I hurried to button the tiny silver buttons on my velvet dress.

On deck it was cold and windy. I peered over the railing at the shoreline, so near and yet so far.

"What are you looking for?" asked Misha, pulling up the fur collar of his leather coat.

"Oh, nothing. I just wanted to see what America looks like."

I didn't tell him I had been looking for another Statue of Liberty. I turned away from the railing disappointed.

"That must be the little boat coming to pull us into the harbor," said Misha. We pushed open the door to the warm smoky dining room. "Oy, have I got a headache. Where's the coffee? Can't a man get a cup of coffee around here?" He slammed his fist on the table.

Jacques stuck his head out of the kitchen and shouted something in French. Then he winked at me and brought a parcel wrapped in brown paper.

"I made you a lunch," he said. "Can't have you hungry on your first day in America."

"Thank you." I took the package and put it on my lap.

"What did he say?" Misha asked, eyeing the package.

"He gave me a lunch." I remembered how hungry I had been waiting all those hours on Ellis Island. "He is a nice man."

"But a lousy cook," said Misha. "They give the second-class passengers the bad cooks. I bet in first class they eat roast chicken off gold plates every night."

I laughed. "In third class, the food is even worse." I remembered the watery stew and soggy bread the passengers had eaten on the Manitou.

"We're lucky there's no third class on this boat. All those swine with their squalling babies." He raised an eyebrow and stared at me. "What do you know about third class, anyway?"

I picked up my glass of tea and drank it quickly. I had to be more careful.

"Did you win at cards last night?" Papa asked to distract Misha.

"Of course. Those Poles are a bunch of peasants. Too bad you don't play. It's not as if you were religious."

The color drained from Papa's face. "I do not have money to waste on gambling," he said coldly.

"We're docking! We're docking!"

There was a clatter of plates as everyone stampeded for the door. Only Papa remained seated, chewing his bread and butter as if the boat were still in mid-ocean.

"Come on, Papa!" I tugged at his sleeve. "Let's get our things."

"Patience, meydele. America will not be there in another five minutes? Of course, whether we will be in America is another question."

Papa swallowed the last of his bread and drank his tea. My stomach was dancing like a groom at his wedding. Finally Papa wiped his lips and stood up.

"Wait, Papa, I almost forgot. I'll meet you in the cabin." I dashed toward the kitchen and pushed open the door.

"Good bye, Jacques," I said to the startled cook. "Thank you for talking English with me."

"The pleasure was mine, little lady. Good luck in America!"

As I closed the door behind me, I prayed I would not be seeing Jacques again soon.

We waited on deck with our suitcases as the tugboat pulled us to the shore. The sky was thick with woolly gray clouds. The wind spit rain in our faces as we got on line to leave the ship. Low wooden warehouses lined the Boston harbor. Unsmiling immigration officials walked back and forth, checking lists and shouting orders. I shivered and thrust my hands into the pockets of my coat, but the cold seeped into my bones and turned my feet into chunks of ice.

"There go the first-class passengers." Misha had managed to wedge his way into the line in front of us. "They think they're better than we are. When I have money, no one will ever get ahead of me again." He gulped from his flask of vodka and offered some to Papa. "Warm you up."

Papa shook his head and wrapped his scarf more tightly around his neck. The first-class passengers were walking down the gangplank. Sailors carried their baggage, just as they had carried the Goldenberg's.

"Why don't they let us down? What are we, cattle that we have to stand in the cold and rain?" Misha stamped his feet.

"Second-class passengers follow me!" Two guards stood on either side as they led us into an enormous wooden building. The wind whistled through a broken window. Inside wasn't much warmer than outside. We added our suitcases to a pile near the door and sat down on a bench.

"Line up for medical inspection!" an official called. When no one moved, he motioned with his arms and repeated himself in a language I didn't understand.

"Papa, I thought second-class passengers didn't have to go through a medical inspection," I whispered.

Papa shrugged his shoulders. "Who knows? Maybe in Boston they have different rules."

When our turn came, I was too frightened to breathe. The doctor tapped Papa's chest and peered in his mouth and eyes. Then he stamped a piece of paper and motioned Papa into the next line. I let out a sigh of relief. Now it was my turn.

"Don't be afraid, little girl." I opened my coat and smiled. The doctor had me turn around, lift my arms, and open my mouth. I tried not to stare at the pair of eye tongs sitting on the metal tray. But the doctor only glanced at my face and waved me on. I ran to join Papa.

"What I wouldn't give for a cup of hot coffee." Misha blew on his hands and peered around.

The immigration center was almost empty. I guessed we were the only ship to land in Boston that morning. A few bored-looking guards stood around with their hands in their pockets. They looked as cold as we felt. The man sitting at this table wore the uniform I recognized from Ellis Island. He had a big black mustache that seemed too heavy for his lean face.

"Name?"

Misha looked at the official blankly.

"Italiano? French? Polish?"

"Yah, Polish," Misha said and began answering the man's questions. Although I couldn't understand what they were saying, the questions seemed to last a long time. The official shuffled his papers, called to another man, and raised his voice. The back of Misha's neck turned red. He yelled and banged on the table. Two guards ran up. Papa took my arm and pulled me away.

"Papa, what's happening?"

"Shhh. Pretend you don't know him. We don't want to get into trouble."

A guard put his hand on Misha's shoulder. Misha swung around and cursed in Yiddish. The guards grabbed both his arms and pulled him out of the chair. Misha yelled like a madman as spittle ran down his beard. The guards dragged him to another room and slammed the door.

I couldn't stop trembling. It was happening again. They wouldn't let Misha into America, and they wouldn't let us in either. We were back in the nightmare.

"Next."

Papa took my arm and approached the official. He sat down in the single chair facing the desk.

"Name?"

Papa shook his head.

The man sighed and tugged at his mustache. "Italiano? Polish? French?"

Papa shook his head again. "Russian. Yiddish. German."

The man turned his head and yelled to one of the guards. "Where's Bernie today? I need a translator."

"Sick."

"Great, just great. Did you try that aid society?"

"It's Saturday."

"I speak little English." The words flew out of my mouth like a frightened bird. My stomach turned over with fear. I looked at Papa. He nodded and gave me a tight smile.

"What is your name?"

"R-raizel," I answered.

"No, I mean this man's full name. Is he your father?"

"Yes, my papa." Here was the moment I had been dreading. What name should I give? If I asked Papa, the official would be suspicious. Desperately I glanced around the room. An old man sat on a bench against the wall, hunched over a wooden cane.

"Altman," I said quickly. "Benjamin Altman." Papa drew a sharp breath.

The official ran his finger down the passenger list. Then he began at the top again. He stopped at a name and looked at me. "I have a Benjamin Balaban and his daughter Raizel. Is that you?"

"Oh no!" I said, pretending to be surprised. I had to make up a good story quick. "The ship man in Antwerp, he make . . . mistake. Balaban name of my aunt."

"But there is no Altman on the list, only Balaban."

"Yes, yes," I said. "Altman name of Papa. Aunt buy ticket. Then she sick. Stay Antwerp." The words were tumbling out like a sack of potatoes. I had never spoken so much English at one time. "We sell ticket. Man in ship office write Balaban, not Altman, maybe."

"Hmmm. Well, it could be. Can I see your Russian passports?"

"He wants your Russian papers," I said to Papa. He took out his identity papers and handed them to the man.

The inspector glanced at them. "What is this? This isn't a passport."

"Papers to show Russian police," I said. "We leave Russia no passports." Now what would happen?

"Well, I can't read these." He took a watch out of his pocket and opened the cover. "Let's get on with it. Your father's age?"

"Twenty-nine."

"Nationality?"

"I do not understand."

"What country are you from?"

"Russia."

"What religion are you?"

"What is 'religion?'"

"Are you Christian or Jewish?"

"Jewish."

"What is the family status? Married? Are there children?"

"Yes. My mama, two brothers, one little sister."

"What was your last residence?"

I shook my head.

"Where did you live before you came to America?"

"In Jibatov in Ukraine."

"What is your final destination? Where are you going to live?"

"America." I breathed a prayer.

"No, I mean where will you live in America?"

"New York." Oh no, why did I say that?

"Then why did you come to Boston?"

"The ticket not so much money." I hoped it was true.

"Have you been in the United States of America before?"

"No." We had been on Ellis Island, but they wouldn't let us into America, so Ellis Island must not be America.

"Your father's occupation?"

"Work?"

"Yes, what work does he do?"

How did you say it in English? "He writes numbers in book." The official raised an eyebrow. "For buy and sell. How much. He writes numbers in book."

"Oh, you mean a bookkeeper who keeps records of business transactions?"

I nodded my head up and down. "Yes, bookkeeper." I had to remember that word.

"Has anyone offered you a job or paid you money to come here? Ask your father."

"He wants to know if you have a job waiting," I said to Papa.

"That is not allowed. Tell him I hope to get a job through Mama's cousin, but I don't have one yet."

"Papa say no. Cousin help find job. Cousin lives in New York."

"All right, girly. That's it." He stamped some papers and handed them to me.

"We finish? We live in America?" I couldn't believe it.

"Sure enough." The man smiled at me. "Say, where did you learn your English? You're going to have a real head start in school. Most of these people can't speak a word when they get off the boat."

"Nice people on boat teach me," I said and smiled at him. Could I really go to school? I wanted to ask him, but he had already motioned to the next man to come forward. Papa got up from the chair and followed me.

"Nu, Raizel?" His voice was choked.

"We made it, Papa! We can stay in America!" I wanted to skip down the vast hall, whirling and running and laughing all at once.

Papa hugged me. "What a smart daughter I have! Come, let us get our things and leave here quickly. They should not change their minds."

As we approached the pile of luggage, Misha came out of the room with his hands tied behind his back. He scowled at us. A guard held his arm tightly.

"What happened?" Papa asked.

"Someone told tales on me, probably those Poles I beat at cards every night. They think I am a horse thief!"

"What are they going to do?"

"Keep me in jail until I can prove it's a lie." He spat on the floor. The guard gave him a shove. "For this I came to America? For this I could have stayed in Russia."

Papa nodded. "Well, good luck to you, in any case."

Misha didn't answer. The guard picked up his suitcase and led him out of the hall.

"Do you think he is a horse thief, Papa?" Even though I didn't like Misha, I felt sorry for him. I knew what it was like to be a prisoner in America.

"For his sake, I hope not. Now ask that guard where we find the train to New York after we deliver the package."

I took Papa's hand and squeezed it. "Papa, there is one thing you should know. On the papers your name isn't Balaban anymore."

"Not Balaban? What do you mean?"

I looked at his face. "I'm sorry, Papa. I was afraid they had our names on a list and wouldn't let us in, so I gave them a different name."

"So I am not Binyumin Balaban anymore? What else must I give up to be an American?" Papa rubbed his bare chin. He sounded more tired than angry. "Never mind, meydele. A name is like a beard. In time you get used to either one. So what is my new name?"

"Altman. I saw an old man and it popped into my mind."

"Altman, nu." Papa sighed again. "Am I still called Binyumin? Because I don't want to be like the man from Chelm."

"Which man?"

"Raizel Balaban—I mean Altman—does not know the story about the man who lost his name? On the train I will tell it to you. I feel like Chelm stories once again."

"I think I've told enough stories for one day, Papa."

"Don't feel bad, meydele." Papa put his arm around my shoulder and hugged me to him. "You did the right thing. Someday, perhaps, you will write down the story of how we came to America. If you don't mind, that is one story I would like to have a happy ending."

And it did.

Afterword

The story of Raizel and Papa's double crossing is not a true story, but many things in it are true. My grandfather, Benjamin Balaban Altman, came to America from Jibatov (usually spelled "Zhivotov" in English), Ukraine in 1905 to escape from the Czar's army. He was rejected on Ellis Island and sent back to Europe. On the boat he met a wealthy Jewish man who advised him to dress in a modern fashion and eat the unkosher food on the boat. The man actually gave him the money to return to America. Who was he? Unfortunately, our family no longer remembers his name or anything about him.

My grandparents died before I was old enough to listen to their stories. My mother, Hannah, told me the story of her father's immigration. Raizel (Rose), Lemmel (Louis), and Shloyme (Shalom) were her brothers and sister. Hannah, Shloyme and her younger sister Sima were born in America. Raizel did not accompany her father to America, so that is one of the made-up parts of the story.

I will always be grateful to that kind stranger who helped my grandfather out of the goodness of his heart. Most of my grandparents' relatives who remained behind in the Ukraine were killed in the Holocaust during World War II.

I dedicate this book to my grandparents, Eve and Benjamin Balaban Altman, whom I never knew; to my loving and much-loved aunt, Rose (Raizel) Altman Goldfield; and to that nameless shipboard angel. Special thanks are due my mother, Hannah Altman Goldberg. Without her help, I could not have told this story.